A Pride & Prejudice Reimagining

Desire & Destiny

Pride, Prejudice, & New Adventures
Volume III

NEY MITCH

DEDICATION AND AUTHOR'S NOTE

Reader, if you decided to pick up this next installment, then right off the cuff, I shall declare you as awesome. Welcome to *Desire & Destiny*, the third chapter to *Pride, Prejudice & New Adventures*, which is a variation to Jane Austen's classic novel *Pride and Prejudice*. This is a **Second Edition** of this novel.

While this one continues with the marriage of Mr. Darcy and Elizabeth as being the focus, this particular part of the series also focuses on Kitty's romantic adventures, Colonel Fitzwilliam's decisions, and Jane Bennet's character development. Also, to make you aware, all references to the royal family of Regency England in this novel are fictitious and did not occur.

As for continuing this part of the series, I realized that I had more to say, as well as being grateful for all those who enjoyed the first two, therefore wishing to give you some more closure to the tale. Thus, I hope that you enjoy this next one, and for those of you who have decided to follow these characters and their adventures to whatever end, then I dedicate this book to you, for I owe you so much just for stopping by.

PROLOGUE

In the pews we sat, as the ceremony ended.

"I now pronounce you husband and wife," the reverend said, standing between Mr. Bingley and Miriam Goldman. "May you be joined together in holy matrimony. And Mr. Bingley, you may kiss your bride."

Mr. Bingley and Miriam turned to each other and kissed, while we all stood and clapped for them.

Turning to us, Mr. Bingley beamed, shining from his happiness with his bride standing next to him. Together, with their arms linked, they walked down the aisle as the piano played the wedding music.

"He looks content," I whispered to Darcy as he sat next to me. "I wish them all the happiness in the world, yet I daresay that I still looked happier."

"I daresay that you did," Darcy replied. "For your happiness was infectious; you made me smile in turn."

"Smiling becomes you almost as much as scowling does."

"Scowling..." He chuckled, taking my hand in his and kissing my palm. "Yes, that is a favorite pastime of mine."

❦

"Bingley," Darcy said, offering his hand which Mr. Bingley shook. "Congratulations, and I hope that you and your bride will be very happy."

Bingley beamed. "Thank you, Darcy. I do believe I have made the right decision in this case. She is my second self, and I know that our time together was no more than a couple of months, but that was all that I needed."

"Time doesn't always determine intimacy between two people," Darcy acknowledged, "for some, seven years cannot do, whereas for others, seven days can be more than enough. I suppose that if I wasn't certain that she didn't make you happy, I would be anxious for your state. But I have instead seen that she in fact is you, and therefore, I shall hope to find your fortune for the better, as opposed to being ruled over by a mistake."

"Mistake? No, I pray not so. For Darcy, though I say it myself, she is the most beautiful creature I ever beheld. And that is saying much, for you and I both have seen Miss Jane Bennet."

"Yes, you must be truly in love with this woman to determine such a thing."

They continued to speak on while I turned my attention back to the bride, who was surrounded by her family. As she was offered congratulations by them, except for her father who still looked wary, Miriam turned her attention towards me. She nodded to her family, moved through the crowd of well-wishers and approached me.

"Miriam," I said. "Oh forgive me, you are Mrs. Bingley now."

She radiated happiness. "Yes. I believe I am. Oh Mrs. Darcy, it is too much! Did you think that it could have ended in such a happy way?"

"I could, and I did." I smiled. "Fortune can favor those of us it seemed least likely to, at first."

"But to have obtained him, it is simply that... he loves me, Mrs. Darcy, he truly loves me. And I am not blind, nor ungrateful."

"I do not understand."

"I know that, despite your pretending to be ignorant of my happy ending, this came about due to your intentions and actions. Mrs. Darcy, Elizabeth, I am not wrong, am I?"

I looked down at my hands and felt the weight of such a declaration, as well as not knowing how to confess my hand in the events leading up to Bingley's willingness to court her. For if I spoke too much, I did myself too much credit, yet if I denied it, I would not satisfy her curiosity.

"I cannot say that I did much at all," I began, "nor can I say that I did little. All I can say is that I had faith."

"Faith?" Mrs. Bingley said, smiling. "Yes, it is a powerful thing. Yet you didn't need to have faith in me, nor care if I was the right woman for your husband's bosom friend. However, you did, and I don't know why, but your faith saved my life. I don't know why you decided to help me; however I will not soon forget it. And perhaps it's best that I don't."

"You owe me nothing."

"On the contrary, I owe you everything. Mr. Bingley is the best of men, for I have grown to see that, and I always will. I daresay, that you must think that the benefits are all on my side in winning him."

I chuckled at the comment. "Not at all. Not at all."

"You do, and in this case, you are right, and I will not argue with you. The gaining of much is on my side entirely."

"Mr. Bingley always has and always will deserve the best of women, and I ask this of you, Mrs. Bingley. You have your goodness now, through him, and while I know that your heart and soul is good, I implore you."

I put my hand on her arm. "You say that you won't forget my helping you now and you suggest a debt to be paid to me. I shall make good on that debt of yours easily. Repay me by being the best woman for him. Mr. Bingley's happiness depends very easily on those around him. Always be there for him, always offer him your love, and stand by him, as he faced the world to stand by you. And that will be enough."

Her eyes were shiny with happiness. "I shall not make him regret it."

"Then you have made your promise, and you owe me nothing. Be happy to be Mrs. Bingley. Be very happy to become so."

❦

All throughout the wedding feast, everyone looked content except for Miriam's father, who looked rigid during the entire ceremony. Miriam's mother however noticed this and clearly took charge throughout the day to dominate the conversation whenever she or her husband was addressed.

"Do you notice his stiffness?" Kitty asked me, whispering under her breath. "Her father looks downright miserable, poor soul."

"There is nothing poor about his soul but misplaced pride," I derided. "He is bitter."

"About what, do you think?"

"The differences between his daughter and Mr. Bingley. Naturally he would not have wanted his daughter to marry so far outside of her class."

"And therefore, only felt pressured to give her hand to Bingley," Kitty finished, "due to Mr. Bingley's good name and wealth."

"Precisely."

Kitty released a sigh. "Well then I do hope he gets over it. And I would be very annoyed if he doesn't."

I began to laugh.

"Have I said something foolish?" Kitty asked.

"Perhaps, yet it was still fascinatingly funny."

"What are you both laughing about?" Jane asked, sitting near us.

"I was saying something foolish," Kitty explained. "Nothing out of the ordinary."

⚜

After the wedding and feast, Mr. Bingley and Miriam joined us at the inn where we were all staying in Philadelphia. Once we reached our bedroom, I could not contain my glee and I overwhelmed my husband and tackled him. Laughing, he fell on the carpet while I remained on top of him.

"And might I be so bold?" Darcy asked. "What is the meaning of my wife overwhelming me so?"

"Well," I started, "I could begin with the fact that I am proud of you."

"What have I done to deserve your appreciation of me?"

"You encouraged Mr. Bingley to follow his heart. Do you have any idea how strong a notion that was?"

"I did not want him to make the same mistake that I almost had done."

"I forgave you for that long ago. Will you not, Fitz, ever forgive yourself?"

"Of course, I will not," he said, kissing me. "I was unfair to you, Elizabeth, and I believe that I owe it to myself to improve always. Though I do believe that being on the other side of the world, away from the pressures of the life and society we have been obliged to walk among, has improved me tremendously."

"Then," I said, "you have no improper pride, and you truly are the best man I have ever known."

We kissed once more.

"And you, my dearest Mrs. Darcy, taste better than my mother's pudding."

I pulled back and gave him a look of surprise. "Your mother could cook?"

"Of course not, yet we still called it her pudding all the same. It was really the cook's pudding, but with the money that we paid her, she was fine with not gaining the credit."

He paused a moment. "I was at first hesitant, Lizzy, with encouraging his marriage to Miriam."

"She is now Mrs. Bingley, dear."

"Yes, she is, and I was hesitant, for we knew so little about her. Yet Bingley is a grown man and therefore able to make his own decisions. With my nature, I would've once objected to it."

"It is a tricky and dangerous business, my love to try to influence the fate and decisions of others."

"Yes, it is. I never would have learned that, had it not been for you, dearest and loveliest Elizabeth."

"And I have one more reason for tackling you to the floor in such a rash manner," I said, brushing my lips against his.

"And what is that, pray tell?"

"I just wanted to embrace you."

"And that, I daresay, was all I needed to hear."

He lifted me up and carried me to the bed.

"My darling Lizzy, I am prepared for anything. For I knew that fate brought me much when it delivered you to me."

"I daresay that I am a lot of trouble."

"Perhaps, yet you are worth every bit of it along the way."

৩⁎৩

After our bodies lay under the covers, spent from the exhaustion and satisfaction that goes hand in hand with being intimate, we remained in each other's embrace, feeling the joy of our skin being pressed against one another and becoming one.

I looked up into Fitzwilliam's face and I saw a troubled expression.

"And..." I sighed, running my hand down his nose and cheek. "What is that look for?"

"Can you not guess my thoughts?"

"Of course not, for they are locked away in here," I said, touching his forehead. "And that is stronger than any safe."

"Elizabeth, we remain here in Philadelphia and I wish to be happy."

"Oh."

"Do you see?"

"Yes, I do. We are so near your cousins and yet so far away from them all the same. United by being in the same city but separated by disagreement and misplaced pride. Family strife is a damned nuisance!"

He laughed briefly and squeezed my shoulders. "Yes, it is. A part of me is content to leave for England without speaking to them again. For Henry to even think he could address you thus, and what is even more gruesome was his inability to accept Jane's refusal of his worthless hand! Dear lord, Lizzy, I deserved for you to have rejected me often in the past, yet I hope that if you ever did, I would have taken it more like that of a gentleman than he did."

"I hope you would as well," I added, running my fingers over his chest. "Yet Henry is a Darcy and, if I might say so, the Darcy pride runs deep, just like the Bennet prejudice runs even deeper. I believe that if I had not fallen in love with you as blindly as I had, I would have loved to have fought with you for everything you had done. I daresay my desire for you kept me from resisting you, even when you deserved it, you wicked man."

"Yes, but do you think, under the same circumstances, I could have acted like Henry?"

"Under the same circumstances, we humans are capable of anything. Yet, I tell you now, resist implacable resentment now, Fitz. The Darcys here have so much good in them, so much happiness and domestic felicity. Do not let your anger for one ruin your resolve in admiring the rest."

"Henry Darcy's parents condoned his behavior at first."

"And my parents condoned Lydia going to Brighton and look what happened. Now she's married to Mr. Wickham, who we both know by all counts will hurt her eventually, all because my parents thought they *were right*. Parents seem to have a blind spot in regards to their children. I acknowledge, even when we have children, we shall be guilty of that crime."

"I hope we need not fear on that score," Fitzwilliam added, "yet that is not something we need to think on for quite some time. I still am getting my *husband legs* in this rocky ocean that is called marriage. Could you imagine me being a father when I have not even found my *paternal legs*?"

I nestled closer against him. "I believe that you would be a great father.

You already look after many under your care with diligence. You protected Lydia, Jane, and you even protected me in the end from all your notions of family loyalties. Any man who can defeat himself has it within him to possess perfect paternal skills."

"You flatter and criticize me all in one." His voice was filled with humor.

"And I have the right to do so, for I am your wife!"

"Oh, you have that right, do you?" He rolled on top of me, moved down and kissed my thighs while running his hand over my breasts. "You use that excuse too often." He kissed me.

"And I always will. Dear me, Fitzwilliam, how I desire you always." We had just made love and I desired him again.

"Oh, do you?"

"Indeed. And you best desire me as well, forever and always, or I shall be greatly annoyed." I made a fake moue.

"I could never annoy you."

"If you stopped loving me, you would."

"And like I said, I could never annoy you."

"Well then, before I fall into you, for I believe myself to be always at your mercy, except for the circumstances when you are at mine, we must remember the purpose of our discussion. Fitzwilliam, we loved our time here in Philadelphia and we loved most of our time with your cousins here."

"Tis true, we did. I found bliss here with you. You might even say that I stole it while I was here with you. I left our problems over on the other side of the ocean. Even at our bitterest times here, between getting verbally attacked for political problems and having to savagely attack those ruffians, I still felt purity here. I felt quite content with the freedom we found."

"And having something to fight for while no society to fight against."

He rose up on his elbow. "What do you mean?"

"You hate not being free."

"You're correct. I want to be liberated. I want to not be judged always. And I wish for the world to not look upon me always and look to either praise or to criticize. Elizabeth, for so long I lived my life under the strict and firm gaze of many prying eyes, who wished to know all that was within me, not because they cared, but because they desired the life that I had. They desired an image and not reality."

"Then why me?" I persisted, quite intrigued by all that he was confessing.

"I do not comprehend again. You are being wonderfully elliptic tonight, you know."

"Why did you choose to fall in love with me?"

"I chose nothing, remember? I did my best to reject you, no matter how much you deserved more than my paltry behavior, for I was quite the worthless libertine. No, no, no. You were brought to me, despite my stubbornness. I could not help but fall in love with you."

"Yes, but you had to have seen many beauties in your time. Many who must've enticed you? What about me was different?"

"The fact that you are different, and you are not afraid of me."

"Is that it?" I chuckled.

"And you love to laugh."

"Many women do."

"And it's often a fake laugh. Yet yours is real. That is it!"

"How so and what is?"

"Lizzy, you were *real*. From the first time I saw you at Almacks and you poured me wine, then when you gave me flowers in the park, you were genuine. You were the truth. I had never met a woman who could encompass such veracity in her countenance while also being light, carefree in her disposition, and optimistic in nature. Your habits and manner lighten my own. Therefore, whenever I looked away from you, I would become lost, and when I chose to reject you, I fell even further."

Darcy rolled me over and began to kiss my back while running his hands over my bottom, massaging me over and over while I moaned into the pillow. He raised his lips, removed my hair off my neck and began to kiss the back of it.

"You must not lose your love for me, Elizabeth," he whispered desperately.

"I won't."

"Then all is well."

"Fitzwilliam?"

"Yes," he replied. His hands stopped moving over my skin.

You can still listen to me while your hands still perform their work upon me."

He laughed at my comment, continuing to run his hands along my body. "Of course. Now, what was it we were speaking of again?"

"Of your family, we were speaking of your family," I whispered, eyes closed and allowing myself to enjoy his touch. "And my fears of you turning from them forever because of one harsh encounter. I do not think we should lightly abandon them and forsake a part of the family who we have had so many good moments with. Whether it is through a letter or by wishing to see them again, we should not leave for England without speaking to them once more. And who knows? Maybe we might need them to help us in the end."

"I cannot see how that is possible, yet stranger things have happened."

"Aye, they have. After all, I am friends to a woman writer who has just published a book named *Sense and Sensibility*. Therefore, all is possible, isn't it?"

"Yes. Everything is. Fine then, I shall submit to your counsel for the moment. But I do not wish to see them just yet. We should write them a letter."

"Shall I write it, or you?"

"You had better do it. I'm afraid if I were to do so, then I would say something offensive."

༺❀༻

Dressed in my robe, I sat at the desk and finished my letter while Fitzwilliam lay in our bed. When I finished, I read it over and then turned to him.

"Well, shall I begin to read it?"

"I am ready for it."

I cleared my throat and began.

"*Dear Cousin Thomas and Emilia Darcy,*

*Many a day has gone by where we look on our memories of our time spent on Canterbury with fondness, for we found much **happiness** in your company. Just as we have found in coming to America, yet as you know, our fortune in coming across the ocean to these lands was not always for the good or even the acceptable. We have been met with anger, prejudice, racial and social injustice, and yet, rather than deter us from loving the land, we are still endeared to it.*

Philadelphia has been the greatest of places, and your company made it so. Therefore, as we look on with all things, we choose to refuse to let our

9

memories of tension erase any memories of being content. We grew to love you, our American cousins, and we did not wish to part under such ill terms.

May we all, despite the anger that Henry Darcy has, not sever all ties. We shall always look on him as family, if he remembers that we are his. And we urge him to look on my sister's rejection of him not as the ending of a story, yet as the chance for him to make a new one for himself.

With one rejection in one quarter can lead to an acceptance from another one more suitable. Another woman will come along, and my sister's actions will allow him freedom to find her. Which he shall. We are soon to leave Philadelphia, for we had returned to see Mr. Bingley wed Miriam Goldman, and now she is to travel with us back to England, where we must acknowledge now will not only be separated by ocean, but by the threat of war. We wish to not lose your love and understand that you have not lost ours. And you never will.

Yours, etc.

Mr. and Mrs. Darcy of Pemberly.

I turned back to Fitzwilliam.

"Well, does that suit?"

He gave me a warm smile. "Yes, very well."

"I can assure you, Fitzwilliam, this is all for the best. For we may never know, but something tells me that if we maintain the connection, they might aid us in some way in the end."

"You do not wish to burn a bridge?"

"I do not know if I have achieved that. All I can say is that I do not wish to build a wall."

"I am very good at building walls."

"Yes. And I love breaking them down in reply."

We rang for Jefferson, and Darcy gave him the letter to mail. Once Jefferson left, I turned back to Fitzwilliam.

"And on another matter, you must tell me how a man like Jefferson came to be in your employ, and why you trust him so much."

"That is a discussion for another day."

"Why not this one?"

"Because I will only tell you when you have known him long enough to forgive him for anything."

"Was he a villain once?" I asked, intrigued.

"He might have been in some ways, yet he was also a hero in many others. Yet the duality of his nature is not something that I must own to knowing all of."

I gave him a fond look. "Then we shall have something to talk about in the future, and I promise not to tell Cassandra and Jane Austen that part of the story."

"Thank you, Elizabeth, that is a great comfort."

I

HOMEWARD

I t's a word, forever used, when describing such a unique sensation, a marked emotion: surprise. Yet surprise is all that can be said when describing my life and the events that had occurred so recently.

Darcy, my sisters Kitty, Jane, Georgiana, Mr. Bingley and I had booked passage back to England with another addition to our company: Mrs. Miriam Bingley.

Our preparations to leave for home were swiftly done and a quiet departure, for while we announced in our letter to the American Darcys that we were leaving along the Delaware River back for Britain, we knew that they would not offer to meet us along the riverfront to bid us farewell.

Therefore, when packed to leave and arrived by carriage to the riverfront, we were surprised to find that there was an unexpected family member awaiting us.

"Deborah!" Kitty cried out. We all turned and there, amidst the crowd, was Deborah Darcy, formally known as Sister Mary Ignatius.

"Oh," Deborah called out, approaching us, "remember that it is Sister Mary Ignatius amongst the outside world."

"Oh, forgive me."

She laughed her quiet laugh. "I am not reprimanding you. I simply am holding to standards and structure."

"Sister Ignatius!" I cried. We all approached her and Georgiana, Jane, Kitty and I could embrace her without shame or shyness.

"It is wonderful to see you all once more," she said, then turned to Mrs. Bingley. "And as for this one, well, I do believe that we have seen each other often, yet we have never fully met. Is this Mrs. Bingley then?"

"Yes," Mr. Bingley began. "Sister Mary Ignatius, I would like to introduce you to my wonderful new wife, Mrs. Miriam Bingley."

"It is a great pleasure to meet you," Miriam said demurely.

"And it is a great pleasure to meet you as well," Sister Ignatius replied. "And I dare say that you have made Mr. Bingley happy, for though he loves to smile often, now he is laughing!"

We all laughed at her words.

"Sister Mary," I said, "you must not misinterpret my words, for they are simply worries, but will you not be in trouble for leaving your convent?"

"Oh, here in some parts of America, we nuns can leave our convents with more freedom than you would assume. Besides, my mission in coming is a noble enough one that even if it weren't permitted, I would still have sojourned here."

"Your presence here is most welcome," Jane said. "It is nice to see you once more, and to know that you bid us a kind farewell."

"I can see what you are feeling," Sister Ignatius added. "You are happy to see me, in hopes that my presence here is a sign to offer the olive branch of peace between both parts of our family. You are worried that my family does still harbor resentment for your refusing my brother's hand in marriage, do you not?"

"We confess that to be true," Kitty said, answering for Jane. "Yet just as Jane is not responsible for any breach in familial bonds, so we do not desire to lose the love that has been gained through such a connection."

"Eloquently spoken," Darcy said. "Dear god, Kitty, you truly were right to reject Mr. Collins, for that would have been quite a waste."

"I shall enjoy that compliment," Kitty replied.

"You have rejected an offer of marriage as well?" Sister Ignatius said, turning to Kitty. "My goodness, while it seems to be the priority for a family of women to find happiness in matrimony, are you Bennet women resolved on rejecting proposals, for that is quite amusing?"

"I confess myself amazed at our stubbornness," Kitty added. "However, where Jane and I have been staunch, Elizabeth and our sister Lydia have made up for our rigidity."

"It is not rigidity to have preferences," I said. "I would have rejected Mr. Collins and Henry Darcy as well. Oh, forgive me for any offense I might have said against your brother, Sister Mary."

"And I have taken none. I know my brother, and he can be quite stubborn and hard of the head. Stubborn enough not to even see that it is not the obligation of every woman to accept the hand of any man simply because he has offered.

"I am sorry for it, Miss Bennet, for I know how he must've taken the rejection, and it does not do any credit to my family in how they cornered you afterwards. We did not show our best sides, only our passionate one. Passion can be necessary, yet in such moments, it was not prudent, and I am sorry for it."

"Thank you for coming to apologize, Sister," Jane said, "yet you need not do so. I feel sorry for having caused any disquiet or disharmony between both families, for it was not my intent or my desire. And now I seek nothing but peace between the Darcys."

"Unfortunately," Sister Ignatius said, "this is the Darcys, and rejecting one on a romantic level is a clear indication that disquiet will follow. Tis' the way of our family. Henry will pine, then feel resentment, implacable resentment, and then, if all goes well, he will be the better man for it."

"Surely my opinion will not be so high in estimation after this?" Jane said. "He will not think happy thoughts toward me."

"No, but nor will he think happy thoughts on himself. My brother is proud, stubborn even, but is just and clear-sighted by the end, as well as wise, in his own way. It will take him awhile, yet in time, he shall learn from your rejection of him, and he will also see that it was a love that was not meant to be. Though, if I know him well, and I do because he is my brother, he will need something else to boost him in the right direction. You have other sisters, have you not?"

"Aye, we do," I said. "Yet between our sister Mary and Lydia, I doubt either of them will ever be to his tastes, touch, or sentiments. Besides, he might never perhaps meet them."

"I cannot help but wonder," she said, sounding mysterious. "Life is simple, but the roads we take that cross others make them all complicated.

"Yet I am simply clucking away like a hen," she said, "and I was wondering, if you would be so kind to give me a service."

"What service could a Bennet do for a sister of the cloth?" Jane asked. "And how might we assist?"

"When you return to England, will you be journeying back into Hampshire?"

"Yes," Darcy said, "for we must return Jane and Kitty to Longbourn."

"Then I offer you no inconvenience," Sister Mary added, "for you shall be passing by Lucas Lodge. Can you be so kind as to deliver this missive to Samuel Lucas?"

She took a letter from her reticule and handed it to Jane.

"I dare say that it is too late to say such words, but I still wish that he knows my mind nonetheless."

"Yet," Jane began. "Forgive me, Sister, I wish that I could help you..."

"However," Darcy interceded, "it is improper for a lady to send a gentleman a private letter. Most indelicate."

"Oh, put a sock in it, Fitzwilliam," Sister Mary chided, making my husband stand even more upright than he usually was, simply out of shock. "Sometimes the bounds of propriety must be breached, for the sake of the truth being revealed, and integrity being found. Believe me, if you were not wed to Mrs. Darcy here, and letting her know your feelings through a letter was the only way that you could achieve your communication, you would toss decorum to the wind as well and give her a letter to tell her your feelings."

"I would not ever have sent a letter and risk her good name!" Darcy argued stoutly.

"Oh, yes you would have," I replied archly. "For if you recall, bending the standards is not something that you are averse to when the occasion calls for it."

"Are you disagreeing with me?"

"Yes. For your not bending under the labor of propriety is something that I always found quite remarkable."

"Well, if you are to disagree with me one moment because you wish to give me a compliment in the next, then I shall let you win this battle for the moment. Though I see the tactic and strategy that you were trying to utilize."

"That will never mean that I shall cease to use it."

"And nor does it mean that I will turn a blind eye."

"Are you both that much in love?" Sister Mary laughed. "It truly is quite comical."

"My husband just said that I was not worth a letter," I added. "I had to rectify the matter." Then I turned to Darcy and pursed my lips. "If we were not wed, then you had better have sent me a letter to show your feelings, and that shall be the end of that."

"I shall let you believe you have won for the moment, just so that I might win in the next."

"And you both are still speaking?" Sister Mary sighed. "Do you both truly realize just how much your perfect happiness is making all around you appear lesser in contentment and domestic tranquility? You really shall make me question my love for my faith over my love for a marital path, and that is hard to do. Now, of all you sisters, is there one who is strong enough and fearless enough to give my letter to Mr. Lucas?"

"Can I be for the task?" Kitty offered. "I have no qualms with falling from propriety under such circumstances. And I dare say that it will be said of me often."

"Nay, you shall not," Jane said. "For I should do so, since I was the first one who was asked, and now I shall make good on that offer by not being such a prude."

Jane took the letter.

"However," Jane continued, "you must promise me, Sister Mary, that there is nothing within the contents of these papers that will harm the emotional security of Mr. Lucas in any way."

"Nay," Sister Mary said. "There is none, and I take no offense in you wishing to know it. I am not afraid to admit that I simply wish to tell him that I never forgot him. And that I pray he is well. And you must promise to never read my missive."

"I promise that I shall not. And I am honored that you trust me with this deed."

"I still have my doubts," Darcy added, "at your presumption, Sister Mary. Please reconsider, for you are, after all, a lady."

"You forget, Cousin Fitzwilliam, that I am no lady. I am a nun! And before I was even that, I was Deborah Darcy. And she was a force to be reckoned with."

I leaned forward and kissed Sister Mary on the cheek.

"Sister Ignatius, thank you very much just for being who you are."

"I knew that you would understand, Mrs. Darcy. Yes, and Cousin Fitzwilliam?"

"Aye?"

"You are lucky to have snatched up your wife here, for I daresay, that if you had married one of her sisters instead, she might have been the one who my brother Henry would have favored in the end. He only claims to like serenity in a woman, yet he has been raised to secretly admire spirit. And he will remember that in the end."

"I know that I am lucky, Cousin Deborah. Believe me to be sincere, I know that I am."

"Well then..." Kitty and Georgiana hugged her as well, and then Jane and I hugged her. She waited on the docks as we boarded our merchant vessel, The Rose. The anchor was raised, and the ship took off. She cried out to us, but at first, we did not hear her.

"What did you say?" Jane asked.

Sister Ignatius then cupped her hands around her mouth and exclaimed.

"And who knows? Who says that we shall never be sisters? I do not know why, but I feel that it will come to pass in some way!"

She waved to us as the ship passed down the river and we left Philadelphia behind.

As she grew smaller in the distance, I turned to Darcy and saw his familiar scowl.

"And what is that look for?" I asked, smiling.

"I would never have sent a letter to you in secret if we were not wed. Believe me, I would never have done so, and that is the last word that I shall say on it."

"Very well, I can speak, therefore. You very much would have, and you know it."

"No, I would not have."

"Oh, you very much would. And you better have."

And that was the first argument we had as we held passage on The Rose, heading homeward back to England.

2

CONVERSATIONS & CURIOSITY

"Oh, no, I would not have!" Darcy continued.

"Oh, yes you would have," I persisted. It had been an hour and we still were debating if Darcy would have sent me a letter if we were not married and yet he wanted to show me his feelings.

"And I must add, dear Fitzwilliam that even if you had not, how is this argument between us nothing less than mute? You claim that to have sent me a letter when I was single was breaching propriety, yet all we have ever done was breach it. How can you debate writing me a missive, when we kissed at Aginfield during a ball?"

He gave me a private grin. "I did more than kiss you."

I laughed. "You would be a terrible attorney, for your words only added to my argument, and did not aid yours."

"It did not aid yours because you are correct for the moment."

I raised a wary eyebrow. "For the moment?"

"Your power over me is too strong at times, and I let you win often. I must remind myself to be harder in the future and not let you win every battle of words we have."

"Are you telling me that you will harden yourself against me?"

He laughed at such a remark. "Never. I am simply telling you to be on your guard. You are a master of words, my wicked wife, and I only wish to keep up with you. And I will and win as many arguments as I can."

"You can try," I teased, "but you will fail."

"I am Mr. Darcy. When I want something, I never fail."

"And I am Elizabeth Darcy," I retaliated, "and I did not fail to win you, therefore what can I fail at getting when I desire it?"

"You desire me truly?" His eyes grew stern, which meant secretly that his passion was roused.

"You know I do. This was why I could never deny you anything, even when I should have denied you everything."

I turned and looked out at the sea as we stood by the railing of the ship.

"Now, to discuss other matters. Your cousin, Deborah Darcy."

"Ah, yes, Sister Ignatius."

"What did you think of her last words?"

"They were nonsensical at best."

"Do you think?"

"She is a very good woman, and I am happy that she came to see us. Yet her words were that of a holy woman with a romantic side. Those combinations do not stir together to become a perfect mixture."

"You admire her, and you know it."

"I do, she must be an oddity."

"She is a Darcy, my love. You are all oddities."

"We are not."

"You very much are. Which makes me overjoyed, for I would not have married you if you were not."

"What purpose for not?"

"To marry a different sort of man is to be constantly surprised and in wonderment. By being married to you, my husband, even the mundane becomes a marvel. The common everyday things become profound. All because you, sir, are not at all normal."

"You are an oddity yourself."

"I thought, according to you, I was wicked?"

"You are wicked. And I suppose that I desire you for your wickedness."

"And that was also a very wicked thing to say."

"Mrs. Darcy?"

"Yes."

"Do not ever change."

I took Fitzwilliam's hand in my own, careless of those who saw us, and kissed it.

"I promise that I will not and never shall."

❦

Throughout the voyage, Mr. Bingley and Miriam spent most of the time with each other, in hushed and quiet tones, speaking in confidence, hiding their desires which were apparent through their physical language, and never wishing to be far apart. One time, as we all stood on deck and they were further near a group of sailors, Jane looked on them as Miriam laughed at something Mr. Bingley had said.

Jane smiled as she watched them. "She laughs a lot."

"Mr. Bingley is a funny man," I added.

"Yes, he is, but Miriam is something more than that. She is naturally happy, which is good for him. They have the same heart."

"Aye, their tempers are so much alike, their attitudes so compliant, that nothing will ever be agreed upon, their natures too giving, that they shall be cheated insidiously by their servants."

"You make jokes!"

"I do, and I can," I said with a laugh.

"And you joke well, for he does have 5,000 pounds a year and liable to live comfortably. Miss Miriam has won with him and is guaranteed to be happy with him. Though if our mother was here, she would say that it made sense. For Mrs. Bingley is a handsome woman, and therefore she would declare that she could not have been so beautiful for nothing!"

"Now you joke, Jane!"

"Yes, I do. And I quite like it."

"Though, you were a bit in error."

She turned to me. "Was I?"

"Yes, our mother would first say that after Mr. Bingley did not wed me, he should have wedded one of you all."

"Oh, that is a just assumption. And to think, what would our lives had been if the reverse had happened? Say Mr. Bingley had proposed to you as she had wished, and Darcy had proposed to me, what a strange turn of events that could have been? But according to Sister Ignatius, she actually believed that you were more suited for Mr. Henry Darcy than I, but his misplaced pride and priorities only confused him."

"I do not understand what could have prompted her to make such an observation," I acknowledged.

"I can and I do, however."

"He criticized me for my views, do you not recall?"

Jane answered, "And you stood up to him. Men such as Henry Darcy only think women like me are suited for them, yet they are in error often, I have learned. Your Mr. Darcy found you, but again, such a curiosity it would be, for our worlds to have been so reversed. Say that you and Mr. Bingley had fallen in love as planned, and then Mr. Henry Darcy and I had wed, as was intended. I would then have been Mrs. Darcy, and you dear Lizzy, would have been Mrs. Bingley."

"Yes, how strange! And how very much unwanted! I believe in the feeling that there is something very strange and erroneous with that picture."

"Yes, there would have been. And yet a puzzlement it is, for one wrong step, and that could have been our fate."

"Are you truly happy, Jane, for turning down Mr. Henry Darcy?"

"Elizabeth, though I still do not have a husband to my name, I could not be happier to have done so. As we said before, I am no Mrs. Darcy. Yet you are. *Yet you are.*"

"Then what are you?"

"I am, simply, Jane Bennet."

❦

"I do not know what to make of us," Georgiana said to Kitty. I was standing near them, but I did not believe they knew that I overheard them. They had just conversed with some sailors. One of the sailors had shown them how to braid the twain for the ship rigging, so they were helping them.

"What do you mean?" Kitty replied.

"We are like seashells in an ocean it seems, and we forever get tossed about."

"I see what you are feeling."

"Do you?"

"Aye, I do. Around us, everything seems to happen to everyone else, and we simply have a small part to play in this epic thing, does it not?"

"Precisely. And I wonder where we shall end up. For the better or for the worse. Yet I do not think our fates to be so very hard," Georgiana said, "at least not when compared to the hardships of others."

"Precisely," Kitty added. "And that is what annoys me."

Georgiana paused in her work. "What do you mean by such a confession?"

"I mean that I feel so poor and plainly made in mind and mentality as of now. In going to Philadelphia, we have seen things that life seems to label us too delicate to see. Does it not annoy you, Georgiana, that much of the hardships of life, we are denied from witnessing?"

"Propriety commands us to be ignorant, Kitty."

"Yes, propriety, that is the double-edged sword. A blessing and a curse, does it not feel so? It protects us from the truth, yet it also denies us the truth, and therefore we are denied the self-advancement that occurs when one is exposed to it. We have seen pain and been almost attacked because of this war that seems doomed to occur. We have seen injustice.

"That is the point, however. Should I have been sorry to have seen it, or happy to be forced into seeing it? To be a gentleman's daughter, our worlds are so small, so miniscule, confined to wait at home, and much of the world I have not seen. Yet now I have seen it. It does make shopping for ribbons and only caring about simple gossip all pointless. Not when I have seen such things and true problems. All that I can say for myself, and it is not an enviable state, believe me, is that I feel that I have been so narrow-minded."

Georgiana had been studying her. "It is not our fault, so do not be hard on yourself. As you say, our worlds are small because we have no choice but to be confined by them. And just so propriety does command us to be ignorant of such tragedies does not make you or I smaller in the world."

"Do you believe so?"

"Kitty, I know so. Nor does it make our grievances when they do ever arise any the less important in our eyes. We have the right to be as all are," Georgiana said. "We should laugh and gasp when something very vexing happens to us. Yet we still have the right to smile, to make merry, find the fun of life, and the small things, the trivialities have the right to make us aggravated in turn. All for one simple reason."

"And what reason is that?"

"That life would be very boring if we never got angry over anything!"

Kitty and Georgiana both had a good laugh over that.

"Yet still," Kitty added, "I am not the same woman, I feel, and the Kitty

Bennet that was, will not be the same Kitty Bennet that returns to Hampshire. I have seen the mundane and the marvel behind it, and the pain and suffering of others does tend to change one. I don't believe that I can go back to sitting in a drawing room and simply sewing or being idle with no hope or choice of any occupation. I want to be of some use. I am not saying that I foolishly want to walk into hardship. I just want to go on an adventure."

"An adventure?"

"Yes, do you never read mythology of any kind, Georgiana? I know that you do, for you are a better reader than I. To read of those knights who traveled across the lands on noble missions, on perilous journeys, to protect their homes, or in search of a grail, or a sword of magic, I wish...I wish that it was in our right to undergo one now. I do not understand what I say. I simply cannot stand still just now. I wish to go to the world. And be a hero of some kind."

Georgiana appeared amused. "You discovered all of this about yourself simply by gathering a larger acquaintance with the world, by going to Philadelphia?"

"Do I sound extreme?"

"Yes, my dear Kitty, but I understand what you are feeling."

"Do you?" Kitty asked, feeling encouraged.

"Yes, for I have actually wished for magic to exist in this world. For so long, I wished to believe that this was not all there was to life, just the comings and goings of acquaintances, the morning, the afternoon, tea, and evening, going from one day to the next, sitting, and waiting for something to happen, and being surprised when nothing happens at all, as it never does. You wish to find importance in your life, do you not?"

"Yes."

"And I suppose marriage must be our importance."

"Yet is it, Georgiana? For so long, I desired my life to be just that. In Hampshire, when the militia camped there, all I thought of was officers in their regimental uniforms."

She brought her hands to her chest. "Oh, Georgiana, I thought they were so handsome! Yet now, all is changed. I find that I could not care one way or the other about them, for they seemed so large and heroic to me, yet they were not. They were simply men in bright red uniforms that didn't always fit them as well as I had thought."

Then it was my turn to chuckle, yet I stifled it and quickly listened in once more, if listening in is what it could be called to overhear a conversation on a ship where you are all out in the open.

"They were not heroes," Kitty continued. "At least, not yet. They were men that I turned into ideals. Yet there must be another ideal outside of the form of another. An ever-fixed mark, something to define us, that no person can be in the place of, and that no nightmare can touch. Should marriage be our only dream? The only thing to define us? Should we have no form, no figure of importance, outside of it? And I do not mean to frighten you, yet what should occur if the dream is not all that we assumed it would be? What if we marry and it is not to our happiness, but more of a hindrance?"

She touched Georgiana's shoulder. "I love my mother and father, yet marriage did not allow domestic tranquility, but rather domestic tension. How was love for your parents?"

Georgiana did not respond at first. She sighed and her brow furrowed as she thought of all it meant.

"It seemed a beautiful bond," she finally acknowledged. "Yet I cannot say for sure. They appeared happy, yet it wasn't the stuff of fairytales or comfort. It seemed to be a formal love, if I am judging accurately."

Kitty nodded. "And while it is wonderful to think that one can find their happy ending in another, I am not always certain that it is possible. Your brother and my sister are a unique exception. Finding each other, despite his flaws and her disappointments and then being bonded so strongly, is a rarity. I cannot guarantee that I should ever be so lucky, and I think that I shall not look to be. For if I do, then I shall find myself disappointed. I am not Elizabeth Bennet. I am Kitty Bennet. And while she had all the rights to an incandescently happily ever after, I confess to seeing myself only allowed to having a simple one."

Georgiana gazed into the distance and sighed. "A simple one. That is all that we can hope for."

"And why we should not cling to marriage as the only source of our happiness, for it is a dream that could easily fall apart or lead to unhappiness. We must find another thing to define us, do you not feel it? We are not allowed to have an occupation, yet we should be allowed to find a purpose."

"Then begin with me," Georgiana stated.

"What do you mean?"

"I mean…Kitty, when we return to England, I shall need a companion, a friend to accompany me so that Elizabeth and Fitzwilliam can have their privacy. Would I be enough of a charity for you?"

"You are not a charity," Kitty said, hugging Georgiana from behind and resting her arms around her shoulders. The watery horizon loomed ahead of them.

"You are my friend and my new sister. I think I should be content to be there for you. And look out, see the swift sunrise as it falls on the distance over the water, creating a beautiful image? It makes one feel all sources of happiness. The sun shines on our camaraderie, does it not? And I shall be merry again, Georgiana, and I shall be happy to follow you anywhere and we can talk about boys, short, tall or ugly, as well as about gowns we would like to have, and enjoy buying ribbons and all."

Both girls leaned over the railing. Georgiana said, "Do not worry of our days not being ever filled with matters of importance. I take part in some charities and visit the poorer homes in the villages in Kent. If you wish to assist in them with me, that would be a wonderful addition, for this way, I would not feel so alone."

"Georgiana, it shall take me awhile to learn how to be a good companion in that regard, yet I shall be honored to assist you."

"Yes, and you shall learn the most profitable lesson of all. Adventures are few and far in between in regards to undergoing them, and whatever heroics we women can obtain, we must do it from home. Yet it is a start. Larger things will come."

"And yet, I still want adventure," Kitty answered with a sigh.

"As do I, in a way."

Mr. Darcy called for Georgiana and she nodded to Kitty, and then went off to see what her brother wanted. Kitty on the other hand, leaned further over the ship's railing and looked down into the water. Just when I believed her lost in thought, I turned to leave, and I heard her shift.

"Lizzy, you were listening in on our conversation, weren't you?"

"Oh." I sighed, not knowing how to lie at the moment. "I was just... just..."

"Listening in on our conversation," Kitty repeated, grinning at me.

"Oh, very well," I groaned, coming from my hiding place and settling beside her. "Yet look on it as revenge for the all times that you did it to me."

Kitty faked surprise. "I did not do it so very often."

"Yes, you did, little sister. You did it every chance that you could own, to the point where I had secrets until I turned fifteen years old."

"Yes, but what you hid with words, you could not hide in your expressions and countenance. I knew that you were in love with Mr. Darcy, even when you told me nothing."

"That is not true," I said archly.

"That, Lizzy, is very true. And he was in love with you, that was also plain, for he tried so very hard not to like you. It really was quite comical."

I studied her long and hard. "Kitty, tell me truly, what has happened to you?"

"And what do you mean?"

"I mean that you have changed truly. You were correct. You are not the same woman who left England."

Kitty gazed out into the ocean. "I have seen tragedy, I suppose, and one is never really the same afterwards, I presume."

"You are correct, one is not. Kitty, on the same day that there was the catastrophe of Henry Darcy's proposal to Jane, we also came upon a slave catcher who was trying to drag a woman and her children into slavery."

"What?"

"Yes, it was awful, Kitty. And the woman had her two children with her as he dragged them out and tried to shackle them. And he would have succeeded, had it not been for Fitzwilliam."

Kitty grasped my hands. "Lizzy, tell me all that had happened."

After I finished my narrative of recalling when Darcy and I protected a Freed Negro Woman and her children from being dragged into captivity by the ruthless slave catcher, and of Harriet Price, the only woman in the street who rallied to our aid, Kitty was taken aback and slightly short with me.

"Why did you not tell me before?" she demanded.

"Because I thought at first, that it was not something that you needed to know."

"Did you not think I was strong enough to handle such a story?"

"No, I simply—"

"Then what did you think? Elizabeth, do you have no faith in me?"

"I do," I faltered. "It is just simply...you know how we were raised. We are so forlorn in regards to giving and receiving proper advice from those that surround us. Our mother and father were so...you know what they are, and I also have a husband whose life can be a pretty drear thing, and how am I to know what he does and does not wish me to reveal what concerns him?"

Kitty nodded in agreement. "Darcy is tight-lipped, true, and I see what you mean when you speak of our parents, but Darcy is stronger than you think, I believe.

"He stood by you when any other man would have continued to mistreat you and not care for your feelings. Darcy is a man who fails, yes, but he sees his failures for what they are eventually, when he is awakened to them. Tell him that I am trustworthy, or at least let me speak to him to show him that I can be confided in. And that I am not so made of softness that I will break under the weight of things."

"You truly wish to be a strong part of this family?" I asked, awed by her resolution. "You are determined, then?"

"I... I just wish to be a part of something. At home, I was never a part of anything."

"What do you mean?"

"Lizzy, you saw it for yourself. I had no identity outside of Lydia for so long. No one thought me of importance, and I now see that I was like a parrot to her, always mimicking what she said. I was a fool, once, yet what was I that I was not forced into being? Our mother worshipped Lydia and Jane, our father worshipped you, and no one worshipped Mary or me, or thought us worthy of any notice."

I felt so badly for her. "That is not true, Kitty."

"It is true, and you know it. Even as sisters, I had no importance for too long. You and Jane were closely bound to each other, Mary kept to herself, and therefore I had no choice but to cling to Lydia out of necessity."

"Are you saying that you bound yourself to her once because you were forsaken of any special attention, not only from our parents, but from me as well?"

"I do not blame you, but if Jane and you had clung to me more, do you think that I would have needed to be bound to Lydia so deeply? It is a strange thing, yet too often I have found the world loves in irony. Those that are more just and right, the world can often care little for, yet those lacking in any moral fiber, the world often praises. Many loved Lydia even when she was a child. Therefore, to bind myself to her was natural for me, but also necessary. It was the only way, it seemed, that I could obtain love myself."

"Kitty," I whispered. "I never thought of your feelings."

"Because we for very long did not confide in each other until Darcy entered your world. Somehow, in some way, his arrival in our lives forced you to see me differently. That is why I can easily forgive how many mistakes he made when you were first acquainted with him. All the pain you endured due to his negligence, Lizzy, and yet it was all worth it for us all, was it not?"

I had to agree that it was.

"Lizzy, our lives have opened. We have seen America, parts of England that I never believed that I would, and I have become something larger than I once was. Therefore, I urge you to allow me to remain with Georgiana when you all return to Pemberly. If I return home, then I will become a ghost again, and will be useless."

"You are not useless," I urged. "You never were. Oh, Kitty, I have failed you quite as an older sister for too long."

"It is fine, Lizzy, and I do not blame you, and you have not failed me. We all became what we became because we had no choice but to. This last year is the first time that we were given a choice in anything, and look what has become of us? And I do not wish to become a villain through idleness and frivolity because the world praised my sister for it."

"You wish to avoid her fate, don't you?"

"I know Wickham married her because he was paid off. And I know that it was Darcy who did it, along with Wickham being threatened by all the Prince Regent's special guards. Georgiana told me everything. No, Lydia may blind herself to the fact that she has been used abysmally and is in a loveless marriage, yet I will not let that be my fate."

"Yes, and I must say that if travelling to America and Derbyshire has done so much to change your outlook on life as a whole, then I wish that Lydia might have had the same disposition to be so easily altered for the better as well."

"Who knows? She might, in the end."

❦

"Dear lord, Mrs. Bingley," I said, looking at Miriam's pale face. "Are you quite all right?"

An hour had passed, and I was surprised to have found Miriam on the deck and not attended to by Mr. Bingley, who had gone off to the necessary room below deck.

"I am well, thank you, Mrs. Darcy," she said when I approached her, though she looked the opposite. "I just believe that I have done my best and failed."

"Failed?"

"Yes, I believe... that I am quite seasick."

"Oh." I laughed in spite of myself.

"Oh, shut it!" Miriam laughed as well, and then covered her mouth as she clearly felt her lunch rise in her throat.

"Water does help actually," I said.

"Water is the problem, I dare say, for it is all around me."

"Actually, though it will make you thirsty, wine helps more."

"You are right! Why did I not think of that?"

I took her arm. "Here let us fetch some."

We walked below deck, went into my chambers, sat down, poured some glasses of wine and began to drink them slowly.

"So, do you feel any improvement?" I asked.

"Yes, I do, thank you. Now if I remain below deck a bit, I shall be fine and quiet and peace in here is most helpful. Yet if Charles were to not find me, I think he will be worried, therefore I shall have to go back on deck."

"You need not worry. Jane saw us travel below, and she has suffered the effects of seasickness herself, and she would be able to make him aware of our location if need be. Though I know that will not stop his present anxiety, for to be a newlywed is to wish to be beside your companion often."

"And that is what frightens me."

Her answer surprised me. "What have you reason for it?"

"Forgive me. I was not very forthcoming with an explanation. I meant that I worry when that feeling ends. That eventual sensation when we no longer are each other's primary concern and intention. I am a very selfish woman."

"How so? We are all selfish in the end, but what way do you mean to call yourself so?"

"I secretly wish to have Charles beside me always. I never want him away from me."

I gave her a sly smile. "I bet that he loves that."

"Yes, very much so. However, when that magic dies out of matrimony, I'm afraid of that impending thing of losing his affection at all."

"All this you think of when your honeymoon has not begun yet?" I asked, chuckling.

"Yes." She laughed in return. "But I had no choice, for this is the first time that Charles has seen me sick, and I know I must look disgusting for it."

"You are frightened that his love will be weakened because he sees you green in the face once? Charles is made of stronger stuff than that, believe me. On the contrary, this shall be a good thing for him and for you."

"How so, do you think?"

"When my sister, Jane, was sick and was vomiting over the edge of the ship we were on, it was not a glamorous sight, and Mr. Bingley was there to see it. Instead of being disgusted, he found it refreshing."

"Indeed! Charles found it so?" Miriam laughed.

"Oh, very much so! He said that it was amusing to see something so beautiful look so... human."

"I simply worry about not being perfect. A man such as Mr. Bingley deserves perfection, and I wish to give it to him."

"Perfection is not possible for anyone to achieve."

"Yet I still wish to strive for it."

"And so you shall and must. Yet when you fall, forgive yourself for it, especially for things you can't control, such as seasickness."

"Yes, you are right." Miriam looked down at her hands, and then up at me shyly. "Yet that is not all that I fear."

"What else then?" I asked, not surprised, for I sensed an apprehension to her other than what she had already confided in me.

"I worry that not only will I be a disappointment to him, yet I will also be an embarrassment."

"You are a good woman, Mrs. Bingley," I urged.

"Thank you for your praises, Mrs. Darcy," Miriam replied, blushing a bit. "Yet when has the world ever cared for such a thing? Mr. Bingley may have descended from a family of trade, yet he is ever so close to being a gentleman in the eyes of the ton of London. And I come from a family, not only still in trade, but one from America. I will never deny my heritage, for it would be cowardly to do so, yet the ton shall call me to spoil with all the things that it shall say of me, and I fear that Charles's love for me might wane under the pressure of it. It would hurt me to see his love for me turn sour."

"I understand your fears. I had the same ones myself, and still do."

"Do you?"

"Darcy's family comes from the most prominent of the aristocracy, and I was a gentleman's daughter who had very low connections on my mother's side that made me altogether unsuitable to good society. I still have not faced the ton myself, yet together, when we are in London, you and I shall face the critical eyes of the masses, and much will be said of us." I reached out and touched her hand.

"Yet, while we need to rely on our own strength to bear us through such a trial, we are not alone in this fight. Your husband and mine are made of stronger sentiments than most and will not forsake those who they have promised to defend. And if the world does not accept us, then they both will have no fear in simply retiring with us to the county they reside in, where we are given a chance to be free of all scrutiny. You have friends here and may that be enough to face the world."

"I believe it is, for your friendship means much to me now." She paused a moment, and then added, "Mrs. Darcy, if I may ask you one more thing."

"Yes?"

"How do you do it?"

"Do what?"

"Live and love Mr. Darcy without intimidation, without fear that you are not up to the task? He and Charles are such large men, great men, and you never cower under the weight of the distinction of being his wife, or of your duties."

"I…I hadn't even thought about it. All I can simply say is that Darcy and I came to each other already knowing our strengths and weaknesses, therefore there was no chance for surprises. Only comfort and understanding. Whatever flaws you have, be honest about them to Charles, and cling to your virtues as well. And you shall never fear losing his love, for you have let him know every truth about you."

"Thank you."

There was a knock on the door and a voice was heard afterward.

"Mrs. Darcy?" Mr. Bingley said behind the wooden door, "I believe that you are keeping my wife from me."

"Yes, I am!" I laughed.

Miriam chuckled. "No, she is not. I was simply desirous of being a tease to you, Charles."

Miriam left my room to enjoy the bond and affection of being with her husband.

❦

After dinner had been served, we all went to our sleeping quarters individually to enjoy the intimacy of our own counsel. Georgiana, Kitty and Jane shared a room, while Darcy and I were in another room and Miriam and Charles were in the other one. Once we entered our sleeping chambers, my husband closed the door and turned to me.

"What is it?" I asked.

Darcy only looked at me with his cold and stern gaze which I learned long ago was a mask that covered his ardor.

"Fitzwilliam, we are on a ship."

"We can be quiet."

I tried to hide my surprise. "Can we?"

"Of course, we can."

Darcy walked up to me, turned me around and began to unfasten my dress.

"You are too stubborn. You know that?"

"No, I do not know that."

Once all my garments were removed, Darcy turned me around and ran his hands down my stomach.

"Can I not undress you now?" I replied archly.

"In time."

Darcy fell to his knees, cupped my breasts in his hands, lowered his lips to them and began to suckle me. My back arched as I did my best to stifle my moans.

"Fitzwilliam, I cannot guarantee that I shall be quiet. For how can I?"

"You must, my dear, for I cannot stop myself just now."

He carried me over to our cot and laid me down on it.

"Why can't I stop loving you ever?" I remarked with a wry smile.

"Because that would be most foolish," he murmured between mouthfuls.

"Oh really?" Breathing was becoming most difficult. "I dare say that you are trouble and have been for quite some time."

"You like the trouble I give you."

"You are never one to underestimate the power of seduction."

"No, I am not." He continued his ministrations.

He laid me down and began to run his hands all over me, then covering my mouth with his and we kissed deeply. Afterwards, I wrestled on top of him, pinning him down, settling myself against the erection in his trousers.

"Did I marry a headstrong woman?"

"Of course you did. And therefore, I am the only one worthy of you."

"Oh, are you?" Though his words were light, there was desire in his eyes.

"Yes, I very much am."

I looked down at his nude body beneath me.

"You are beautiful," I sighed, gently rocking against the pleasure that was building.

"You think so?" He expelled a sharp gasp of pleasure.

"Yes, I know it. And when you are shirtless and wearing nothing but breeches and your boots, I daresay that is my favorite look on you."

"You fantasize about me, admit it."

"Does the knowledge of that make you happy?"

"Yes, very much so."

"Then you have arrogance to your list of many sins." I tweaked a nipple.

"That doesn't do to me what it does to you, my love. Yet you tease and torment me."

"Yes, I do."

"Do you take pleasure in it?"

"Of course, I do." My breathing was becoming a bit labored.

"And why so?"

"Because, being tormented, my brilliant husband, leaves a very wonderful glow to your cheeks. I believe that it is the only thing that makes you blush."

"Lizzy..." His voice was husky.

"Yes?" I replied, running my hands down his chest.

"I want you to adore me now," he said, caressing me in between my thighs in my most intimate of places. I sighed, happy for him to remember that touching me there was my favorite of intimate embraces.

"How much adoration do you wish to have?" I could barely concentrate.

"Much."

"I think you are everything that is amiable and worthy."

"That is too tame," he whispered hoarsely, rubbing me faster. Yet, under his attentions, I began to lose myself utterly, falling out of focus, being rocked between crests of pleasure and ecstasy. The heat was beginning to move through my blood.

"I cannot focus. You are too persuasive and overpowering!" I breathed, trying to remain quiet. "When you touch me so, I lose all logic and control."

"Actually, that is better suited for adoring me. Now you must continue."

"I... oh, Fitzwilliam, this feels wonderful." Then he grabbed my breasts with his other hand and caressed me.

"And I never tire of it."

"Why do you never tire of it?" I tried not to come too soon.

"Because I cannot help but desire you always."

"You do?"

"I wish to always have you to myself." His voice was gruff with heated pleasure.

"Is that all?"

"No, it is not."

"What more?"

"I want to become one with you. I want to please you always. I must have you now, Fitzwilliam. I must have you take me, and you had better love me always."

"That is still not sufficient for me, Elizabeth." He teased my nipples with his fingers. "You must prove to me your passion before I proceed."

"I never want to be away from you. I want you always beside me. I never want to leave the bed, and I dream of you when you are away, Fitzwilliam."

"And what do you dream of in particular?"

"With me on my back, my legs around your neck and you making me ache for you."

"Oh, that is where your mind leads, then?"

He then rolled me over, wrapped my legs around his neck, leaned in and began to kiss me in my softest of places. This time it had been my turn to cover my mouth for I could not help the cries that escaped me.

The joys of such contentment never were or would be a fear or disgusting action in my eyes, for how could it be? How could such a beautiful act lead to anything less than a blissful event?

I pressed my hands on Fitzwilliam's head, running my fingers through his hair and then, when my body was spent, my whole form shuddered. Fitzwilliam raised himself up and smiled at me.

"You must not stop," I said. "Please continue to do as you ought."

"Why?"

"Because I am lost without your touch."

His smile was impish. "You are that desperate for me?"

"Yes. And I will not let you leave this bedroom until you have made me yours. Until you have taken me once more and made me the happiest of women."

"Now that was the perfect amount of adoration."

He then wrapped my legs around his waist, pressed himself within me and then we became one.

After we had reached our pinnacle, he lowered himself down next to me. His shoulders pressed against my chest, and I held him.

"I made you content?" I asked.

"Yes, very much so. Your words were precisely what I sought."

"Why did you need my worship just then?"

"Because...I suppose that I felt quite insecure."

"Did you?" I asked, feeling concerned. "What for?"

"For I think on all that we have left behind and what we look towards. I have lost our family in America now, I arrive home without much to show for it, and I will need your support now, Elizabeth. Now more than ever."

"Then take my strength," I said, "and continue to know that you have it. Yet Fitzwilliam, we did not lose the American Darcys. Believe me. Once Henry overcomes his rage, they shall look to us again, and they shall feel a desire to reconnect. And think of not where we have been, but of where we are going. You still have to take me to Pemberly, do you not?"

Darcy's face broke out into a genuine smile.

"Yes, I do. Oh, Elizabeth, you shall love it there! For there, I am at my best. There I am perfectly content, and you shall be happy."

"You make it appear as if it has your soul in it."

"It does. And it always will. Very soon, it shall have yours."

"Then I shall not be happy until I have seen it, in some ways."

"And what did that mean?"

"That I am always happy, as long as I have you beside me."

"Oh, well, that is very good as well, and would have been the only answer that I had accepted."

"What need you have now, my good sir, to be so naughty?"

"The need of any husband to want what is his to want, and then relish in victory afterwards."

I gave him a side long glance. "You look on me as a trophy?"

"You are a prize, I do regard as such, I admit."

"And why is that?"

"Because, you are the reward a man receives for doing the correct thing. For loving the right sort of woman. For choosing to be a good man. I was not once, and I would have gotten Anne de Bourgh for a wife. I am a good man, and now I have found you."

"And you shall never lose me."

"I had better not."

"Now, onto matters that you shall not like to hear."

He groaned and closed his eyes. "Oh, must we talk of such things?"

"Yes, we must," I teased, "for now that I have you susceptible to my charms, I am going to use it to my best advantage."

"You shall take advantage of me?"

"Yes," I replied, "out of vengeance for all the times that you had done so to me."

"Very well, she-devil, continue."

"Why thank you, spawn of Hecuba, now I shall begin."

❦

"Oh," he replied, "that is what you wish to talk about?"

"Yes, I know that Georgiana has already asked you, but I just wish to convince you as well, to let Kitty join us at Pemberly."

"I have heard my sister's arguments on the matter; therefore I am curious as to what yours would be."

"Practical. If Georgiana has a companion, she will not be lonely, and we shall be left to our own devices, because they have each other. And also, Kitty has been improving in mindset and in spirit every day that she has been away from home, to the point now where I worry that if she returns, she will not blossom into the woman that she is clearly on her way to becoming."

"Kitty is a very good sort of girl, that is true, and I admit that she is often under-appreciated. Yet why not Jane as well? Jane and you seem to be the closest."

"Jane is my bosom friend as well as my favorite sister, this is true, but Jane is a very independent sort of woman in her nature, and I know that when she returns to Longbourn, she will be fine and collected, for she always is. And Kitty is Georgiana's match for a comrade."

He raised a wary eyebrow. "And you are lying to me, my dear."

"What?"

"Yes. Or at least, you speak in half-truths. It's true, Kitty is Georgiana's favorite, it's true that Jane has a strong and serene will that will hold her firm, and therefore she does not need Pemberly in the way that Kitty does, yet that is not your overall objective, is it? You wish for Kitty to come so that you can begin to become the sister that you now wish you could have been to her."

My mouth nearly dropped open. "I don't understand how... Fitzwilliam! Were you listening in on my conversation with Kitty earlier?"

"Yes, I very much was." His answer was smug.

"You devil."

"Oh, as if you are innocent yourself in this matter," he said with a grin. "For before that, you were listening in on Kitty's discussion with Georgiana."

"You were listening in on that as well?"

"Yes, I was watching them, just as I was watching you as you were watching them. I believe that was double spy work on my behalf, and I congratulate myself for it."

"You watch me?"

"Yes, I do."

"You love me that much, do you?"

"Yes, yes I do."

"Then I forgive you."

He slanted me a glance. "I never apologized."

I pinched his nipple.

"Very well, I apologize," he countered, wincing.

"Very well, I accept."

"Yet, I am right, am I not? You wish to now become the sister you should have been to Kitty before now. A more devoted one. One who wishes to protect her from bad influences, and from falling from all that is good in her."

"Since travelling with her to London, when we worked in our father's factory, to going on holiday with her in Derbyshire, Fitzwilliam, I have seen a strong woman. And maybe even stronger than myself."

"I do not think that is possible to be."

"Fitzwilliam, remember, no matter what you did once, I could never deny you anything, or reject you."

"That is not weakness, my dear. You simply could not despise or turn from me because I was so marvelous a specimen of a man."

I pinched him again.

He winced again and chuckled. "Right. Sorry."

"Beloved, I can tell that you are anything but sorry."

"You are correct. I am not. I am very proud of myself just now, and my pride should be my downfall, yet I cannot help but enjoy it."

I smiled at his admission. "I can see that. But you are not wrong, so enjoy being correct again, O' arrogant one. Kitty's soul is a strong one, and it must be saved. And I didn't begin to be a more attentive older sister till last year, so I shall continue the progress that I have made."

"Then for the sake of your sense of debt, Georgiana's comfort, and for Kitty's permanent reformation into an amazing woman, yes, she can become Georgiana's companion and accompany us to Pemberly."

"Thank you, Fitzwilliam." I kissed him on the cheek.

"It is no inconvenience to me whatsoever. And I do like Kitty. She reminds me of you."

"Does she?"

"Yes. In truth, of all your sisters, she looks the most like you."

"Should I be concerned?" I replied, feigning anger, but just a slight bit.

"Am I losing my hearing, or are you sounding jealous simply because I am agreeing with you that your sister is a remarkable girl?"

"Oh, well... no."

"Yes, you were! You were getting jealous because I was giving your sister praise."

"Very well, but only a mere little."

"You lie again. You were really angry, and terribly jealous."

"Only a mere little!"

"Stop lying, woman. You don't like it when I give applause to any other woman but you."

I rolled him over, placed myself on top of him and began to run my hands further down his stomach, making him shudder.

"Very well, I do not. You may offer small compliments to them here and there, yet you must devote yourself to me completely when it comes to true praise. And I am a jealous woman, so there!"

"Oh, are you," he said, raising himself up and kissing me.

"Usually not, yet in your case, very much so, it seems. And I will not suffer any other woman to be higher than I am in your eyes."

"No woman shall ever be."

"Swear it!"

"I swear," he said, his eyes alight with amusement. "That I shall not ever think any woman higher than you."

"Very well, I am satisfied."

He gave me a cheeky look. "No, you are not. You want more than that. You want me to begin praising you now."

"Yes, I do," I whispered, bashful. "Am I so wicked?"

"Yes, very. Yet no more than I, for a moment ago, I demanded your adoration."

"Then you must not leave me ever unsatisfied, for I satisfy you often. Perhaps, I see, our flaws go hand in hand, and it is our imperfections that tie us to each other."

"Yet one virtue wraps itself around the flaws."

"And what virtue do we claim to have?"

"Loyalty, Elizabeth. We have loyalty."

"Too true. Even if I lost you irrevocably, I still would wait, I suppose. Loving another doesn't seem possible anymore. You do quite eclipse them all."

"Yes, even in my wickedness, I am enough for you."

Darcy leaned into me and we kissed, and then made love once more.

࿇

I looked down at my husband's sleeping form as he rested his head against my neck. I wrapped my arms around his shoulders and continued to study him.

He is perfect, I thought. *The perfect man, though filled with imperfections. What spirit lay beneath this complex character that he was? Need drove him, yet so did desire. So much so, that he would forsake any world or image in the end that did not encompass a bond. His very form and figure left nothing to be desired, not only from a physical view, but from a soulful one. His body seemed to encompass the truth. Even at his worst, he symbolized all that was best in me.*

All I had was my strength. The strength that would keep him company when left to his own wonderings and dark thoughts. The strength that would make him wrestle with the side of himself that was dark and fearful. I did not deny that I married a man with a red heart; bold, brave—but severe. Frightful, and under the right circumstances, an emotional weapon. Yet through all that darkness that was in him, there was a light. An inextinguishable light that a woman, who in love with him, could not help but walk towards, as if it was a path we must walk down.

That I must walk down.

I could never be with any other man but him, for he was in the very depths of my soul. He was the stones beneath the earth, and I was Darcy! He was forever in my mind, my heart, my subconscious, connected to me always, knotted to me so that he would never break away from my emotions. How did he get caught there? How did this love, this unbreakable and imperfect bond ever come to be? Even if Darcy had turned me away as he had once done, my mind would always chase him. For it would have always been my way. I would always chase after my Mr. Darcy.

Very soon, heavy under the weight and reflection on the day, of the many conversations and curiosities I had experienced, my thoughts turned toward Pemberly, to think of what the place was that possessed Darcy's soul to such a degree, and would I find our connection even more bound there.

❦ 3 ❦

THE INTERMISSION

After a little less than a month at sea, we arrived in London.

When we reached town, I took comfort in our arrival, for it was the next best thing to being at home.

"Oh, Mr. Darcy," Jane said as we rode in our carriage. "Is there any way, while being in London, may we see the Gardiners?"

Darcy nodded. "Of course. You did not think I would deny you such a luxury, did you? As a matter of fact…"

And here, Darcy leaned out of the carriage window. "Jefferson!"

"Yes sir?" Jefferson said from the carriage driver seat as he sat with the coachman.

"When we arrive, may you write a letter for me as invitation to the Gardiners to inform them that we should like them to dine with us when we settle into Grosvenor Square?"

"Already done, sir. When we arrived, I wrote a letter under my own name telling them you would like to receive them at your townhouse this Sunday, for I knew that we would have settled by then."

"Of course, you did." Darcy released a contented sigh, and then he turned to me. "There, all is in hand." His expression changed when he noticed all of us looking at him, incredulous. Did Jefferson truly know Darcy's mind, mood and intentions even before Darcy knew them himself? How strong was their bond and what had formed it?

"Oh," my husband uttered. "What can I say? It's Jefferson."

I decided to test a theory.

"Jefferson?" I asked, leaning my head out of the window of the carriage.

"Yes, Mrs. Darcy?" Jefferson said, turning from looking at the road and tipping his hat to me.

"By any chance," I began, "do you know the weather for the rest of the week?"

"Oh, well, I believe the rest of today shall be sunny, tomorrow it shall rain, then the next day it shall be sunny at first then rain in the afternoon, and the two days after that, it will be sunny but the cold will be deplorable."

"And you are certain of this?" I asked, archly.

"One can never be certain with nature and the weather, ma'am, but I believe that I am correct. Now let us find out, shall we?"

"Yes, let us."

I leaned my head back into the carriage, looking at my husband.

"What are the chances that he is inaccurate?" I arched an eyebrow at him.

"Very little, my dear. Very very little."

❦

The next day it did rain, then the next it was sunny at first, but rained in the early evening. I could not begrudge Jefferson for being off by only a couple of hours, however. Once in Grosvenor Square, I immediately felt comforted, for we were so close to being home. We arrived on Friday, Mr. Bingley and Miriam went to Bingley's townhouse where they would dine with us the next evening. When we arrived at Darcy's townhouse, we were greeted by the servants of Fitzwilliam's household, who this time I greeted them as not just a guest, but as their new mistress of the house, Mrs. Darcy, their employer's wife.

I decided, rather than press my authority, to act as I had when I had first entered it as nothing but a dinner guest and meet them all with the same harmless congeniality I had before. In truth, I did not care to press my pride forward and exert myself on them as of yet, but rather, was content to watch Georgiana, and follow her example on how to run the household the way that Fitzwilliam was used to it being so.

I did not wish to change the way he was used to living, and letting his sister take the lead as she had done so before would be a wonderful way to easily learn all that I should. Besides, I had married Darcy for the sake of being his wife, not for becoming the ruler of a household. One brought the other, but I would take pleasure in the first, and learn the trade of the second by necessity and from a desire to make him proud of me.

"I remember this place." Kitty released a sigh when we entered, twirling around. "And for a time, I never thought that I would see it again. Oh Jane, so many fond memories we had here!"

"Did you?" Jane said, for this was her first time in Darcy's townhouse and she took it in with serenity and sweetness of temper. "And I see that you enjoyed it. Mr. Darcy, you have a lovely home here."

"Thank you, Miss Bennet, and I hope you shall enjoy your stay here."

"I believe I shall, sir."

For a brief moment, I worried about not thinking Jane should come with us to Pemberly, yet I knew that she did miss Longbourn. In truth, we all did in one form or another.

"I should show you our home," Georgiana said, "yet I know you want to retire."

"But," Darcy began to object, "routine must be attended to Georgiana and—"

"Fitzwilliam," I interrupted, "I am of your mind in all things, but this is my last chance to be selfish, and from after this day forth, I shall always wish to be in harmony with your devotion to protocol, yet now I wish to enjoy your company for it is your company, and not the home that it is in. We all just wish to sit and be peaceful and content. Georgiana can show us your home tomorrow, and show me all that will make you happy, but for now, let us all go to our bedrooms, change our attire, and sit by the fire where we can enjoy being in your home because we are sitting by you."

Darcy looked around us all and saw four women looking up at him, imploringly, smiling. His will, though always one of strength, now weakened. How could he say no to us? For even he knew that his iron determination was no match for four women who looked at him so.

He shrugged his shoulders and sighed. "Very well. Yet tomorrow, routine will be obeyed."

I kissed him on the cheek, took his hand in my own and we all followed the maid who took us to our individual rooms. Kitty and Jane would stay in adjoining rooms while Georgiana had her own. My husband led me to our bedroom where he made it quite clear that we would share rather than us having our own rooms. I agreed, happy that he knew it was how I always wanted it to be.

When we were alone, he turned to me.

"You are so lucky that I was hoping you would want us to retire this way."

"I know, but it wasn't fully luck. When I want something, I seek it and fight for it. You know enough about my frank manner to know that if I desired you, I would have no scruples of fighting to persuade you even in front of our family."

"You must attempt to not use my weakness for you so much again, Elizabeth."

"Yet I will. Once more, as always."

"I love you."

"You had better."

"Shall I ring the bell and have my servant draw a bath for all of us?"

"That would be splendid. Yet may we take our bath first, before our sisters do?"

"Yes and wait, do you wish for us to take a bath together?"

"You do not wish for me to bathe you?"

Darcy immediately blushed and looked down. "I have never had a woman bathe me before."

"Well as your wife, I shall be happy to be the first, and hopefully the last."

"Then the first and the last you shall be."

In the bathtub, soaking in hot water, I sat atop Darcy and ran a hand towel over his arms and chest, and he had his hands wrapped around my thighs and bottom.

"This feels nice." He sighed and closed his eyes

"I am happy that it does. Yet more so, I am happy that my impulses tell me true with you. I was worried that when we married, I would not understand nor learn how to please you, yet it comes so organically. Pleasing you seems natural and my instincts take over more than thought and long deliberation."

"Then you were made to love me, it is settled."

"Oh, was I?"

"Elizabeth Darcy, you very much were. And it feels nice."

"Does it? Tell me why it does." I continued to bathe him with the cloth.

"My life, for so long, was quite a dreary thing, a somber one, and with all my wealth, it was a constricted one, where all I did was under the steady and stern gaze of servants and the ton. And having you now, so full of liberty, it is pleasing to know that something like you was made for me in particular."

"You are a spoilt man," I teased, washing down his thighs.

"Elizabeth," he said, his voice lowering, sounding desperate and serious, "you must never stop."

"On the contrary," I said, looking him in the eye. "I have to stop bathing you sometime. When your skin starts to wrinkle is a good sign."

"That is not what I mean. I mean, I want you to always spoil me."

I shook my head and smiled. "I can do that. For I know that it shall not go to your head and be the ruin of you."

"I want all of you to do so."

"What do you mean by all of us?"

Fitzwilliam closed his eyes and leaned against the copper tub.

"What you said earlier," he began, "when all four of you looked at me and you said that you wanted to just be around me. The look in all four of you as you expected me to agree to such a plan, well, it reminded me of when I sat with you all at Longbourn, with your family, the Austen sisters and Miss Jane Austen telling us about her book, *Sense and Sensibility*. All of you were just happy to be near me for no other reason than you wanted my company. You wanted me for me. That is not something I am used to. Call me selfish, yet I liked the sight of you all wishing to be around me for the sake of me only and no other reason."

I studied his beautiful features. "Did it make you feel stronger?"

"In a way, it made me feel more at peace. And peace, well, it is a form of strength."

I lowered the rag and looked deep into his eyes.

"Then you need us?"

"Yes. I need you in love with me. And I need their love for me as well. I suppose, it is family. I desire more of it that is congenial."

"Then you shall always have it. And I was being sincere, as were they all. We like your presence; it is all that I can say by way of explanation. Your presence amongst us makes us feel the presence of your mind and, well, you are home itself, Fitzwilliam. When we all look upon you, you make us feel like we are home... and I now believe that our skin is wrinkling, and we are done bathing."

"Mr. Darcy," Kitty began as we ate dinner, "while we are in London, will we see any of your family?"

"Oh, that is a comical story."

"How comical?" Kitty urged. "And if you decided to say that it is a long story, then I shall say the only thing I can to persuade you to continue."

"And what is that, Miss Kitty?" Darcy chuckled quietly.

"I will say that we are eating dinner, and therefore we have plenty of time."

We all laughed.

"Very well," Darcy conceded. "And you need not worry, for it is not a long one. When arriving to London, Jefferson proposed that it would be wise to invite my Aunt and Uncle Fitzwilliam, the Earl of Matlock, to the dinner that your Aunt and Uncle Gardiner will attend. I agreed and sent the letter already."

"Oh." I pressed a hand to my heart. "Fitzwilliam, that was a perfect idea, and our aunt and uncle will be most gratified."

"I wish I could take the credit, but it was Jefferson's idea."

"And that is another story that you have not told. The Curious Case of the Valet named Bartholomew Jefferson."

"Now that is a long story that is too long for dinner."

"You are intentionally not telling us something," I commented archly.

"Am I that bad of a liar?"

"Yes. I shall let you forego that story now, for something tells me that Jefferson's story is his story and when I wish to know it, I should ask him."

"I suppose that if any has the right to tell it, he does."

"Then back to your family, will the Earl of Matlock bring any of his three sons to dine as well?"

"Your uncle and aunt had three boys?" Jane inquired.

"Yes," Georgiana added, "they had six sons in total, yet one died of pneumonia when he was a child, and the other two died in infancy."

"Six boys initially?" Kitty was incredulous. "So they were a male case of our family, but plus one. I wonder if the circumstances were reversed, how our mother would have felt under such a case."

"Probably suffering less from her ever-present nerves!" I added.

"All too true," Kitty agreed. "And less inclined to marry us off to whoever seemed even the slightest bit suitable. That would have been a great comfort!"

"Kitty," Georgiana said, "then is it true? That your mother tried to coerce you into marrying my aunt's clergyman, Mr. Collins?"

"Oh, dear lord, Georgiana! Not only is it very true, yet the method I chose to escape that fate was not so glamorous. I climbed up a tree and refused to come down until they allowed me to refuse him."

"Truly?" Georgiana laughed.

"Yes, truly, and I'll tell you the whole tale of it."

Kitty then told the whole story of the disastrous 'courtship' Mr. Collins offered her and Georgiana enjoyed the tale while Darcy only pretended to act indifferent about the subject when in reality, he loved hearing the story and was hanging on every word.

When Kitty finished her narrative, Jane sighed.

"Imagine how it all could have ended otherwise," she speculated. "Say that he was wiser and more attentive to the truth, he would have seen that Mary was not averse to wedding him, yet instead of witnessing her preference for him, he shifted his attentions to you, Kitty. Yet if he had sought Mary all the while, she would have married him without a doubt, she would be Mrs. Collins, Longbourn would stay an entail that remained in the family, and Kitty would have never climbed up a tree."

"It could have ended even more different than that," I added, enjoying thinking of the paths not followed but potentially could have been. "If you had not been engaged at the time, surely Mr. Collins would have probably thought to have courted you, Jane."

"Very true, Mr. Brocklehurst, in all his villainy, was good for saving me at something." Jane's smile was pensive. "Yet while pondering the roads that could have been taken if our lives had been altered, we also must thank our mother in your circumstance. For if she had not been so bent on you and Mr. Bingley becoming intertwined, then she would have encouraged Mr. Collins to pursue you, which he might have done in Kitty's stead."

I laughed at that scenario. "Yes. Our mother's machinations were good for something in that case. Her convincing herself that Mr. Bingley and I were headed for courtship resulted in her dissuading Mr. Collins to think on me."

While I lifted my fork to my mouth to take another bite of food, I somehow felt a stern gaze upon me. Almost sensing disquiet, I turned to see my husband's gaze fixed and troubled.

"Your mother," he began, "had encouraged a match between you and Mr. Bingley?"

His eyes said everything. He was angry.

"Well," I stammered, "well, yes, yet Fitzwilliam, there was never any sincerity or evidence to her assumptions. You have met my mother, and you know how she quickly makes matches with no truth to them."

"Yes, yes," Jane added hurriedly, realizing that her jest had led to her acknowledging something that she didn't even know would affect Darcy in any way. "Our mother simply saw them dance together at the assembly and quickly began to devise a scheme that never had anything else in it but her hopes and dreams."

"Yes," Darcy replied, and to which we all saw the disturbance in his eyes, for her explanation did not settle his objections alone. "Yes."

Jane looked at me, clearly feeling guilty to have caused any doubts or tension to a dinner that had none.

I looked back at her, trying to communicate that I was not angry.

Kitty looked at Darcy quickly, then at Georgiana.

Georgiana looked at her brother, a little vexed at his response.

Darcy looked down at his food and ate with more alacrity.

We all looked at him, but he would not look up at us.

And I was frightened.

And there was nothing that I could say at the moment.

"Well, then," Georgiana began, trying to diffuse the tension. "Fitzwilliam, you forgot to mention if any of our cousins will join our Aunt and Uncle for the dinner party."

"Oh, yes," he replied, doing his best to come out of his gloom. "The eldest, Henry Fitzwilliam, the son and heir will attend, but not Acton, who is the youngest. Due to Henry's inheriting Matlock and all the wealth of the family, Richard and Acton have had to become men of profession, and Acton is going into the church as well, and taking Holy Orders, where he will inherit the parish on our Uncle's estate and begin his own services when he finishes his studies."

"Then," Jane added, "Colonel Richard Fitzwilliam, the middle son, is not wishing to join us?"

"He is still in the service and is training a new regiment that he oversees. He is not even in London, but in Northampton now, at camp."

"It is strange," Kitty added. "Yet all this talk of a man who I have and always will hear much about, but have not met. It makes one wonder if he will live up to the legend."

"Does he have a legend to his name?" Fitzwilliam asked, looking slightly jealous of hearing the intrigue that the Colonel had to him.

"Of course he does," Kitty replied confidently. "For a few reasons."

"And what would those reasons be?"

"For one, he is your cousin, whom you favor, and favors you, which makes him seem worthy. For he has your good opinion, which is not so readily bestowed, and makes it more worth the earning. Also, he was the means through which you realized that Lizzy was and forever would be the perfect match for you. Therefore, how can I not see the wonder that is him?" Darcy looked at Kitty, smiled gently, feeling the compliment she gave him keenly, and then looked at his dinner plate.

"My cousin is a legend," he acknowledged. "And is a good man who has it in him to make others good. And he has fortune on his side. It seems to be in his destiny to have it, even if he did not inherit the wealth of his family's name. Any war cannot kill him. Therefore, you shall meet him soon, I feel it."

"Then I hope to think him as good and amiable as any other whom I am open to getting to know."

"And," Jane added, "I am certain that we shall love him, almost as readily as Elizabeth learned to love you. As we all wish to love you."

Darcy rested his eyes on me, and I smiled encouragingly. He felt more confident with all the compliments he was then receiving, and his demeanor did improve for the rest of the evening.

After dinner, we sat in the sitting room by the fire briefly, before we all retired to bed. Once we entered Darcy's bedroom, I turned to him as we closed the door.

"Fitzwilliam," I began, "before any silence reigns on you, I wish to remind you that I love you and—"

I was overcome with Darcy's embrace, for he rushed to me and kissed me savagely. Then he turned me around, unfastened my dress as quickly as he could, to the point where he ripped the buttons clean off and ruined the fastenings. When done so, he tore all my undergarments off, removing my stockings and all doing so with swiftness I never thought possible of him. When I stood bare, he lifted me up and threw me on the bed. He only removed his own jacket and shoes before he simply unbuttoned his trousers, climbed on top of me and drove himself within me with an urgency that showed his purpose.

I wrapped my arms around his shoulders as he rocked back and forth within me. There was no delicacy in his actions at the moment; all that remained was his passion and the rashness from possessing what he deemed to be his own. Yet his desire to establish his dominance did nothing to deter me from enjoying his passion and his urgency. There was still a beauty to it, for it was pure. I enjoyed him still. And I adored him even more.

When he reached his full arousal, his back arched, and his seed was spent. He did not get up and remove his clothing however, but only rested on top of me as I ran my hands through his hair.

"Elizabeth..."

"Fitzwilliam. I love you."

"And I know it. I do. You have always given yourself to me. And yet, within me is this fear, this voice that keeps crying out, like a frail voice out of the shadows. Is it true, did your mother really intend you for Bingley?"

"He danced with me at the assembly, Fitzwilliam, and his open nature made him appear as if he was offering me his attentions. Therefore, my mother, in her haste to unite me with a suitable husband, naturally clung to the idea that Mr. Bingley would be perfectly suited for me. Therefore, to answer you simply, yes she did plan me for him."

I felt Darcy's body grow tense.

"Yet you must understand," I hurried on, "it wasn't out of partiality for him only. You must remember, you did everything to make it appear as if you despised me, and you succeeded, making me despise you in turn. If you had offered me encouragement from the beginning, she would have leaned toward you."

"Elizabeth... did you ever wish for Mr. Bingley to have shown you special attention?"

"Fitzwilliam..."

"Elizabeth, please, answer the question."

"Over time, I cared for him not at all, yet in the beginning, when you seemed to not care for me, I thought of the idea of him, yes."

"Ah..."

"Yet I very quickly learned that I did not like him, nor did he like me. It was all simply soft flirtation that ended even before it could have begun."

"He liked you in return, Elizabeth."

"What?"

"Yes, at first, he found you attractive. He wanted you to remain at Aginfield because a part of him desired you. And I, in my wickedness and desire to keep you from the attentions of any man, while also hypocritically not offering you anything as well, did my best to make him find you unsuitable."

"You…you slandered me?"

"I did not sully your good name. I simply tried to dissuade him from finding you desirable."

"You tried to ruin me?" I gasped, lifting his head. "At the time, you refused to acknowledge your love for me! You did not give me a chance! Yet if your friend, Mr. Bingley, had offered me something, had truly wished to seek me out, and if I had reciprocated his sentiments, then you were willing to separate us, all so that your heart could not be wounded? The very heart that you shut away of your own free will?"

"Elizabeth, I…"

I pushed him off me and sat up. "No, Fitzwilliam, I will be heard! Are you telling me that your first intention to me was not only to *not* make me an offer of marriage, yet it was to defame me in the face of another man who did? Who if you had never come to your senses, could have saved myself and my family from destitution, and saved my heart from never learning love? Fitzwilliam, you could have been the ruin of me and my family."

"I…"

I crossed my arms over my bosom. "Please tell me that you see that!"

"I do… I do see it."

"Is this the man I have found perfect despite his flaws? A man who would have willingly separated me from a potentially happy ending, exposing his friend to the world for caprice, and me to its derision of disappointed hopes. And involving me to misery of the acutest kind? Do you deny it?"

"I do not deny it."

I turned away from him. "Then I must despise you now."

"You must not, Elizabeth. Do not turn from me."

"You are mistaken to think the mode of your declaration spares me any concern I might feel in denying you my forgiveness now, for memory of when you did not behave in a more gentlemanlike manner!"

"You hate me now?" he whispered harshly, half angry and half in sorrow. "Elizabeth, you wouldn't."

"I would. Are men so easily led, and they have no will of their own? Those who are good-natured, such as Mr. Bingley are ruined by being influenced by those who are bad."

"Take care my love," he replied, his eyes turning dark in the candlelight, hollow with anger, "that savors strongly of bitterness. Bitterness toward me."

"I feel it now."

"Then perhaps you married the wrong man! Perhaps you would be happier with Bingley!"

"I never said that!"

"Then what are you saying, wife!"

"That I want you to always care how your actions affect others. You once had such a selfish disdain for the feelings of others and called it integrity. I gave you my heart from the very beginning. Even when your manners impressed me with proof of your arrogance, your conceit, and your implacable resentment, you were always in my mind."

I sniffed back unwilling tears. "And now, to find out that you sulk at a table because you are angry to find that I once opened myself up to a different path. A path, that if you had accepted me from the start, I would have never thought to walk down. And then, if that path would have been a sincere one, you would have ruined it, all for the sake of ceasing your jealousy and your iron pride?"

I dashed away tears of anger and frustration with my fingers. "Did you never care about how you almost ruined my life? For you almost did, too many times. I forgave you for all of them, yet I do not know if I can forgive you now. For I know that you, in the name of all that is righteous, have it in you to ruin a life and not care for the mess you make of it afterwards. Now leave me."

"Elizabeth..."

"I said leave me! Before I sock you, Fitzwilliam."

Looking resigned and forlorn, my husband Fitzwilliam rose up off me, fixed his clothing and walked to the door.

"I was never worthy of you, Elizabeth," he whispered. "I know that every day. Yet you promised that you would never turn from me. Please remember that promise."

He left me alone. At the sound of the door closing, I leaned into the pillows and began to weep.

How had I come to love such a man? The depths of his pride were profound; his blindness to how he could inflict such permanent damage to another person was frightening. He could hurt people, and then call it necessary afterwards.

Yet I wanted him still. Even at that very moment, I felt that I missed him beside me. Love truly, in all essentials, was the enemy of logic and reason. I could not remain angry with him when every part of my soul cried out to forgive him. Yet was I right to? Or was I to not forgive? To let the conflicting voices cry out in my soul, tearing me in two as I remained in a state of confusion.

Darcy was the earth beneath, every rock and bit of soil beneath my feet. And I could not deny that he was what made all feel steady. Yet my life was steady before him, and that autonomy that I possessed, surely I could find my way back there again.

The answer was hidden from me however, and I knew that I would not sleep that night, for the indecision was the enemy of slumber. For the moment, there was an intermission to my bond to him, a break in the consistency of it, and tomorrow, I would wake, and another act would begin. Tomorrow I would decide which way my mind leaned. Would I love Darcy tomorrow, or would I choose to never trust him again?

❧ 4 ❧

FIGHT AS LONG AS WE LIVE

The next day, I awoke, and felt strong in my stance. I stood up, wrung for the maid and she helped me dress. When I felt that I was presentable, I inquired about where Darcy was, and she said evenly that he had slept in the adjoining bedroom that was made for the mistress of the household, but he awoke early and had taken an early morning ride. At present, he was in his study, with Georgiana. I thanked the maid, and when finished, I left and went downstairs toward the study. However, when I reached the door, I heard Georgiana's voice from the other side of it.

"What did you do?" she cried from within.

"Georgiana, quiet yourself and remember decorum."

"Yet you do not. I saw the look in your eye, and I know that you did not sleep in the same room, which leaves me to deduce that there is tension between the two of you. And I know that you caused it. Fitzwilliam, you cannot be angry with her for liking Mr. Bingley. He is charming and engaging, whereas you are a harder man to get to know, of your own choosing. Fitz, even I liked Mr. Bingley once."

"Dear god, does everyone like Charles?"

"That's rich, coming from the man who clings to him so desperately as a friend."

"I see your point."

"Fitzwilliam, all that I am saying is that you cannot blame Elizabeth or

55

her mother, for holding any design on that score, for it was clearly a temporary sentiment with no validity behind it."

"Georgiana, it is more than that. I hurt her terribly, and there was a point where I had almost ruined her life."

"Tell me something I do not know?"

"What?"

"Fitz, you are always almost ruining Elizabeth's life. For some reason or another, you make it a habit."

"When did you learn to speak to me thus?"

"When I gained five sisters and realized that there was nothing in you to fear."

"You... you feared me?" he replied, sounding hurt.

"Everyone does. Fitz, you have such potency to your demeanor that how could I not feel some slight awe at you? Yet now I realize that, seeing what another family life is like, standing up to you is healthy. Not simply for me, but for you as well. You cannot have your own way, Fitz. And for too long you were allowed to."

"It is different this time."

"How so?"

"Georgiana, I do not believe that she will forgive me this time."

"What do you mean?" Georgiana asked, startled. "Of course she does. She *is* you."

And that was when I decided to knock on the door and announce myself.

I entered after the fourth knock.

"Good morning all," I said. "Georgiana, did you sleep well?"

"Yes," Georgiana said, looking at me, her face pale as a ghost. "Yes, I did."

"I am glad to hear it. Good morning, Fitzwilliam."

"Morning, Elizabeth," he said, looking like stone.

"Well, forgive me for interrupting what I'm sure was a very integral intercourse between a very devoted brother and sister, yet Georgiana, would you forgive my rudeness and ask if I might speak with your brother alone?"

"Yes, of course, Lizzy."

Georgiana walked past me and left.

"You have a brilliant sister," I said, when we were alone.

"Yes, she is. Did you sleep well, Elizabeth?"

"Of course not, and you know that I did not."

"Yes, I suppose. If it is of any consolation, I did not sleep well either."

"That is of some comfort actually. I spent most of the night in deliberation, of whether I should remember my promise, or whether I should turn from you, which I have discovered, I do not fear in doing so."

"You would abandon me?"

I chose not to answer his question but continued telling him my conclusion.

"I have reached a decision of what I should do. I know which path I choose to take."

Darcy's eyes narrowed on me, out of fear.

"Elizabeth..."

"You shall let me finish, Fitzwilliam."

He glanced at his shoes. "Yes, yes I will."

He stood there frozen, as did I. Fear overwhelmed him, and I knew where his apprehensions lay, in a delicate balance of expectation but anxiety of what was going to come next. Would I admit to him that I would never trust him again, that we would be wife and husband in name only, but never again in harmony, or would I forget as well as forgive? Would we rise above this, or fall into the darkness of our path's separation and the bond broken?

I walked up to his desk, where he stood on one side, and I sat in the seat that was opposite, looking up at him.

"I made a promise to you once," I began, "that no matter what, I would never turn from you. As you had so reminded me the night before."

"And?"

I breathed out evenly, choosing my words carefully.

"And to that I hold," I answered. "I always will hold. Fitzwilliam, you had hurt me once, but not only will I forgive, but I will forget it. You are a part of my soul, and I will not be severed from it because of a past mistake that you made."

Darcy closed his eyes, his shoulders relaxed, and he rested his hands against his desk.

"Elizabeth, have you no idea how frightened I was?"

"Yes, I do. I wanted you to be frightened."

"Did you?"

"Yes, very much so."

"So, all this torture you had me endure..."

"Oh, do not complain to me of this 'little' bit of torture I had you endure,"

I exclaimed, raising up my arms for emphasis, "First of all, you deserved it. Secondly, it was miniscule compared to the suffering I endured when I thought you would never propose to me. And thirdly, it was the only way that I could think of you ever learning from your mistake."

"How so?"

"Well, think on it. Fitzwilliam, if I only got angry with you for a little, then you would feel no more than a slap on the wrist and might fall back into your old ways. Yet if you learned to fear such a response to your actions, then you would feel as if you were burned by fire, and you would not want to make the same mistake twice. You would learn—you must. While I prefer you infinitely to your cousin, Henry Darcy, you and I both cannot deny that you and he are similar. You make the same mistakes of not seeing how your actions have a negative effect upon others, and that the damage can be irreparable. Think on it. When we met, you were engaged to your cousin, Anne, but if you had been single, do you truly not think that you would have found something else to hinder your cause to love me? You, who once weighed so much by the master power of Gain, Society, status and position amongst the ton? You, Fitzwilliam?"

My husband looked down at his hands and I gathered the resolve to continue.

"Oh no, there is a chance that you would still have hardened yourself against me, and I know that somehow. Therefore, learn now, more than any other time, that you must not be so keen to act without regarding the feelings of others or your offenses against them. And your good opinion, once lost, should not be lost forever, if the person did nothing to gain it in the first place."

"You are worried that I will make the same mistake."

"I am worried that you will not ever open yourself up to the fact that you can be wrong. And I do not wish for that to stop you from letting the right one in again."

My husband looked shaken.

"Oh, do stop looking so broken." I stood up, then sat on his desk, whipping my legs over it, crawling toward him and then standing up in front of him while I ran my hands down his chest. Instinctively, he wrapped his arms around me. "For after all, it's not as if I am perfect either."

"No," he agreed, "you are not. You are close to it, but even you have your moments."

"Yes," I said, willing to allow his critique of me, for I believed that he needed to say it to feel more confident. "And I will have my moments where I will falter in regards to sound mind and judgment, and then it shall be your turn to forgive me and help me find my way to a more correct path."

Darcy sat down and pulled me onto his lap, where I let him hold me as if I were a child. Indeed, I quite liked it when he did that.

"Yet I must assure you of one thing."

"What is that?" he asked, his brow arching.

"Fitzwilliam, we are going to argue again, it is our way. With two stubborn individuals in love with each other as we are, emotions are going to run and flow deep and disturbed sometimes, but I shall never change toward you. I will always love you, be bound to you, be loyal, and I will never turn away from you. No matter your flaws or mine, steady I shall always be, therefore, no longer should you fear to lose me in any way. No matter how angry I get, or sullen, I will remember my desire for you always. You shall never lose your wife."

"Oh, Elizabeth. You swear this?"

"I do, and it's a swear that I shall easily hold to."

I took his face in my hands and fondled it while he smiled gently.

I sighed. "Ah. There you are. Fitzwilliam Darcy, the man who is content with himself."

We kissed passionately, and I rubbed my nose against his.

"Falling in love with you was easy," he whispered. "Having you fall in love with me was surprisingly easy as well yet maintaining your love shall be hard."

"Stay loyal to me," I said, "and it shall be maintained."

"Then it shall stay in turn. And yet," he said, running his hand under my gown, and wrapping his fingers around my thighs, "that doesn't stop the fact that you did torture me a bit with your silence last night."

"Oh, just a little torture."

"A mere little is still much with you." He pulled my dress down below my chest, exposing my breasts and he began to kiss them while I rested my head against his hair and sighed in happiness.

"You were right to marry me," he said, "for you saved me from much and I would have been lost without you."

"Indeed, I was right to do so. And your love is something I will always fight for, and fight for as long as we live."

❧ 5 ❧

BLESS BE THE TIES THAT BIND

D arcy spent the rest of the day appearing lighter, more content, and his mood affected us all. Kitty asked him if we could all take a turn in the park, for she wished to be out of doors for some reason. I always welcomed a good walk, as all ought to recall from my notorious long miles walk to Aginfield Park. Jane and Georgiana were wishing for one as well, and Darcy was quickly learning that his desire to please us was something that had a very strong hold on him.

We at first wondered if we should call on Mr. Bingley and Miriam, yet we knew they would wish to keep to themselves, for they were newlyweds after all.

Therefore, we went to the park, and Darcy would every now and again come across an acquaintance of his and would introduce us. Jane received the most attention after me, for her beauty was breathtaking as well as stately.

We soon found ourselves invited for many tea-times to a Mrs. Sofia Knightly, a Miss Amelia and Miss Soarse Kensington, who were twins that had just come out into society a summer before. It was made clear that they once had a soft spot for Mr. Darcy, and once had designs on him. I accepted their invitation out of politeness, yet my jealousy got the better of me and I secretly did not like them at all. However, many offers had to be postponed once Darcy made it very clear that we would only stay in town briefly.

As we walked through the woods, with our sisters talking together amiably, I took Darcy's arm.

"Too many of the women we have met today stared at you with fond admiration and secret disdain for me," I whispered. "And while I should be flattered that they recognize your regality and beauty, I do not deny that I wish to claw their eyes out."

"Do you?" He laughed, and then stifled his reaction.

"Yes, very much so. I know that they did not know of my existence once, but it does not keep me from an irrational and implacable resentment for them wishing to have once coveted what is mine."

"Oh..." he said, hiding his grin.

"Yes, and I have no shame in admitting it to you."

"Why, Mrs. Darcy, are you irrationally jealous and covetous of me?"

"Yes, very much so."

He gave a contented sigh. "How flattering. I do not, nor will not ever reprimand your obsession over me, even if it sounds indelicate."

"I know. Though our sins go hand in hand. As a man, your mistakes are that every man is still a child in some ways. To be a woman is to let our emotions make us very much imbalanced sometimes and takes us long to find our way back to the road of logic. Therefore, I find it amusing, and we may be called even."

His laugh was triumphant. "You are possessive of me! That is an insanity that I do welcome, if you reveal it to me only."

"I will always reveal it to you only. Especially since I see that it makes you feel special."

"Oh yes, my darling Lizzy. Very special."

We walked on through the park, and the day appeared to have brought us much peace and gifts.

The evening fell, and we waited in anticipation as all that we hoped for came.

First it was Aunt and Uncle Gardiner and when they arrived, all was met with warmness and familial bliss.

"Jane!" Aunt Gardiner cried happily when they arrived, and we received them in the hall. "And Elizabeth, Kitty, and Miss Darcy, it is wonderful to see you all."

"Aunt and Uncle Gardiner," we cried, rushing up to them and practically tackling our aunt in an embrace. Kitty pulled Georgiana in the embrace as well and we all hugged while Fitzwilliam and Uncle Gardiner shook hands. Such public displays of affection were neither common nor customary ever, yet we were so happy to see our aunt again that it overwhelmed any care for prudence.

"You missed us, I see," Uncle Gardiner declared, smiling merrily. "And Mr. Darcy, I daresay that I have never seen my nieces happier."

"Then I can claim myself content that I have done right," Mr. Darcy replied as we entered the sitting room and had tea, as we waited for the rest of the company to arrive, which was not long. Not five minutes after they arrived, Darcy, who had been waiting by the window, saw the next carriage and we all went down to see the butler open the door and we rushed out to meet the Fitzwilliams, the Earl and Lady of Matlock.

※

Earl of Matlock was as I remembered him. Large, prominent and direct. When he and his wife stepped out of the carriage, his eyes immediately sought me out.

"Ah, there is the woman who caught my nephew, and her gaggle of sisters."

"And it was a worthy conquest," I added. "And I believe that I have made good work of it."

His gaze stayed on mine. "Still direct as ever, I see."

"In reply to the equally direct."

"Upon my honor," said another man who looked similar to Colonel Fitzwilliam as he stepped down from the carriage after his mother. "I heard legends of your forwardness, Mrs. Darcy, yet I did not believe the tales to be true."

"And her forwardness is a virtue," Darcy replied, coming to my defense. "The very best of them."

"Especially in your case," the man replied. "For where you are involved, anything less would not be worthy of you."

"Ladies of Longbourn," Mrs. Fitzwilliam began, already annoyed with how the turn of the conversation had taken, "this is our eldest son, Henry Fitzwilliam."

"Ladies," Henry Fitzwilliam said, bowing. "I am honored to make your acquaintance."

We all curtsied.

"And this is their Aunt and Uncle," Mr. Darcy added, "Mr. and Mrs. Gardiner."

Henry bowed to them as well and then said, "More new acquaintances. And each as pleasing to meet as the next." He added, "Mr. and Mrs. Gardiner. Now, to the Bennet girls. I have heard rumors of your beauty and for once, gossip was correct."

"Yes, the gaggle of pulchritude," Lord Fitzwilliam added.

"As much as I enjoy being found pleasing to the eye," Kitty said, smiling, "I had never thought my sisters and I would be labeled as a 'gaggle'. Nay, we are more like a 'pride'; for I daresay we have more in common with lions than geese."

"My word!" Lord Fitzwilliam exclaimed. "You're a cheeky one as well."

"Cheek and wit go hand in hand, sir," Aunt Gardiner replied. "And wit must always be welcome."

"As does truth," I said, coming to Kitty's defense. "To be a Bennet woman, one of five daughters, is to always speak your words up sharp, for only then will you be heard."

"You despise silence?" Henry Fitzwilliam seemed amused.

"Only when words should be used in their place," Georgiana added, "and we use many words."

"And this is the influence that the Bennets have on my niece?" Lord Fitzwilliam said. "I shall enjoy this supper immensely."

"And yet," Henry Fitzwilliam said, looking on Kitty, "I wonder, of your 'pride' of sisters, which one roars the most?"

"That one is not present," Kitty said. "But she is Lydia, the youngest of us. Yet I wish to believe myself a fierce thing to behold, and hopefully I shall make up for her absence."

"Something tells me that you will," Henry Fitzwilliam replied, amused.

"Oh, let us sit down," Lady Fitzwilliam said. "And Henry and Lord Fitzwilliam, you shall restrict your words to pleasantries so that I may get better acquainted with the Gardiners and their nieces. For I quite like the company."

I gave her a warm smile. "You like us. That is very pleasing to hear."

"I do. Isn't it an amusing thing?"

We all entered and began to inquire about all that had occurred in London in our absence. Yet as the conversation untwined, I noticed that Henry

Fitzwilliam casually but smoothly seated himself beside Kitty and began to engage in simple intercourse with her. I could not hear what they spoke of, yet it was soon made apparent that he enjoyed her company, and she enjoyed his as well.

After no more than ten minutes, Darcy, who was waiting for the last arrival, sighed when he saw another carriage pull up at the window. The doorbell rang again, we all went to the hallway as the door opened and Mr. Bingley and Miriam arrived, yet they were not alone.

I flinched at the sight of her, though quickly regained my composure as she entered in all her finery and smiled at us with her superficiality that she clearly had practiced for the occasion.

"Mr. and Mrs. Darcy," Caroline Bingley cried. "What a pleasure to see you again!"

I groaned inwardly, but it was an addition that could not be helped. And turning to see Mr. Bingley's expression, he secretly felt that it could not be helped either.

"Forgive me for being deficient in telling you of our addition to our party," Mr. Bingley began. "Yet my sister, Caroline, has been so wonderful as to grace us with her company and I simply forgot to mention it."

I knew that Mr. Bingley had not forgotten anything, but simply Caroline added herself at the last minute and bullied Charles into bringing her along. Dear lord! What a tedious woman! And the fact that she for too long liked Darcy did not do anything else but lessen her in my eyes. Yet the idea that he now was mine to have and hold, rather than in her clutches, was most amusing and it brought a smile to my face as I approached and curtsied.

"Miss Bingley," I said. "You shall make a wonderful addition to our party and it is no trouble at all to add a place for you." I raised up the bell and wrung for a servant the way Georgiana showed me to do and then ordered another place to be set at the table while everyone else began to converse.

The table was reset with alacrity, we were called into dinner, and we all took our places in the dining hall, seating ourselves in the way that Georgiana recommended us to be arranged. Darcy sat at the head of the table, I sat to his left, with Miriam to my right, Aunt Gardiner next to her, Mr. Bingley next to our aunt, and Caroline Bingley next to her. On the other side sat Lord Fitzwilliam, then Lady Fitzwilliam who never liked nor followed the concept that a husband and wife could not sit next to one another at a table (I secretly admired her for that)then Henry Fitzwilliam, Kitty, Uncle Gardiner, Georgiana, and Jane.

The first course of the meal was served, and we all began to eat politely. When I was a child, I sometimes wished that we humans could eat with our hands when it was quite convenient, and it was a practice that I secretly desire till this very day.

"So," Lady Fitzwilliam began. "I very much want to know how your holiday was in America?"

Darcy looked at me with concern, and I knew he did not trust himself to speak kindly on them. For our last encounter had gone so ill, that his opinion on the American Darcys was marred by prejudice. And as I had said before, his good opinion, once lost, often is lost forever. Therefore, I found it only fitting that I begin the narration.

"I enjoyed it immensely," I allowed. "And I quite loved Philadelphia. We went to New York as well, yet Philadelphia I preferred more. It had all the benefits of a cosmopolitan life, while having some luxuries of a rural one."

"How so?" Uncle Gardiner began. "I have never had the good fortune to go to Philadelphia, therefore how can it encompass both the country and the city within it?"

"It was designed for that purpose," Miriam interjected. "When William Penn founded the city, he designed it to have such a design where there were buildings spread out yet making sure there were parks and large areas of grass to keep it free from becoming too congested. It was a brilliant scheme."

"He learned from living in London, no doubt, to not repeat our mistakes," Mr. Bingley added. "The Great London Fire, for example. If buildings were not so close to one another and fire was to erupt, it would not destroy most of the city because much was spread out."

"And going to Philadelphia seems to have given you immense profit, Mr. Bingley," Henry Fitzwilliam commented, "for you have come back with a lovely bride."

He gave Mariam a warm look. "Yes, I have profited immensely."

"Yet, it should go hand in hand with my own profit,"

Miriam added. "If he was lucky to have come to America, then his coming shows that I was fortunate in someone of England deciding to come to my city."

"Yes," Jane added, lowering her fork. "For while it is wonderful to know that a person can walk toward fortune, it is also nice to know that fortune can walk towards you."

"Yes," Miriam answered, "it is a happy lesson to learn."

"You suggest then to believe that a happily ever after can be found in more than just storybooks?" Henry Fitzwilliam asked.

"Of course, they can," Kitty answered, perplexed at the question. "Do you not believe so?"

"Love can be obtained," Henry argued, "but I've often found that the concept that is the love we have come to admire, the love found in novels, plays, and poems are unreachable and unreal. It is either made blissful and flawless, or of comical proportions."

Kitty gave him a coy smile. "Then let it be for those of us who see flawlessness in something flawed or think comedy can be quaint and still filled with affection and let us keep it."

"And what is left for me then? To not keep it?"

"If you don't wish to keep it, then let it alone. The pursuit of love, of the ideal kind, is as you put it, a dream that is most unlikely to occur. Yet I have seen it obtained," Kitty said looking between Darcy and me, "and even in its smallest and most stressed moment, it makes the mundane a marvel."

She directed her narrative toward Henry. "A novel, play or poem can encompass true love, for it is a matter of the heart, however temporary. Have you never felt that sort of love, that even though not perfect from without, it still feels a phenomenon from within? That is what novels, plays and poems do, Mr. Fitzwilliam. They take that feeling that is an internal feel and turn it into an external force. It is its own reality."

Clearly interested, he asked, "And what happens when it does not become obtained?"

"It then becomes an unfulfilled dream that as long as you were brave enough to have it, was worth having it all the same."

Henry looked on Kitty, wondering at her, and it was hard to determine whether it was a look expressed through amazement or confusion. Or both. Yet when his expression became too intense and long, Kitty looked down, blushing.

"Well then," Uncle Gardiner said, eyeing Henry with suspicion and wishing to turn the subject to safer topics of discussion, "I am waiting in suspense to hear about the American Darcys."

"Yes," Aunt Gardiner encouraged. "What were they like? And did they meet your expectations?"

"Yes," Georgiana began, "I did quite like them immensely. They are enormous. Oh, what I mean is that there are so many of them. Cousin Darcy and his wife, Emilia, have many children, and they are all so different."

"Were they pleasant and mannerly?"

"How could they be?" Caroline Bingley scoffed. "Americans lack respect for the importance of good breeding."

Kitty, Georgiana, Fitzwilliam, Jane, Mr. Bingley and I all turned to Miriam, who was the only American in the room.

"It is true," Miriam added, "that good breeding is not always first and foremost in all of our minds. Yet whether it is for the better or for the worst can be determined by the perception of the individual. For breeding and the circles one moves in, that is important to some. Yet for the rest of us, such restrictions are meaningless, and the soul and spirit of the person is all that matters. And to have such freedom, to marry as one wishes, without fear or care of what others will say, that is not something that all of us have the luxury of obtaining, yet when and if we do, we have the right to chase it. And it ought to be chased."

"A fine notion," Mr. Bingley added, looking at his sister coldly. "Love found through liberty is always more to the benefit of one found through restraint."

"Restraint leads to order out of chaos, Charles," Caroline said.

"Or it leads to affection that is forced, and not organic," I argued. "For to be confined to select a soul mate from a narrow grouping that does not consider compatibility of mind, mood, or disposition between a man and woman, but only considers breeding and position as well as consequence in the world as what matrimony should be based upon, is harsh."

"And to base a bond on such qualifications," Darcy added, "while it may suit some, it should not nor ever be the only grounds for marital bliss."

"Oh." Caroline Bingley smiled fetchingly. "When you put it in such a way, Mr. Darcy, with such wording and sound argument, then I find I am quite converted to your way of thinking."

And that was the final word, and the only word, that Caroline Bingley needed to be persuaded! My husband merely had to support me, and all was agreed upon. I smiled gently and said nothing, but secretly found the inner idea to kick Miss Bingley, and the idea made me chuckle to myself. For despite it all, she still felt a desire for my husband.

Knowing her mind, which was one who must not have enjoyed losing such a splendid conquest, she probably still believed she could obtain him somehow. I did not fear her, for she was no threat to me, yet I feared for Darcy. I always felt that it wasn't just a mere attraction with him, but that she had a secret obsession over him, and rather than releasing him from her mind once he no longer was single, she still desired him.

Yet it was not love that she had for him, that much was certain. But rather, it was the idea of love, and the fact that she, as so many other women before her, viewed my husband as a conquest, a trophy of the greatest kind. And that kind of obsession was of the most dangerous sort often, for it was one that was made through mistaken intentions and misplacement.

⊗⊗⊗

"One of Cousin Thomas and Cousin Emilia's children is a nun," Jane added. "Her name was Deborah Darcy, yet now she is Sister Mary Ignatius. And to show how small the world can be, she was acquainted with a neighbor of ours in Hampshire, a Samuel Lucas."

"She knew one of the Lucas boys?" Aunt Gardiner said. "Now is that not a surprise indeed!"

"Yes, and she was quite a favorite of ours. She was full of life and vitality."

"And who were the others?"

"There was Felicity," Georgiana listed, "Victoria, Esther, Helena, Samantha, and then there were the two sons, Joseph, who was the younger brother who is married, yet the eldest, named Henry Darcy, is the sole inheritor of Canterbury estate."

"And does he have any family?" Lady Fitzwilliam asked, "For I never get the chance to fully know of the details of that side of the family."

"Oh, no he is single."

"Single?" Caroline Bingley perked up, to no one's secret surprise. "And what manner of man is he?"

"He is tall," Kitty elaborated, "of handsome build, yet I am not sure if he is handsome or not. I prefer men to have a softer look and his features are more of the stern sort."

"Strength in appearance and firmness of manner can often display good breeding. I should dearly like to meet him."

"Yet that may not come to pass," Lord Fitzwilliam said. "Not for either of us. I would like to engage in reconnecting with that branch of the family, and I would, if it were not for this accursed war that looms over our heads between us and America."

"War for a second time with our one-time colonies!" Caroline cried. "It is pointless and should not be born. Such trouble it is."

"It is a trouble that could have been avoided," I added, "if naval impressments were illegalized, yet it was not. Or if the colonies did not wish to pursue land in Canada, but they do. And now the effects are most likely irrevocable. Something should have been done to avoid this drastic step that is to be taken, yet apathy toward the solution was what it was met with."

"And," Darcy added, "with Napoleon being a constant threat to this new danger, the times shall be harder."

"We shall still have many comforts," Caroline said. "And society will not be hindered or deterred."

"Yet our soldiers suffer thus," Kitty interjected.

"They are soldiers," Caroline retorted. "And now they shall have use in their posts, though my heart does go out to them, believe me. Now, Mr. Darcy, can you tell us of this mysterious cousin of yours, the other Mr. Darcy, who lives across the Atlantic and seems quite the enigma."

"He is no enigma, but a man who is devoted to being a bachelor at present."

Caroline waved away the comment. "All men are devoted to being a bachelor until they meet the right woman. It's grown to the point where I wonder if the word bachelor was invented to be no more than a euphemism for: man who wishes to appear indifferent to love, for only by not looking for it does he believe he can find it."

"While it is possible for the word 'bachelor' to be translated in many ways by those who wish to find more meanings to it, in this case, I believe myself to be accurate. Henry Darcy does not wish to marry at present, for he has grown to have quite a sour perception toward the idea of matrimony."

"And what sour perception is that?"

"That he is neither good enough nor deserving of it."

"Oh, Mr. Darcy that is too cruel!" Lady Fitzwilliam said.

"Indeed Darcy," Henry Fitzwilliam said. "I can never understand why you are determined to go through life displeased with everything and everyone in it."

"And I can never understand why you are determined to approve of everything and everyone that you meet," Darcy replied, smirking at his wit.

"Well," Henry said, smiling gently at Kitty, "you shall not make me think ill of some people."

Caroline laughed, albeit a bit forced. "Indeed, he shall not. And though I have not met this Mr. Henry Darcy, I shall dare your disapproval, Mr. Darcy, and declare that he is a dear sweet man, and if I were to meet him, I should not object to knowing him better. You see, Mr. Darcy, I am not afraid of you."

"I would not have you so," was my husband's curt reply.

"For after all," Caroline answered, smiling sweetly, "this cousin of yours, Henry Darcy, is after all a Darcy. And the name, by its very nature, commands all that is best in life."

"If any name were to do so, I am happy that it would be mine. Yet a name is a name."

Again the brusque wave of her hand. "Oh, names can sometimes be all that matters."

My husband did not look at her but continued to eat his food, hiding his disdain for her.

"Yet," Henry Fitzwilliam added, looking at Kitty once more, "what is behind the name also is of value. Such as a beautiful smile and artlessness of manner."

Kitty smiled gently at him, blushing and looking down at her food.

The rest of the night passed casually, and we were all able to enjoy each other's company, for we quickly learned not to care much for all that Caroline Bingley said, and therefore the evening was a small kind of accomplishment, I supposed.

However, I could not overcome my anger at her for disrespecting Miriam in such a way. For not only did she offend a guest in my husband's home, but Miss Bingley also insulted her own brother's new wife. What a foolish thing! And yet it seemed only fitting to come from a woman by the name of Caroline Bingley!

Yet, while I could host the evening with grace enough with the assistance of Georgiana at my side, I could not help but every now and again spy Henry Fitzwilliam out of the corner of my eye. He was never far away from Kitty, and if they were on opposing sides of the room, he would secretly stare at her in a way that was not so secret.

By the end of the night, it was clear...

Whether as a passing emotion, or a desire to gather a permanent one, Henry Fitzwilliam was taken with Kitty.

⚜

"Well," I said, lying beside my husband in our bed. "What do you think?"

The dinner party had ended three hours ago, and now the house was silent as our guests had left and the rest of us had retired to bed.

"I think that it is now clear more than ever before." Darcy released a sigh. "That Caroline was always in love with the name of Darcy, and not the man behind it. Though she is now more a fool ever than before, for not only to develop a curiosity toward Henry Darcy, but to also even think she could win him. Henry Darcy would despise her on the spot. For whatever my feelings toward him, even I have to admit that he is smart enough to recognize the Caroline Bingleys of the world and see them for what they are."

"Yes, her aims are pointless. Yet I am happy she has directed them to a different though equally pointless target. Now you are at liberty to only be admired by me. And in your case, I am quite selfish with my admirations."

"As you ought to be, yet dearest, I observed another scene tonight that I feel deserves some discussions on."

"You are thinking of your other cousin, the other Henry, but now on the Fitzwilliam side."

"Yes and, oh dear god, both of their names are Henry!"

"Yes, but this time it is over a different Bennet. You wish to speak of Henry Fitzwilliam's constant attentions to Kitty this evening."

"Yes."

"He is your cousin, and therefore you know him better than I. Does he flirt often, or are his attentions so marked because he truly finds her attractive?"

"It is hard to say. Henry Fitzwilliam has had his flirtations in the past, yet what man has not? He is by no means a rattle or a rake. Yet very rarely have I seen him look on a woman the way he gazed upon Kitty, and Kitty, if she likes him, said all the things to fascinate him. Yet if she does not care for him, then she did herself no favors."

I turned toward him. "I know Kitty and while she once flirted while paired with our very flirtatious sister, Lydia, Kitty was never so blatant about it. She was not flirting with Henry, I swear it, Fitzwilliam."

"Oh, I did not mean that she flirted with him. On the contrary, she did the exact opposite. She was honest, curious, but not intrusive. She was sincere in full, and it is not something that he is used to."

"So, he was enraptured by her because she did nothing to make herself appear enraptured?"

He ran his fingers along my cheek. "You never did anything to enrapture me. You simply were sincere as well. For there is nothing more deceptive than the arts that women use to entice me."

"While I believe that we women have the right to show men our affection and flirtation, when harmless, can sometimes simply be a natural product of being blinded by our feelings. Yet your confession shows a hidden truth of the male species. Ah! I now see how the minds of men work. You are enticed only by those who never seek your good opinion, but only those who do not seek it."

"Ironic, isn't it?"

"Yes, very," I answered wryly.

"Aye. The idea to not trust a woman who tries too hard, while to be drawn to one who does not try at all. It is all so confusing." He indeed sounded puzzled.

"However, with Kitty, she did not flirt with him, and it made her lovely in his eyes. Yet I know Kitty well enough to know that her demeanor was too calm, her expressions too casual. Your cousin Henry Fitzwilliam is charming, and she might grow to like him, but she has no initial feelings. If she did, she would have shown it more, as well as possibly, as you put it, try too hard."

I felt his nod of agreement against my cheek. "Perhaps we think on something that has no real substance to it. He could have simply been interested in her because she was a novelty to him, and the next morning, he would have forgotten all about her."

"I hope so," I answered, "for I fear, that for him to attach himself to her is a complication that we do not need."

"No, we do not."

"Though I confess myself surprised. With Jane being five times as pretty as the rest of us Bennet sisters, I thought he would have favored her first."

"You do Kitty and yourself ill, Elizabeth. In truth, Kitty and you look similar, and you are a unique beauty. One that a man can feel comfort with. Jane is stunning, yet her beauty is so stately that for some men it is either too overpowering or it feels cold like perfection often appears as."

He drew me closer. "You were meant for a man such as myself, one who admires a distinct and different sort of beauty that is remarkable. Kitty is meant for a man who wants an artless woman who is both lovely and easy to understand, while also being comfortable to be around. Kitty and you both express comfort and humanity. That is what he sees in her."

"Ah, well, let us sleep on it and discuss it further on the morrow. For I cannot deny seeing the pattern. We left one cousin of yours named Henry in America disappointed by one Bennet girl, and I would hate for history to repeat itself with this Henry Fitzwilliam."

"Yes, my dear. Bless be the ties that bind, and those ties are family conflicts and the vicious cycles that continue them."

❧ 6 ❧

COMPLICATIONS

A nd the next day proved to be the addition of many new things to consider.

First, at a suitable hour, we were visited by Henry Fitzwilliam himself, who asked to call on us and sit with us for an hour. Yet his intention became very clear, for when he joined us in the sitting room, he spoke with us all at first, but then he focused on Kitty and began to engage her in small conversation. Kitty returned it with ease and grace, not encouraging him shamelessly, but also, she was clearly flattered by his attentions and therefore met his conversation with alacrity and offering him all her attentions.

And that was encouragement enough for him.

When Henry Fitzwilliam finally took his leave, he promised that he would call again very soon, and then he was off on his horse. When alone, I turned to Kitty.

"Well," I began, "Kitty, you are no fool. You know why he has come."

She sighed and made a little moue. "Yes. While I at first thought his attentions to me were meaningless, I shall not deny it now, nor blame myself for my pride being affected."

"Are you comfortable with this?"

"Elizabeth," she said, her confidence slipping, "it is strange. At one time, I would have loved the idea of a man on his way to being violently in love with me. And yet now, I don't understand. I should be happy, and yet, I am frightened. I know I sound foolish, yet I don't know what to feel truly."

"You are not being foolish. You simply are growing."

"We are passed our prime years," Kitty said. "And very soon, I shall be labeled an old maid if I do not marry. And yet, the idea of that does not frighten me. It no longer frightens Jane either. I…forgive me, for some reason I wish to be alone now with my thoughts. I need to take counsel and wonder what and where my mind is."

"Do not feel as if you should have all the answers now," I said, offering my solace, "for all that we know, there is nothing even in motion yet."

"Thank you." Kitty sighed, feeling instantly lighter. "That is a great comfort."

Then she ran up the steps and to her room. Just as I left her and began walking toward Darcy's study, the door opened, and he emerged.

"Lizzy, I have received some letters and they pertain to you. Come in and read them."

"Very well." I entered his study, sat down, Fitzwilliam handed me two letters and I saw that the first one was from Colonel Fitzwilliam.

Dear Fitzwilliam,

How does married life find you, my taciturn cousin? I trust you are in good health, as you ought to be. Again, I congratulate you on your most happy event, married life will suit you well, and you must tell Elizabeth that I look forward to seeing her again and meeting the rest of her family, which I have been remiss in doing, not because of wish, but by obligation. As a soldier, my life is not my own.

You must also inform Elizabeth that I wished I could have been at your wedding, and it was a great wish to be so, yet now I can make up for it. Write to me to tell me when you are to return to Pemberly, for I have been granted leave from the army, due to the lack of action on the battlefront. Napoleon is not on the move at present and shows no signs of being so. And therefore I am allowed to go on holiday. For both economical and familial reasons, I was hoping to visit you at Pemberly, where I was hoping you would receive me and not look on my presence as an intrusion.

However, even if you write to me or not, I shall still arrive in Kent in a few weeks' time, for which I am certain that even if you are not there, Mrs.

Reynolds will receive me and let me enjoy playing head of the household in your stead.

Ergo, by your will or not, I will come to Pemberly and be sure to nag my serious cousin.

Hope you are well,
  Colonel Richard Fitzwilliam

"Who is Mrs. Reynolds?" I asked Darcy.

"Oh, she is my housekeeper for Pemberly."

"Oh, still! Colonel Fitzwilliam is coming to visit us in a fortnight. We shall be at Pemberly by then, shall we not?"

"I hope so."

"What do you mean by hope?"

"Read the second letter."

I opened the second letter and blinked. "This is from the royal court!"

"Yes, yes, it is."

Opening the paper once more, I began to read.

Salutations Mr. Darcy of Pemberly,

By royal decree, you have received the great honor of presenting your new bride, Mrs. Elizabeth Darcy, at court, where she shall be received by the Prince Regent and her royal highness, the Queen of England.

Another invitation has been sent to the household of Mr. Charles Bingley, which is to also accompany you, along with his new bride as well.

Your arrival and presentation is meant to proceed in two days' time.

By your leave,
  Lord John Grant,
  Royal advisor to the High Court

I closed the letter and looked up at my husband. "The Prince Regent knows that we are married?"

"Well, it was in the newspapers, and it was put in prominently."

"And he knows about Mr. Bingley's marriage to Miriam."

"Yes."

I turned to him, puzzled. "Does that not strike you as fast?"

"Not where the Prince Regent is involved. The Prince Regent only appears to surround himself with sycophants, but he does have eyes, ears, and spies all around the city. He probably was informed of our arrival through someone who spied us as we came into town."

I stifled a shiver. "That frightens me. I do not like the idea of our actions being forever watched."

"They are only watched if it is a necessity."

"Yet I do not understand, why does he care about me being presented?"

"Because it will amuse him, no doubt. After all, he in many ways is the reason for why I ceased to be a fool."

"He had something to do with it all?"

"I sense that as time wears on, history will have many things to say about the Prince Regent, but none will be about us."

Fitzwilliam went on to tell me about how the Prince Regent had actually urged Darcy to pursue his love for me against all odds, and I found it all the more amusing how a man like Darcy and he, who were so different and at odds, should also be in each other's debt over and over.

"Well, since I do owe him," I acknowledged, "of course I shall look forward to it. Besides, it was only a matter of time before I would have been presented at court. Yet is it solely myself, or shall my sisters also join me?"

"They may as well."

"Then matters have grown more colorful, for the Prince Regent is involved, and where he is always concerned, there will always be interesting complications to it."

THE PRINCE & HIS PERSONALITY

Gowns that were suitable had been bought and fit to us the next day, and I, along with my sisters, Georgiana, Mr. Bingley, Mrs. Miriam Bingley, Lord and Lady Fitzwilliam and their son, Henry, found ourselves at St. James Court, where we entered to a crowd of the highest of society, from Earls, Knights, Ladies, members of the royal court and the royal family. At the head seats sat the Queen of England, along with her son, the Prince Regent.

It was all so dazzling! Almost like a dream.

Darcy took my hand and as we walked forward, being announced, I turned to my husband.

"Such strange thoughts come to one at such a time," I whispered.

"Such as?" he whispered back, barely moving his mouth.

"I was just thinking, of Sir William Lucas, and of all the times that he mentioned St. James Court. Now I am suddenly in it!"

We walked forward and were announced.

"Your highness, Mr. and Mrs. Darcy of Pemberly."

I curtsied as Georgiana had shown me and was amazed to find myself in the presence of the Queen of England. Beside her stood her son, the Prince Regent, and he was as I remembered him. He met my eye and smiled at me knowingly, but his smile, as always, was a half-smirk. Forever he loved to look as if he knew something that you did not.

After I curtsied, I rose and proceeded to back away, for words usually were never to be spoken in such a case. Therefore, there was nothing left but to be shocked when the Queen spoke first.

"So, Mr. Fitzwilliam Darcy, this is the woman that you have chosen for a wife?"

I turned to my husband who was momentarily surprised at her speaking as well but covered it with grace and ease.

"Yes, it is your majesty. I have found myself fortunate."

"And does she think so as well," the Queen said, turning to me. "One of the most sought-after men in England, are you proud, Mrs. Darcy?"

"To become the wife of Mr. Darcy," I began, "one feels a whole range of emotions, and pride and fortune are just the beginnings of them, your majesty."

"And what," the Queen added, "is the middle of them?"

"Contentment," I added, smiling. "And affection. For love must render itself to such states, if one is fortunate, and fortune was something even you admit that I now possess."

"And pray tell," the Prince Regent interjected, "what is at the end of this list?"

He looked on me, with a twinkle in his eye, and it was the same twinkle he once had when he spoke with us in the gardens at the celebration of King George's returning of his sanity, though we all knew that he was going to go mad again. At the time, I had thought that look signified that he was up to some mischief, yet now I knew that it only meant he felt the satisfaction on being on the inside of a joke, while most were on the outside of it.

"There is no end," I replied. "For with matrimony, two become one, your highness, and never are they unraveled from one another."

"Indeed."

I turned back to the Queen. "I thank you for your invitation to court, your majesty, and your notice is most keenly felt. As well as it shall not be quickly forgotten."

She raised a rather humorous eyebrow. "It had better not be forgotten at all, for I am the Queen of England."

"And you are much loved by the people."

"I am, to my face. Yet behind my back is another matter. Well, Mrs. Darcy, welcome to St. James, and to all the ties that such notice brings along with it."

"Thank you, your majesty."

My husband took my hand and began to lead us away.

"And Darcy?" the Queen said.

"Yes, your majesty," Darcy said, turning to her and bowing his head.

"You have found your Mrs. Darcy now."

"I have, your majesty."

She looked at him keenly.

"Well done," she said at length.

"I know. Yet I thank you."

As the ceremony commenced, Darcy was summoned to the side of the Queen, who had a private matter she wished to discuss. He looked at me with worry, not wishing to leave me alone, but he was compelled. When he left my side, I went to stand in a corner, and was surprised to find that someone was standing over my shoulder. I turned and was not surprised to find the Prince Regent looking down at me.

"Congratulations, Mrs. Darcy, your presentation has gone well," the Prince said to me.

"Thank you for the compliment, yet I must ask, was this all your doing?"

"Partly."

"Forgive me for not being afraid of asking why you would do this for my husband."

"You ask very direct questions of your Prince. How impertinent."

"You welcome impertinence, your highness. You always have."

"And what makes you say that? You hardly know me."

"I know that you and my husband, while being very different in manner, personality and mind, you are one in soul. You have the same core and essence. He loves spirit, and despite appearing as opposite, you admire it as well."

"Oh, do I? And these decided opinions, from the country lass who has no rank to her title, except for the one she married into."

"You are just saying that to hurt me, not because you actually feel such."

"You claim to always know my mind. I should be disgusted by you."

"Are you?"

The Prince Regent looked away from me, and then looked back and his eyes contained the same mischievous look to them that I had become familiar with.

"I do not know what I feel."

"Well, I know what I feel."

"And what is that? I am intrigued to know. For your mind is like a safe and I wish to unlock it."

"I feel gratitude for you, your majesty. For it is your shift in manner, your secret desire to be a good man that made you encourage my husband to follow his heart."

The Prince, now seeing me heartfelt and serious, dropped his smile and blushed, becoming bashful suddenly. "I do not know what your reason was, but it was not one of design or self-advancement. You simply did a good deed because you wanted to do... a good deed. And because you fell into the danger of being a good man, I was given the best of fates. Now you can pretend that it was of some clever scheme of yours, but it was not. You simply wanted to give someone, a woman you barely knew, a chance at fortune. And for that, you have done well."

"Yes, I suppose that I have."

The Prince looked around the room, and his eyes fell on my sisters and Georgiana.

"Tell me something, Mrs. Darcy, are your sisters anything like you?"

"I cannot say, yet you can always rely on us Bennet girls to be Bennet girls. For better or for worse. That being said, I have my courage, and I shall always keep my wits about me."

He cocked his head. "And what does that mean?"

"That I am their sister, and I look after my other sisters. And those who plan to do them mischief will want to think otherwise, for I am a stronger force to behold than they would believe."

And then came the familiar smirk that the Prince had perfected so well. I was testing him, and that was something he was familiar with, and therefore enjoyed more.

"I am insulted, Mrs. Darcy. I am harmless."

I gave him a knowing smile. "You are a Prince, which means you are anything but."

His smile was rather sardonic. "Yes, you are correct. I am anything but. Yet as you said, I am a Prince. And what is Mrs. Darcy in the face of that?"

"Mrs. Darcy. And she always will be."

"I am happy that you enjoy your fate," he said, taking my hand and kissing it. "And your fortune. Now good day, country lass."

He bowed his head to me and walked away. Coincidentally, as soon as our discourse finished, the Queen was finished speaking with Darcy, and he joined me.

"I may have been speaking with the Queen," he said, "yet I never turned my eye fully from you. What did the Prince want with you?"

"You need not worry on my account, Fitzwilliam, for it is of no matter. He just wished to be cynical and witty and was taken off guard with my reaction."

"And what was that?"

"I thanked him for bringing us together. And my sincerity was too much for his sensibilities, for when dealing with a man who is used to either being met with extreme charm and flattery, or witty sarcasm, the one thing that always disarms them the most is warm sincerity, for he could not make a joke on it."

"And what was his reaction, I wonder?"

"Hesitation and a desire to turn our conversation to more cynical levels. He tried to hide that he had a heart. In that, he is not unlike yourself."

"I hide my heart?"

"You did, once. But unlike him, you finally allowed yourself to find it. And that is where you differ."

"I owe him, but I do not trust him."

"As you ought not to. As I owe him, but I do not trust him."

"Are we on accord in this, Elizabeth?"

"Yes, I believe that we are."

"Then I need not worry. For you know our Prince all too well, even though you have only met him twice."

"And twice was enough, for as seven years might not be enough to determine knowledge of a person's character, seven hours can be more than enough for others. In the case of the Prince Regent, seven minutes is all that I need to determine a first impression of the prince and his personality."

❧ 8 ❧

FROM LONGBOURN TO PEMBERLY

The next day we made all preparations to leave for Hampshire. While Jefferson made all the arrangements of the staff to pack what was needed and to close the townhouse while we were away, Jane, Miriam, Kitty, Georgiana and I spent the next day at our Aunt and Uncle Gardiner's home. We escorted our uncle to his factory where he showed Miriam some wonderful imported fabrics he received from Israel.

"My goodness!" Miriam cried, enjoying the fabric, and asked if she might purchase some of it. Our Uncle Gardiner, who had not expected the offer, was delighted, and began to tell her of the time he had went to Israel to establish a connection in trade with another factory.

"In Jerusalem, the architecture was unlike any I had ever seen before," Uncle Gardiner confessed. "And to this day, it has left a powerful impression on me. I am fond of history, of good building design that seems filled with memory, and there was much there."

"I have never had the good fortune to visit the Holy Land and make such a pilgrimage," Miriam said, "and it has always therefore been a curiosity and a fascination."

"Fortune has changed for you I dare say," Uncle Gardiner answered, "For Mr. Bingley, who is by all accounts a very agreeable and wandering man, might be persuaded to step outside to take your hand and forever be your companion in going there."

Georgiana laughed and clapped her hands. "He will, and even more easily convinced if he hears others desire to join you. Mark my words, if Fitzwilliam would want to join him, Mr. Bingley would be open to it."

"I sense a scheme coming on between you women then," Uncle Gardiner answered, his smile just a little bit wicked.

"Uncle," I said, "there is always a scheme afoot. Nothing can be done for it, for with all the time we ladies have on our hands; our thoughts become a constant activity."

৩⁜৪৩

As we returned to Gracechurch Street, we regaled Miriam and Georgiana about how Kitty and I worked at our Uncle's factory whenever he had need of us, or work that we could easily learn to do. Miriam, who was raised to value having an occupation of some kind, enjoyed hearing of it, and therefore left a profound sense of satisfaction over all of us.

Since Mr. Bingley so hastily fell in love with her, there was always that great apprehension that he had made a frightful move, and as often so, the hasty strike goes oft astray, for it forces one to move too quickly, putting less thought in the aftermath of our decisions. It was that same decisive manner of leaping before looking where one steps that led to Darcy proposing to Anne de Bourgh, even when he did not love her.

Yet now all had proven well. Miriam Goldman, now Miriam Bingley, was the perfect match for Charles. She was artless, open, and not quick to judge or criticize, appreciated those of professions and thought having an occupation was not only beneficial to one's finances, but also to one's sense of purpose and identity. Work, and the happiness in doing it, could define a person and make them feel of use.

"It all comes down to liberty," Miriam had said to me in confidence. "Both occupation and lack thereof can present their own freedoms. To be allowed to have hope and choice of an occupation allows a person to be free *to* be of more independent nature, yet to not work is to be free *from* having to slave and toil. Therefore, it all comes down to which liberty a person desires more in their individual state: the freedom *to* do something, or the freedom *from* having to do something. Yet that is what it all comes down to: freedom. And to not have such a thing, that is the greatest loss of all."

"I know your mind," I said, "for I have seen the fruits of both. A friend of mine is a writer, and her very happiness, her soul and her spirit are filled by her stories."

"You know a woman writer?" She smiled. "Truly?"

"Yes, her name is Jane Austen and she is a friend of the whole family. Yet her pursuits also form a sisterly bond. While she writes her stories, her sister, Cassandra Austen, edits them. It was Cassandra who had suggested that her sister's first novel should be *called Sense and Sensibility*, for before that, it was called 'Marianne and Elinor'. Therefore, one forms her identity around the occupation of writing, and the other finds contentment in reading it."

"That is a wonderful way for two sisters to bond."

"And they do, all the better for it."

"Has your friend written any more books?"

"She completed another novel, *Northanger Abbey*, yet she does not plan to publish that one yet."

The more we grew to know Miriam, the more it became clear that she wished to always try to deserve Mr. Bingley, as he would always try to be deserving of her, which made them a perfect pair in the end. Mr. Bingley, by sheer accident, had done right for himself and had done right by Miriam, despite his lack of comprehension in seeing that he almost made the same mistake of turning from her in the way that Darcy once made the mistake of turning from me.

And yet, it could be successfully argued that had it not been for Darcy and I falling in love and marrying, then there never would have been need for him to have gone to America. For the whole intention behind doing so was for us to find another part of the family that would embrace our union. Yet since we did marry, and there was need to go to America and meet the other Darcys, Mr. Bingley accompanied us and therefore he was able to meet the love that would define him hopefully. Hope therefore was kindled. Happy ending had begotten happy ending.

The next day came soon enough; we were packed and ready to depart. Mr. Bingley and Miriam would naturally remain in London, where he would present his new wife to the delights of the town and we were all off to Hampshire.

The journey home was without mishap or delay, we reached Hampshire, had

Jefferson leave us so that he could peradventure to the Drunken Prince Inn and order us some rooms, and we proceeded to Steventon.

Along the way, we passed Aginfield Park, which was the country seat of Mr. Bingley.

"Before we left," Darcy said to me in the carriage, "Mr. Bingley said that he planned to cease renting it and give the estate up entirely, for now that he was married and settled, he would like to find an estate closer to Pemberly, in Kent."

I tilted my head and glanced at him. "You would like that, wouldn't you? To have your bosom friend so close."

"It would make me happier I confess with ease. Therefore, as soon as there is a suitable purchase of it, he will give the place away."

"Do you remember, that is the place where we first danced at the ball?"

"I do. I was in love with you, yet too afraid to do much about it except toy with your affections."

"Don't despise yourself, Fitzwilliam; it is too early in the day to do so."

I looked back at Aginfield and sighed wistfully.

"Then its fate is undecided, for then who will occupy Aginfield Park?"

We turned around the bend and the view of Aginfield disappeared behind some trees.

We reached Steventon and then came upon a familiar sight.

"Longbourn!" Jane nearly shouted. "For as home is where the heart is, so can be one's comfort. All the adventures we have undergone." She turned to me. "And though fun, moving and full of diversions, now that I look on the place, I now see that I missed it very much."

"I comprehend your feeling," I said. "Longbourn is more than just our home. It is a character in our lives and it has a hold on our identity that is very strong."

As we approached our house, the door opened and our hearts swelled as our flighty mother escaped it, followed by our father and Mary, along with our most devoted of servants: Hill.

Despite the fact that I was never her favorite child, I could never deny that my mother loved me, yet just sometimes forgot how to show it. Therefore my emotions did lift at seeing my parents.

"We were so worried!" she cried. "When you had not arrived earlier, we thought that you had an accident on the road, your carriage had been turned over or you had been attacked by robbers."

"Oh nonsense, Mother," Kitty said as we exited the carriage. "We have made very good time."

"Oh well, my wonderful girls!" our mother cried, embracing us all. When she released us, she beheld Darcy and Georgiana.

"And my new son-in-law! And my new daughter-in-law as well, as a result! Oh, please let me kiss you," she cried, kissing their cheeks.

Our father smiled, finding the scene comical. "Well then, let us all get inside before the very highwaymen robbers that Mrs. Bennet worried about attacking you on the road decided to now jump out of the bushes and take their chance."

"Oh nonsense!" our mother cried, swatting father on the shoulder.

We all followed our parents inside as she continued. "Now we are to the Phillips this evening, for it could not be helped. You know that once we received word of your coming, she could not deny a dinner party. Mind you, I have no desire to be going here and there at night. I'd much rather stay at home and rest my poor nerves."

We entered Longbourn and it was wonderful to see that our home had not changed at all. And nor had our family. Mary immediately began to inquire about the sights and findings we found in America, mother immediately wished to know of the Darcys and if there were any single men in the family. Here she turned a significant eye to Jane, but not to Kitty, who I believed that she lost faith in once she turned down Mr. Collins. Our father said nothing, knowing that there was no point in trying to speak when our mother was.

Darcy, to our utter surprise, spoke the most! He answered all of Mary's questions about what we saw in America, from Philadelphia to New York, and as for my mother's inquiries, he informed her that Joseph Darcy was married. But he smoothly avoided mentioning Henry Darcy altogether, and thus spared any discussion our mother could have begun over his marital status, or avoiding Jane having to accidentally let slip her refusal of his hand.

By the end of his description, Jane breathed out a sigh of relief, knowing that her rejection would be a secret never made public in Hampshire, locked away from her mother's scrutiny, and she would never have to suffer criticism and our mother's censure for denying a man who would have given her all the comforts the world had to offer. For this was the second proposal that Jane had rejected, and our mother had barely enough nerves to have survived the first one. A second one, where there were no impediments to her judgment, would have made our mother possibly suffer from a stroke.

Yet, soon after our arrival, we were interrupted by Hill, who entered and let us know that she saw Cassandra and Jane Austen coming down the walk, which meant that they were coming to visit us.

"How insufferably rude," our mother cried. "For you have not been home for more than an hour, and they are already come to call."

"Oh, who cares?" Mary cried. "We've known them all our lives, so why should we have to stand on ceremony with a family that we are so well acquainted with?"

"Precisely," I said, standing up with alacrity. All of us stood in turn and exited the house to see Jane and Cassandra approaching.

"Well!" Cassandra Austen said. "We clearly were not in error when we decided to make a hasty visit. Our mother saw you pass as she was walking home and immediately went to let us know the news that you had returned."

"And we tossed timing to the winds," Jane Austen added, "as we do in many things."

We all met pleasantly, Jane and Cassandra followed us inside and we began to tell everyone all about our time in America once more, not fearing repeating our narrative, for the sisters were happy to hear everything.

When we were done, my sister Jane decided to begin an errand that she promised she would uphold.

"Well, Austens, if you would not mind joining me, I was wishing to visit the Lucases today, for I have to deliver a missive."

"What sort of missive?" our mother asked critically.

"One that I promised I would deliver in confidence," Jane whispered. "And I feel as if time has been wasted enough by the time that has lapsed between it being written and when it was meant to be read."

"You are delivering a letter written by another?" our mother said, suspicious "That is most improper."

"What is necessary is never improper, Mother. That much I have learned by crossing the ocean. So," she said with such serene finality that no one would argue with her, "shall I have any companions who would like to join me?"

Her response was met with Kitty, Georgiana, the Austen sisters, Darcy and I all wishing to escort her. Our mother was most put out for knowing that all her guests wished to take a walk so soon after coming, then was consoled by our father who had only one thing to say:

"My dear, they will only be walking half a mile to a house they will spend little time in yet will be our children for the rest of our mortal lives. In the end, who do you think will get the most time, for I firmly believe the Lucases will receive the least in this case."

As we walked, Jane Austen looked at Jane with suspicion and my sister noticed this.

"What is it?" Jane asked.

"You have changed," Jane Austen replied. "You are not the same Jane Bennet that I remember."

"How do you see such an alteration?"

"You spoke just then with finality and firmness. Your serenity is still present, yet now there is something underneath. Vitality. How do you account for it?"

"Simple and plain. I traveled and earned a point of view."

"Ah, I did not see that self-discovery coming."

"No," Cassandra Austen said, "nor did I."

We arrived at the Lucases, were met by Sir and Lady Lucas, who met us well with kind wishes and eagerness. To our good fortune, their eldest son and heir, Samuel, was there and he welcomed us as well.

When we announced to Sir William that we had all been presented at St. James Court, he went on to regale us with many stories about his presentation into knighthood there. For to this day, his elevation to the position was still too keenly felt and was all he mostly knew how to talk about.

Yet while he continued to speak about his own experiences and inquire after the Queen of England and what we thought of her, it was the perfect chance for Jane to speak with Samuel in private. Out of the corner of my eye, I saw her hand Samuel the letter, to which his expression dropped from one of casual good humor, to one of curiosity and surprise.

"Excuse me, Father," Samuel Lucas said, standing up and concealing the letter. "Yet I shall return presently, and only have a quick matter that must be attended to."

He left, Lady Lucas wondered at him, but continued her polite inquiries about our holiday.

A couple of minutes later, Samuel Lucas returned, looking red in the face. He sat down near Jane and whispered something to her; she looked at me, and then said something to him in return. Afterwards, Samuel looked at me as well, came to a decision and stood up.

"Mother and Father," he began, "I am so delighted in seeing the Bennets and Darcys once more that I have wondered if they would be so kind as to take a turn with us here in our gardens? Mother, you have made such improvements on the garden, and I wish for them to see it."

Lady Lucas looked at us all, uncertain of if this was a welcomed offer, and we all acquiesced with eagerness, which made her feel more comfortable.

It was all agreed upon, and we found ourselves following the Lucases to observe and admire their grounds.

Once we began to leave the room, Samuel Lucas approached me before Darcy could take my arm.

"Mrs. Darcy, we have planted harebells, and I know that they are a particular favorite of yours, therefore I was hoping I could show them to you especially."

I looked at my husband, who eyed Samuel Lucas with animosity, and I nodded to him to imply that all was well.

"Thank you for being attentive, Mr. Lucas, and I should like to see them."

Taking Sam's arm, I allowed him to lead me to the grounds. While the rest went along and followed Lady Lucas, with Darcy not going too far from me ever, Sam led me slightly away from the throng and began to speak.

"I hope that you enjoyed your time in America, for it seems to have brought fruitful ends in regards to your experiences."

"It has, but Sam, we have been friends long enough for you to be frank with me instead of speaking in formalities. Besides, I am not certain that we have much time before my husband will lose his patience with you taking me away."

"Fair point."

"Why do you seek me out as opposed to Jane? For it was her duty to have given you the letter."

"And she tells me that it was you who Deborah Darcy spoke most with."

"Sister Ignatius, you mean?"

"Yes, but I wish to call her Deborah, for that is the name that I knew her as."

"Does knowledge of her being a nun hurt you, or give you resolution?"

"It gives me both. She has given herself back to God, and I should admire her for that. I am respectful of that."

"Sam, I know what you are feeling."

He sighed and shook his head. "No, Elizabeth, believe me, you don't."

We walked on a little further.

"When Mr. Darcy came here to Hampshire," I asked, "did you know that he was Deborah's cousin?"

"I did not. The name Darcy, while not a frequent last name to come upon, still did not faze me. For Mr. Darcy's legacy here in England seemed like such a distant thing from the family that I had met in America, that I could not make the connection. And yet, the world as it seems, is very small. And fate as it seems, has a very wicked sense of humor."

We walked on a little further before Sam chose to speak again.

"You must think me foolish, Mrs. Darcy, for thinking hard on a woman who I have not had contact with for over three years, but our past loves are like shadows behind our shoulder. They never really leave us, yet we sometimes forget them, so when we are reminded that they were there, those shadows rise up and we remember all that we forgot. The emotions re-emerge and are awakened."

"So, you loved Deborah Darcy, then?"

"You've met her, so you've seen the exceptional creature she is. Oh yes, I loved her."

"Then why did you not do anything about it?"

He raked his fingers through his hair. "I was a fool. Believing that the pressures of the world were more to be adhered to than my own heart. And now she is lost to me. Although, it is better she be lost to her faith than to another man. My vanity would be burdened the worse if it were otherwise."

"When she wrote to you, if you do not mind my asking, what did she tell you?"

Sam looked ahead, gathering a wistful gaze.

"That she had never stopped loving me. And that she forgives me for the decision that I made."

"That is very strong of her, and yet, she is of the nature that can endure much and still find something to smile about."

"Yes, she can. And forgive me for everything, she does. Though I am not sure that I can forgive myself. And perhaps, it is best that I don't. Yes, yes, it is better that way."

"Sam..."

"But you must forgive me, Mrs. Darcy. Would you do me the honor of assisting me?"

"How can a Mrs. Darcy help a Mr. Samuel Lucas?" I teased.

"By remembering your one-time softness toward me. Twice in my life I have lost out on two exceptional women due to my inaction. Deborah Darcy and the woman that was once Elizabeth Bennet."

I looked down and blushed, growing nervous. I knew that there was a time when Samuel Lucas had fancied me, yet I had since regarded it as nothing serious or certain. Rather, I thought it merely a passing attraction that we both had for one another. Yet now I learned that it was merely fleeting on my side and was easily extinguished by time and experience. With Samuel Lucas, it became clear to see that he had felt something deeper, more substantial, and thus showing how complicated life could often be.

"Sam, your feelings were a mere innocent attraction," I began.

"They were not, and you are aware of this," he said. "I had for too long relied on knowing that you would always be present, always at home, and then when you married in such a fashion, I secretly swallowed my lost opportunity, and never let you see my disappointment. Yet this idleness of my nature, this failure to act on my impulses has proven to be the downfall of me. Forgive me, Mrs. Darcy, for it is very ungentle to speak so, yet you must know; I loved you once. And I would have done something about it, if I had not been so weak as to be remiss in making decisions that would affect my future. Just as I would have married Deborah Darcy, for she was the only love that ever reached me besides you."

"Mr. Lucas," I whispered, "your confession is not unknown, but only unexpected. I am flattered beyond all measure, yet we must not speak of such things again. And while I do not wish to silence you on the matter because I do not value your words, I simply do so to keep you from saying more that will commit you to past regrets. Your inaction and indecision has led to some happy results. I have found my second self in Mr. Darcy and Deborah would never have found her calling. You gave us another path, we walked down it, and we found the best of lights as our destination. And so, in some strange way, we must thank you."

"Yes, I must look at it that way."

"Though I do understand your need to tell me your feelings at last, for it was a desire that was never spoken by you. Yet, now you are learning to find your voice and wish to begin by making a change."

"Precisely, and I shall be brave. If you ever had any feeling for me, or any pity for my forlorn state, then do me this courtesy; if you ever are in communication with the American Darcys again, could you send Deborah a message for me, through your missive?"

"At the moment, contact will be hard pressed and it will be rare, yet if it be so, then I shall write to your sister Maria, and she shall send me a letter containing yours, which I will send to Deborah as your intermediary."

"Thank you, Mrs. Darcy. That will mean the world to me."

The next second, we were met by my husband who came around the corner of the walkway, stared at Samuel Lucas sternly and then looked at me with quiet finality.

"Mr. Lucas, I hope you enjoyed my wife's company, now I must ask that you return her to me, thank you."

After Samuel Lucas left us, and I knew we were out of hearing, I turned to Darcy.

"Tell me the truth, Fitzwilliam, how much did you overhear?"

"All of it."

"You have got to cease doing that."

"No. Never in your case."

"I see your reasoning."

"So, the Lucas boy was in love with you. Between him, Mr. Bingley and myself... how many men you have enticed."

"I can't help it!"

"I know, yet I must be firm now. I never want you to be alone with him in any way, and if ever we return to Hampshire after this, I will not ever allow you close to him in company."

"While I don't like the way in which you think you can order my life, I understand in this case that you have a right to."

He appeared relieved. "Thank you for not arguing. And I don't mean to order your life... I just simply wish to—"

"To protect me."

"Aye."

"And I will let you, because it is the right emotion for you to feel. Yet from now on, you must consult me rather than order me. I will listen to you, Fitzwilliam, as long as you give me the right to be heard as well."

"Very well."

"See, there you are." I smiled, kissing his hand. "And now we seal this accord with our promises."

That night, we attended the dinner party at my Aunt and Uncle Phillips home, through which our aunt felt all the satisfaction of having to celebrate being connected to such an illustrious person as my husband.

"Oh," Aunt Phillips cried, "Mr. Darcy and Miss Darcy! You are very welcome in our home."

"Thank you," Darcy said, bowing. "And I feel the compliment keenly."

Georgiana curtsied as well.

"And now we are family," Georgiana began, "making you our aunt as well."

"And a great pleasure it is," Aunt Phillips said. All around, others approached us, and four families had been invited. They all came, and they congratulated us on our wedding while demanding news of America and what were the Americans views on this supposed war that might occur between our countries.

After conversation, dinner was served, and while we all ate, Aunt Phillips began the news that I should not have been surprised to hear.

"My dear sister," Aunt Phillips said to our mother, "have you availed the newlyweds about the assembly that shall take place in two days' time?"

"No, I did not!" our mother cried. "Yet I was waiting for the perfect opportunity to do so."

At that moment, Kitty began to cough, for she drank some water which she swallowed incorrectly.

"Oh, for heaven's sake," our mother cried. "Don't keep coughing so, Kitty; have you no compassion on my poor nerves?"

She swallowed and her eyes watered. "I don't cough for my own amusement."

Our aunt ignored the last sentences spoken and continued her subject as if she had not been interrupted at all.

"Then I am happy to have beaten you to it. Mr. Darcy, Miss Darcy, Elizabeth, Jane and Kitty! At the Red Lion, there shall be an assembly, and I'm certain that if you were to stay till then, it would be a great honor to Hampshire, for we can have the dance in the honor of your returning to Steventon."

I shook my head and smiled. "Oh, aunt, we should be old news at this point!"

"And you know how Hampshire is, Lizzy," our father said. "A wedding can happen almost a year ago, and people shall still be talking of it."

"So, what do you all say?" Aunt Phillips asked. "Will you all remain in Steventon for the assembly?"

I looked around the room at all the expectant faces, then back at my husband who I was worried at being irate for feeling pressured to do something that he may not have wanted to do.

He lowered his fork, lifted his eyes, turned to our Aunt Phillips, and began his reply.

❦

Two days later, as we entered the assembly room, I whispered, "I still am surprised that you accepted this scheme with such ease." As we had done so, with me to his left, he in the center, and Georgiana to his right, we walked into the room to immense clapping from all the other occupants at the assembly.

"A part of me realized that I had no choice," he whispered as we walked down the aisle as people bowed to us.

"You could have come up with a lie saying that we were needed in Kent for some reason or another," I said, "for even you, in all your love for honesty, could have fabricated some tale or another."

"No, that is not what I mean. I mean that I remember the first impression I made on the people of Hampshire, and it became quite a fixed opinion of me that I was the most disagreeable man in the whole of the world. Therefore, I now see that I must rectify that first impression and give the people yet more chances for offering me a second one."

"And that second one is all that you need. The people shall love you, Fitzwilliam, for you are worthy of it."

We reached the other end of the room, and everyone began to converse again, and moved in preparations for the next dance by finding a partner. Darcy, without any fear or restraint, immediately secured my hand for the first two dances.

The dance began as we all lined up, and I was amazed as always, for my husband, though despising the amusement in general, was quite possibly the best dancer that I had ever seen.

"And you hate dancing!" I laughed.

"Right now, I am quite content."

"You are happy in knowing that you are improving people's opinion of you even more?"

"No, I am simply happy in my choice of a dance partner."

I blushed.

"You look beautiful, Elizabeth."

"As opposed to being tolerable, but not handsome enough to tempt you?" I teased.

"Yes. I really was wicked."

"And you have repented by correcting your past. You did not dance with me at the first assembly we had and called me tolerable. Now you call me beautiful, I am your wife, and I am the first woman you danced with tonight. You have quite undone history, showing that it is possible to do so. My dear husband, you are an eclipse."

"Am I?"

"Yes, for you are a natural phenomenon."

After our first two dances, Darcy danced with Kitty, Jane, Mary, yes, he coaxed Mary into dancing, Maria Lucas, Miss Long, Cassandra and Jane Austen.

He did his best to speak with as many as he could in innocent small talk, and it was made easy when he talked of us being presented at court, for this way, Sir William Lucas could add his own experiences of receiving his knighthood there, and being under the weight of the presence of royalty and the best of English aristocracy. Darcy, learning how to be happy with Sir William's volubility, began to let him do the talking while he sunk into comfortable silence next to me.

Before the night had ended and we all called our coaches, Jane Austen pulled me aside.

"Your husband is bent on improving people's opinions of him."

"He understands that he would do more to make friends than enemies."

"And he has been made all the better for your union, and out of my selfishness, I can say I profit from it in one thing."

"And what is that?"

She gave me a knowing smile. "I can always remember that I danced with Mr. Darcy of Pemberly. That was not something that I would have ever thought likely."

"Jane Austen, I warn you now, that if you gather a soft spot for my husband, it will put a strain on our relationship, and you shall not be a match for my defenses," I said in a nonthreatening way.

"I would never feel for him. I simply feel for the experience. And I am well acquainted with your daring and courage, Elizabeth. It is a rare thing to have. So, when do you go into Kent?"

"We leave in two days' time."

"When you see Pemberly, write to me of how you see it. I have heard much of the estate, yet I cannot envision it, and I wish to."

"The idea of it intimidates me."

"Why so?"

"It is said to be magnificent. Do I deserve such grandeur?"

"Yes, you do," Jane Austen said, her smile warm. "Enjoy Pemberly, Elizabeth. For it is your new home."

�

The day of our departure came and went speedily, yet not a moment too soon, and we were on the road again.

In our carriage, Georgiana, Kitty, Darcy and I had left the Drunken Prince Inn. Next, we went to Longbourn to express our farewells, to which our father smiled complacently to hide his sorrow at losing us again to other paths being taken.

Our mother was slightly hysterical at having a home that had only two daughters left to give her company rather than the traditional five, even though to marry us off had been her intention all along. She was forgetting that in her momentary desire to end the feelings of having an emptier home.

Jane stayed behind naturally, yet all had been arranged already, and Kitty was companion enough for Georgiana. When we had begun our journey once more, travelling from Longbourn to Pemberly, I felt our road lay at our feet, and another chapter of my life was beginning. To Pemberly. To Pemberly!

❦ 9 ❦

MRS. REYNOLDS

Looking out the window, the light from the sun in my eyes, I squinted and then turned away from the brightness. I looked at my husband who sat beside me. Next to him was Georgiana, while Kitty sat opposite me.

Darcy however was looking out of the window, smiling.

I nestled close to him. "You look happy."

"I am. We are now entering the borders of Pemberly."

"Really?" I perked up and began looking out the window. "Yet where is Pemberly house?"

"Oh, it is in the middle of the estate."

"Yet I do not see it." Then I turned to him. "My husband, precisely how large are Pemberly's grounds?"

"Large." Georgiana chuckled, answering the question for him. "It will be awhile before you see the actual house."

The carriage drove on and we passed many beautiful woods, smaller farms, and hills.

"This really all belongs to you?" Kitty asked, her eyes wide as she looked out of the window.

"Yes," Darcy replied.

"I confess that I never knew a man could own so much," she answered on a sigh.

"Nor I," I replied, looking at him fetchingly. "Do you own the whole world, I wonder?"

"I should hope not. The responsibility would be astounding, even for me."

We drove on for quite some time, to the point where I wondered if we would reach the house before suppertime, then Darcy leaned forward.

"All right, now prepare, for we shall turn around these set of trees and you shall see."

Just then, we turned and as the branches cleared away, there was Pemberly!

"Upon my word," I gasped, my heart in my throat.

Across the field, where there was a wonderful garden, rested Pemberly, which was quite possibly one of the most incredible homes that I had ever seen.

My mouth fell open, as did Kitty's.

"How is it possible..." she exclaimed.

"How indeed," I said, amazed.

Large and well placed, it was a house that represented all that was beautiful and good in the English aristocracy.

"Perhaps my house," Darcy quibbled, "renders even my worst flaws a little less repulsive. So how do you like the house, Lizzy and Kitty?"

"It is wonderful." Kitty gasped. "I have never seen its equal."

"Indeed," I began. "I have never found a place so happily situated, so perfectly made and complimented by nature. I like it very much." Then I turned to my husband. "And you were never repulsive!"

He chuckled and then we drove on.

The closer we got to the front steps of Pemberly, the more impressive it grew and not less. And when we reached the entrance, we were met by all the servants who were lined up with one woman at their head.

"They are all lined in such a way to meet me?" I said. "And I find myself worried, Fitzwilliam."

"Why so?"

"I wish to be the best mistress for them."

"And you shall be. Believe me, you shall be."

Jefferson opened the carriage door, Darcy stepped out first, then he helped Georgiana down, and then it was my turn. I looked toward Kitty.

"Here I go," I said.

"Yes, here you go. And there you are."

I took Darcy's hand and slowly emerged from the carriage. As I stepped down, all eyes fell on me and their mistress was now being glimpsed for the very first time.

As Darcy helped Kitty down, I moved toward Georgiana gracefully.

"There are so many of them."

"Yes, our staff is large."

"And I shall oversee them. I wish to learn all their names."

She gave me a warm smile. "You have the rest of your life to do so. It took me five months of my life to do it, therefore worry not."

After Kitty stepped down as well, the woman who was in the very front of the lineup of servants came forward.

"Master Darcy! It is wonderful to see you again and dear Miss Georgiana."

"Hello, Mrs. Reynolds," Darcy said, taking my arm. "I have finally brought you all a mistress. Might I present you to my wife, Mrs. Elizabeth Darcy, and her sister Miss Kitty Bennet."

"Mrs. Reynolds," I said. "I am honored to meet you, for I have heard much about your superior house holding skills."

"Thank you, Mrs. Darcy," Mrs. Reynolds said. "And I am very pleased to meet you as well. For so long, we hoped Mr. Darcy would find a mistress worthy of him, and yet it appears he has done so. Now let me show you to the sitting room, where we have prepared tea and cakes."

We curtsied to the servants and then followed her inside, where tea was set up and Mrs. Reynolds made many inquiries about our journey.

Realizing that we would like to change clothes and freshen up, she arranged to have maids show us to our rooms afterwards, and then proceeded to escort me to my room, which surprised me.

"Will Mr. Darcy and I not share a room?"

Mrs. Reynolds looked to Darcy with apprehension, but he only stood up firmly.

"Mrs. Reynolds, forgive me the oversight, yet I can lead Elizabeth to our bedchambers, for while we have adjoining rooms, we shall sleep in the same chamber."

"Very good, sir."

Darcy led me to the bedroom, and we took a route to which I was worried that I might forget the pathway of, but I was enjoying everything all the same.

"It is all truly remarkable, Fitzwilliam! Every part of the house I have seen so far is exquisite."

"Tomorrow I shall have Mrs. Reynolds give you and Kitty a tour of the house to get you better acquainted with everything. Yet when you appraise the house, and find anything not to your liking, then you can speak to me about any alterations that you might like."

"If you insist, yet I didn't come here to not recognize things that should not be changed, however. I came to be your wife, and as of now, all that I have seen is a home meticulously designed, whether it is at the hands of your mother or your grandmother. Nostalgia is a powerful thing that has a great hold on us all. I would never tear that from you."

"You respect my feelings."

"They are worth being respected above all things. Do I compliment you too much?"

"No, continue to do so."

I hid a smile. "Yet, thinking on what you have told me of the past, I cannot believe that one time you would have quite given up this great estate if your family had not approved of me."

I paused briefly. "Fitzwilliam, the compliment of your potential sacrifice is keenly felt within my spirit, and no one has loved me to such a degree. I would not have you give up a place that not only is of such beauty, but also is so dear to your heart. Therefore, in honor of your willingness to sacrifice your happiness under the shades of Pemberly, I am willing to accept your home as it is, and not change a thing."

"Thank you. I do like it as it is."

"I know you do. You were just not telling me because you wanted to show me that you valued my opinion, and that was also a nice gesture."

When we entered our bedroom, Darcy opened the door and led me in.

"And this, Mrs. Darcy, is where we shall live and be happy."

"Fitzwilliam, I know that we shall be."

❧

The next day, Mrs. Reynolds led Kitty and I around, giving us a tour of the house, while Georgiana also joined us.

Darcy was called away to see to matters of the estate, inquire after his tenants and read all letters that Jefferson laid out for him to peruse.

If I had all the talent in the world of describing wonderful architecture, design, and stateliness of a home, then I would do so, yet it is not my talent or my purpose, therefore I shall simply say that every room was as I described it: wonderful.

Eventually Mrs. Reynolds led us to a portrait gallery which held many paintings of the Darcy ancestry, but along the wall, she led us to a long portrait which turned out to be...

"Mr. Darcy!" I exclaimed, forgetting myself.

There was a wonderful life-size portrait of my husband staring down at us. I moved toward it instinctively and gazed up at it.

I was overcome. "A wonderful likeness. It has captured him to the very life."

"Very soon he shall wish for a portrait of you as well," Mrs. Reynolds said.

"Oh! I have never had my portrait taken before. It shall be a new experience."

Mrs. Reynolds looked on me with amusement.

"Well, I believe that he shall love the likeness of you being drawn."

I smiled gently and looked at the portrait once more, feeling the love I have for my husband almost deeper than it was before.

Later that evening, when I was helping one of my maids chose which gown I would wear for dinner, there was a knock on the door and the maid, named Lucy, opened it.

"Oh," Lucy said. "Mrs. Darcy, Mrs. Reynolds wishes to speak with you."

"Oh, let her in, Lucy."

Lucy moved aside and then Mrs. Reynolds entered.

"Mrs. Darcy, I am sorry if I did not come as soon as you wished, but I had to tell the staff that Mr. Darcy wanted his bath to be drawn for you all immediately after dinner. For you all wish to retire after you eat as opposed to enjoying each other's company in the sitting room."

"I understand the delay then," I offered, and then I turned to Lucy. "Lucy, I trust your judgment, you can pick out my gown for me."

"Really?" She answered, beaming, and then regained her serenity. "Very good, ma'am."

She went to my closet and began to look through it, leaving Mrs. Reynolds and I alone.

"Mrs. Reynolds," I began, "I shall be candid. I do not know the many experiences of being a wife, for this is the first time that I have been one. Yet one thing I have often heard of when a man first brings home a mistress, is that in her desire to please her husband, she tries to dominate the hired help, particularly the head of the household staff, which in this case is you."

"Oh."

"Yes, and while I will be firm in my position as I learn how to become so, I do not come with misplaced or improper pride. Nor do I come with a desire to change everything in the name of establishing myself as the matriarch. I know what I am. And I don't wish to define it by being petty or controlling. Your opinion is of importance to me. I will come to you for advice, and all I want is to be the best mistress to Pemberly, and for Mr. Darcy above all, because it is deserved of you all."

"Begging your pardon, Mrs. Darcy, but are your words spoken out of sincerity?"

"Yes."

Her face lit up. "Then that makes me glad."

"Also, if you would be so kind, I would like you to introduce me to the servants individually. A few everyday would suffice, so that I may learn their names and their personalities. I wish to display no coldness in my coming."

"That is a wonderful ambition, mistress," she said. "And if I may be so bold, speaking plain shall be best now. Mrs. Darcy, am I correct in assuming that you fear causing a bad first impression?"

I lowered my head and felt a blush. "Yes, I do not fear admitting to it."

"Then that is all well. Power should mostly be in the hands of those who do not desire it, and if you do not walk around always desiring it, you shall be a good mistress after all. I have been looking after Mr. Darcy since he was a child, and he was always good-natured. Yet I have always learned that they that are good-natured when they are young are good-natured when they grow older. For so long I worried that he would bring home a mistress who did not cherish him properly, and yet it has been made quite plain that you do favor him a great deal and that will be enough for you to be all that you must be."

She took a step toward me. "Embrace him always, Mrs. Darcy, for he relies very much on those that are closest to him. And because you have shown yourself to be on the way to being a fair and generous mistress, the servants are prepared to love you. If I can give the young mistress any advice, I give you this: win their hearts and you will have their loyalties."

She bowed to me and began to leave.

"Thank you," I said. "I shall endeavor to do so."

"Oh, it shall not be so hard, for you have already won half the battle quite easily."

"How so?"

"Oh, you already won part of their hearts when you first stepped off that carriage and they all saw that you were not Miss Caroline Bingley! That was our greatest fear of all."

I chuckled, happy to see that Miss Bingley was good for something. The example she set was so low that she made me appear as the perfect model.

And that was the beginning of my acquaintance with Mrs. Reynolds, the woman who had looked after my husband since he was a boy.

✣ 10 ✣

THE ARRIVAL

Over the next few days, I shadowed Mrs. Reynolds and learned all that I needed to know about the running of Pemberly, except for the time when I got lost wandering through the house and needed a servant to show me to my bedroom.

I also joined Darcy in meeting the tenants on his estate, seeing their farms, and watching him overseeing their concerns. I did my best to pay close attention in case I ever needed to take his place in maintaining the grounds if he were to ever be absent. I knew very well that Darcy relied on my inner autonomy and independence, therefore for me to take initiative and gather a love for the ways and workings of Pemberly would be most satisfactory to him.

Kitty and Georgiana did not join us often, because of the unspoken rule we all had of them doing their best to leave us to our company of two. And to that, they held well, and were able to maintain each other's company quite easily.

When finding out that Georgiana was a wonderful horsewoman, Kitty expressed a desire to learn how to be an equestrian. She asked Darcy if she could use one of the spare horses for practice, and he offered her the mare named Daedalus. He offered to show her how to ride, but Georgiana promised him that she and all the stablemen who worked on their grounds would be more than enough of a teacher and guide to her. Kitty, happy to still find some way to occupy herself while also not being in our way, declined his offer and only asked him to come out and inspect her form and progress once she felt that she made any.

For horse-riding takes much work and begins with simply feeding, cleaning and looking after the horse, building a relationship between horse and rider. After four days of constant work, Kitty was ready to try her hand at the horse-riding. Therefore, with the help of the stable hands and Georgiana's assistance, Kitty and Georgiana rode out together and trotted in the pasture.

Darcy and I came out to see her second day on horseback and it became clear that Kitty actually had it in her to be a remarkable horsewoman! She looked naturally comfortable on the beast, not fearful of the horse's mass or strength, but also commanding it in a way that made it willing to listen.

"Horses can actually be quite lazy," Fitzwilliam said to me as we watched Kitty ride alongside Georgiana. "And not listen to you if you don't use an imperative tone. Therefore, for the horse to listen to her so quickly is quite magical. Elizabeth?"

"Yes."

"When we are given more free time, would you let me teach you how to ride?"

"While I shall always be a great walker, and while I also admit that riding a horse frightens me a bit, over time, I believe that I can overcome that fear and be willing to be taught. Forgive me for not getting over my apprehensions of the sport immediately, but give me a year, and if I survive being mistress of Pemberly in that time, then learning how to ride a horse will seem like a small feat. And you will teach me when that day comes?"

"Of course, I will."

"Then I shall one day be up for the task."

I turned back and looked at Kitty as she laughed at her horse, Daedalus, jerking his head back and forth because a fly flew into its eye.

⚜

Unfortunately, with the sweet can come the sour, and one day, as Kitty and Georgiana were riding their horses, they got caught in the rain and came back to the house drenched from head to toe. It was quite amusing, though Darcy was a little vexed by the matter; he soon saw the humor in it. However, Georgiana woke up the next day to find herself sick with a cold.

Kitty and I sat with her, the doctor was called, yet the cold only worsened to a fever. Kitty felt terrible for the illness hitting her new best comrade, and her feelings, mingled with guilt, made her apprehensive about seeing Darcy.

However, after the third day, her sickness began to abate, and Kitty began to feel lighter and less at fault.

❖❖❖

"My dear," Darcy said while we lay in bed that night, "I have received word from Colonel Fitzwilliam."

"Oh, I worried about him. Did he not declare that he would arrive to Pemberly over three weeks ago?"

"Yes, and I worried when he did not arrive, so I sent a missive to my uncle at Matlock. He wrote in return that Richard was well, he was simply delayed and that he would write to me soon. I had received a letter yesterday, and Richard states that he shall be here on the morrow, yet he is not sure of what time he will arrive. I have sent instructions to the servants to keep an eye out for him and allow him entry immediately. He is coming from the continent, Elizabeth, where he led a sizeable militia in one post, but was lucky enough not to have led them into battle against Napoleon's forces."

"Yet I fear for him, Fitzwilliam. The French can always attack, and while war naturally is a danger, it is undeniable that the Colonel will one day face a lethal force."

"Yes, we worry for him. Richard was born lucky. That much is true, yet even luck can run out."

"All we can do however is make him comfortable while he is here," I said. "And offer him all the ease of being amongst family. Therefore, tomorrow morning, I shall make sure that his room is ready, and all the preparations are made for his arrival."

"Thank you."

"And would you be so kind as to tell me what he prefers to eat, so that we can have his favorite dish for dinner?"

"He and I eat the same things, so you need not worry about that. Nor do you need to vex yourself about making after-dinner entertainments. He simply loves hearing music being played, conversation and playing cards. His taste is simple and easy to appease."

"That is very good, yet when you refer to his loving music, you refer to Georgiana, correct? For I fear that you will make me play."

"Oh, of course I shall make you play, and he will encourage me. I might even make you sing as well."

I gave him a playful swat. "That is a terrible thing to do; you would quite frighten away our new arrival."

"Your singing voice is lovely, Elizabeth. And even if not so, Colonel Fitzwilliam has had to endure much on the battlefields. A woman's singing voice, even if she were awful, would not frighten our new arrival away."

"Then Colonel Fitzwilliam," I said with a laugh, "prepare yourself."

❧ II ❧

AT FIRST SIGHT

While Elizabeth Darcy was learning the ways and workings of Pemberly and becoming acquainted with the residents of the estate, there was another heroine on the grounds who must be attended to, and therefore, for the sake of glimpsing another event that was to occur, we must look to the one who it pertains to. Therefore, Elizabeth remained speaking in one room with Mrs. Reynolds, while Kitty, who by accounts is equally essential in the unfolding of many events, was elsewhere and soon was to meet the arrival.

When confirming that Georgiana was well, but needed solitude from her rest, Kitty left her room and was uncertain of what activity she could engage in. She thought to go to the library and read, yet she was never a great reader of novels, unless they contained the fantastic or the metaphysical, which were books that were not always considered acceptable to young ladies, who were recommended to bend their minds to more moral and theological views.

"When did it become lesser important or erroneous for us women to be amazed at the Legend of King Arthur and the Canterbury Tales." Kitty sighed as she walked through the large hallways. "Give me elves, dwarves, swords of magic and wizards any day as opposed to Fordyce's Sermons!"

However, while she was certain that Mr. Darcy would willingly allow her to find and read such books, she was still too intimidated by him to enter his study and request anything. The only reason, after all, that she had learned to begin riding was because of Georgiana and it was Georgiana who had asked Mr. Darcy to give Kitty a horse.

That is it! I can practice on Daedalus.

Realizing that surely there would be no blame on her part for riding without an escort, for the stablemen would be looking after her, Kitty went to her room, got dressed in her equestrian apparel, and then made her way down to the stables, where Nicholson, the main stableman, was awaiting her.

Smiling a fetching smile, she approached Nicholson.

He returned her smile. "Good day, Miss Bennet. Come to ride I see?"

"Yes, though I am missing my trusted companion, I still wish to continue my studies so that when she does recover, I shall be improved enough to run afield with her."

"You have great expectations."

"Am I wrong to do so?" Kitty asked innocently.

"There is nothing wrong in doing so, but I would exercise caution in that regard."

"You are afraid that I will fall?"

"No, I'm afraid that you will not forgive yourself if you do not improve at a swift pace. I have seen it often enough where a person tries to improve at something, particularly equestrian skills, they don't learn as quickly as they hoped and so they give the matter up entirely, feeling discouraged. To excel at something takes time, and you show great promise."

"I promise that I shall never get discouraged. I want to believe that I have it in me to forgive myself for looking the fool while I am learning something, as long as I get there in the end."

"Very good, Miss Bennet, you have the perfect disposition. Now let's prepare Daedalus for you."

The saddle was placed on the horse's back, the stirrups and the rest were added. Kitty took her whip in hand, allowed herself to be helped on the side saddle and then Nicholson watched her trot around the enclosure, making sure that she was moving at a suitable pace. As she continued to ride along, learning how to turn the horse to have Daedalus change directions, a rider approached from across the field. Kitty did not think on it at first, simply assuming it was one of the many farmhands who was running amuck for leisure, yet then the rider grew closer.

Nicholson moved forward protectively as the rider neared, yet when the man's identity became recognizable, Nicholson laughed.

"Well, I declare, Colonel Fitzwilliam!"

Kitty turned her horse around and beheld the Colonel growing closer.

Ah! So at long last, I meet the Colonel.

"Good day, Nicholson!" the Colonel said, approaching. Kitty urged Daedalus forward and trotted toward the Colonel who slowed his horse down, stopping at the beginning of the enclosure. He turned to Kitty and called out.

"Mrs. Darcy, I see that you have become quite the equestrian! And..."

Then his eyes narrowed, and he realized that he was in error.

"Oh, uh—"

Kitty's laugh was sparkling. "You have the correct family yet the wrong Bennet sister. You mistake me for my sister, Elizabeth, who is now Mrs. Darcy."

"I," he faltered. "Yes, I did."

"Your mistake is proper and understandable," Kitty immediately countered, seeing his embarrassment at being in error, "for she and I do look similar when I think on it."

"Yes, very much so."

"The benefits and deficiencies of sibling resemblance."

"There is no deficiency in this circumstance," Colonel Fitzwilliam answered. "Your sister is quite remarkable and therefore I am already disposed to find you everything that is amiable and worthy."

"You cannot do me such a wrong, for that will be most unfair."

"Unfair? How so?"

"To meet one sister and admire her is suitable, yet to transfer your thoughts and admirations on that one to another is frightening. What if I do not live up to my sister's image? What if you think she is the very emblem for femininity? Which means, that no matter my virtues, I am sure to disappoint, and you are certain to be disappointed."

He sat back in the saddle and crossed his arms over his chest. "You are an odd creature."

"I do not know what I am, for all I can say is that I am not my sister Elizabeth."

"Then we have gone so long into our conversation," Colonel Fitzwilliam said, dismounting his horse and approaching Daedalus, "and we still have not been formally introduced."

Kitty turned to Nicholson.

"Nicholson, would you do us the honor then?"

"Of course, Miss Bennet," Nicholson said, helping Kitty from the horse before Colonel Fitzwilliam could get the chance to do so. "Allow me to introduce you, Colonel Fitzwilliam, to Miss Kitty Bennet. And Miss Bennet, this is Colonel Richard Fitzwilliam."

After Kitty dismounted fully, she turned to Colonel Fitzwilliam and curtsied while he bowed.

"Colonel Fitzwilliam," she said, "it is pleasing to at last meet the man who I have had the good fortune to hear so much about."

"Good things or bad things, did you hear?"

Kitty smiled at him gently, yet her expression was unreadable.

"I shall not answer that question."

"And why not?" Colonel Fitzwilliam asked, perplexed at her rebuttal.

"Because I find it more amusing to leave you not knowing what I have heard, and therefore you must spend much of your time wondering, in misery, of what is said of you."

"Are you implying, Miss Bennet, that so early into our acquaintance, you are trying to torment me?"

"Yes, very much so."

"And why is that, I wonder?"

"Because, despite our differences, Elizabeth and I have one thing in common."

"And what is that?"

"We are sisters."

Colonel Fitzwilliam opened his mouth and closed it, not knowing what to make of the woman who stood before him. Elizabeth was a marvel of a woman, he knew this all too well, yet Kitty seemed to be a novelty; she was a mystery.

"Now," Kitty said, moving forward, "I have kept you from everyone else in the household. Nicholson, thank you for remaining with me. May you return Daedalus to the stables?"

"Yes, Miss Bennet, and Colonel, I shall take Hector as well, if that be your pleasure."

"Yes, Nicholson, thank you."

Nicholson led the horses away and Kitty and the Colonel were then left to accompany each other around the house and to the entrance.

"Well," Kitty began, "I should think it my duty to discuss rank."

"Oh, my position in the army of our Majesty's Militia."

"Oh, forgive me. I was referring to a more personal circumstance. You heard Nicholson refer to me as Miss Bennet, yet that is only due to the absence of my eldest sister. Jane is the oldest of us Bennets, then came Elizabeth until she wed your cousin, then our other sister, Mary, then me and lastly the youngest, Lydia."

"And so, you are the youngest but one?"

"Precisely. Therefore, if we Bennet girls were to be compared between sheep and goats, Jane and Elizabeth would be the goats, and I would still just be a sheep!"

Colonel Fitzwilliam laughed at the reference, comprehending the wit behind it.

"And yet," Kitty said, "while it was natural for you to see Elizabeth in my features, I knew you immediately. You resemble your brother very much, and yet you also look different. The Fitzwilliam look is there, but you are still unique."

"I shall take that as the best of compliments. Yes, I received word that you have met my brother. And while we look similar, only time will tell if you think our minds, spirits, and personalities differ."

"Do you see similarity in that regard to your brother, or do you see yourself as different from him?"

"It is the nature of siblings to think themselves different than their brothers or sisters, therefore I wish to believe that I am unique, as you say, yet I am not a sound judge. Surely, the desire for distinction amongst siblings is something that you can relate to, or were you superior to us other middle children in that you did not feel that way ever, Miss Bennet?"

"Oh, I felt that way all too often and perhaps I felt my station too keenly. For so long I let the desire to stand out render me into foolish predicaments, until I learned the valuable lesson."

"And what lesson is that?"

"Do not try to prove yourself different, or remarkable, but only allow yourself to be those things. And when you achieve it, whether the world sees your achievement or not, then you have obtained victory, and then you are unique."

"Then I shall endeavor to not try in that regard."

"You've already shown the fruits of not trying. Even if I wished to look at you as another version of Mr. Henry Fitzwilliam, you have already proven yourself different in one way."

"And how is that?" Colonel Fitzwilliam asked, highly amused and despite himself, intrigued.

"You rode to Pemberly across the fields, and not down its road, which is why you came upon me instead of being met first by the rest of the household."

"Are you surprised with my deciding to come by an indirect route as opposed to taking the road?"

"Yes."

"And what does that show you about me?"

"I cannot say entirely, not because I have no ready opinion, but because I wish to see if you will tell me yourself what you think it says about you. What do you think it means, Colonel, that you travel over the fields and not along the road?"

Colonel Fitzwilliam looked ahead and attempted a clever way to phrase his answer.

"I think," he began, "that it shows I feel very much at home at Pemberly, that I can come and go in such an unmannerly way and still be forgiven. Yet therein lays a hidden distinction; I desire ties that are so comfortable that I can be in error and the people can still find me amusing."

"Anything else, or have you covered everything about yourself?"

"I suppose I am missing more internal discoveries, yet I can say that it shows, when allowed, I am not afraid to be..."

"Different?"

"Yes, different. Which I suppose is a wonderful thing for us middle children to have."

Kitty cocked him a glance. "I wonder how different our experiences as a middle child were. Yet whether your upbringing was fortunate or merely well enough, I daresay I had it the harder."

"How so?"

"I am the middle child of five sisters."

"And I am the middle son of three boys."

"Three boys... three men, who born under such a rank, have been given the best of an education, has been given a better understanding with the ways of the world, and have been granted luxuries, and are still, as the world has offered, men, and are allowed to be granted more enjoyments. Yet to be the middle of five girls, eventually Colonel, one feels the limits of one's life."

"Limits?" He turned to her. "Miss Bennet, your limits are more than mine, tis true, yet when I unfold my life to you, you shall see that we both are fortunate in some ways, and yet also suffer in others equally."

"You are suggesting that we are similar in our fates?"

"Oh yes, Miss Bennet, very much so. And since my stay here will fortunately be for a month, more than an ample fortnight, I will show you just how similar we are."

Kitty and Colonel Fitzwilliam reached the steps of Pemberly and she turned to him.

"Whatever discoveries you wish me to learn of, they shall have to wait till I am able to get you comfortable enough to speak with me in such a way again."

"That shall not be hard, Miss Bennet. For I by no means would withhold any pleasure of yours."

"That is a very polite response, Colonel."

"It was sincere however."

Kitty walked up the steps first and then she turned back to him, smiling.

"Yet remember that while you have no choice but to call me Miss Bennet in the presence of others, when we are not surrounded by many others, you must call me Kitty."

"Must I?" Colonel Fitzwilliam laughed. "Why *must* I?"

"Because we are cousins now. And I want you to be comfortable around me."

"Yes," he whispered, "we are cousins."

The front doors to Pemberly opened and Mrs. Reynolds exited.

"Colonel Fitzwilliam, you are arrived at last! Yet let me see if I have this right: you travelled across the fields again instead of the road, didn't you?"

"Of course, I did," Colonel Fitzwilliam replied charmingly. "I did so just to vex everyone and put them on their guard."

"And it never works, for we are used to you. And you have met Miss Bennet here."

"Yes," Kitty said, "he has met me in full."

"Well then, come inside you both, so that the occupants of the household can all give proper introductions."

Colonel Fitzwilliam moved aside and allowed Kitty to enter first, smirking behind her as they did so.

❦

To say that heartfelt "hellos" were offered was to say the least. Upon his arrival, Colonel Fitzwilliam's presence caused much warmth and affection to be displayed. Darcy, upon seeing his favorite cousin arrive, immediately felt and appeared lighter in mood, Elizabeth was overjoyed, Mrs. Reynolds grew even more maternal over him than she was over Darcy, and Georgiana came from her sickbed to sit with the rest of the family in the sitting room and be given some tea.

"Oh dear, Georgiana," Colonel Fitzwilliam said. "It is awful to see you unwell."

"It is of little matter," Georgiana said, "for I am quite over the worst of it. A few more days and I shall be as I always was. And probably still as inclined to not be afraid of the rain."

"You sound as if you don't wish to learn from your mistakes, Georgiana," Darcy said.

"One can get sick from the rain, Fitzwilliam, but it should not deter their courage to face nature at her most torrential again."

"Thank you, cousin," Georgiana said. "I am made of stronger stuff than most. I shall recover and be the better for it."

"Now," the Colonel said, looking between Darcy and Elizabeth. "You both look well, thus, I must say. Married life suits you, Fitz, and Mrs. Darcy; it only makes you appear more beautiful, if that were possible."

"Thank you, Colonel," Elizabeth said, "and while I should say that this is too much praise, I am disposed to enjoy it."

"You should."

"Richard," Darcy began, "I was told that Kitty was the first that you came upon."

"She was," Richard said, turning to Kitty. "And she left a marked impression."

Darcy turned to Kitty, smiling at her.

"Did you now?"

"Yes," Kitty said. "For I found myself referring to us Bennets in a very bestial light once more."

"Oh, so you have done this more than once?" Colonel Fitzwilliam laughed.

"Yes, this time I compared us to sheep and goats, while the first time I compared us to a pride of lions. Colonel, the lion reference was directed to your brother when we dined with our family at Grosvenor Square."

"And what was his reaction?"

"He was taken aback by it."

"Then I pride myself on being different, for I was not taken aback."

"Then what was your reaction?" Mrs. Darcy asked.

"I was simply wishing for an explanation, and when given it, it made perfect sense, for Kitty explained it well, without explaining it at all."

"And what was it?" Darcy asked.

"She simply said that she was a Bennet woman, and somehow that was enough explanation for me."

Everyone laughed.

⬥

After an hour, Georgiana had to retire to her room to gain some rest, and Kitty and Elizabeth escorted her there. When she was placed in her bed, Elizabeth left Georgiana in the care of Kitty while she attended to the cooks to arrange what dinner would be served. When alone, Georgiana turned to Kitty, who sat in a seat and looked at her friend in amusement.

"Well," Georgiana said, "now you have met my cousin, Richard, and what do you think of him?"

"It is hard to tell after so short of an acquaintance," Kitty began, "for one cannot make an accurate portrait of a person at first sight, yet I can honestly say that I have fallen in love with him."

12

WHAT IS IRRATIONAL STILL OUGHT
TO BE DISCUSSED

G eorgiana practically fell out of bed. "You what?!"

"I know," Kitty said, "it is quite unprecedented."

Georgiana, out of surprise at the moment, began to stutter.

"Did I truly hear you correctly, Kitty?"

"Sadly, yes."

A smile escaped Georgiana, despite herself.

"Well, this is amusing to say the least. Yet in between you meeting him in the fields to entering Pemberly at his side, what happened to spark interest?"

"I cannot say for certain," Kitty admitted, "and I shall be the first woman to admit that nothing I feel is logical. It is something that is felt at the whim of the moment, and very well might just be a feeling of the second, yet I do not think so."

"Then try and give me one reason that you feel this... bond?"

Kitty paused a moment and then answered, "I feel immediately comfortable around him. In a way that I have never felt with another man before."

"Well, my cousin does have that effect on women in general."

Kitty nodded. "And I am not surprised. He is charming to say the least. And while charm is dangerous, where both genders are involved, being reasonable is not something that attraction always bends its way toward."

"Attraction never bends itself to being reasonable," Georgiana groaned. "And that's what makes it so vexing and tedious to say the least."

"Precisely. When I walked with him, I immediately wished to get to know him. And what's more, I am the last woman to be suited for him."

Georgiana gave her a quizzical look. "What do you mean?"

"I mean that it is my everlasting sad twist of fate to always feel deep affection for men who either will never love me or would never regard me as worthy to be fallen in love with."

"Kitty, you must not think of yourself so meanly."

"It is not mean to see a pattern that rules your life," Kitty answered, "and do not fear. I shall not let it lead me to fawn over him in a vulgar manner. I would have done so once, yet now that I know what love is, or at least what infatuation is, I know that it is not something that is meant to be rushed into, no matter how quickly one feels it. I know he may very well never fall in love with me."

"If he does not, Kitty, promise me that you will not fall into dejection when you become broken-hearted. I know how it feels to fall in love quickly and then to be ripped from it and rejected. While I did not do anything to expose myself to the world for being foolish or insipid, I still did not handle it as well as I should have."

Georgiana settled against her pillows. "And the only reason no one ever saw me break down and cry, throw something out of pain, or humiliate myself was because I shut myself up in my room after that and suffered the indignity of being used and abused in secret."

Kitty's look was sympathetic. "You fear me exposing myself to the world and then shriveling up and becoming a bitter crone for it."

"Yes, I do fear that."

"Then your concern for my sanity flatters me, Georgiana, yet you need have no fear. I am not in any danger. I foolishly like him so short into knowing him, yet I know that it is an irrational thing and I shall not make a mockery of myself. I shall keep it a secret between ourselves, and enjoy the feeling of being infatuated, and be ready for when nothing comes of it."

"That is a wonderful outlook on it. Yet, Kitty, what of his brother? You know as well as I that Henry did feel something for you."

"I know," Kitty said, growing quiet and losing her confidence. "And I don't know what to do in that regard. Henry has grown fond of me, I have grown fond of his brother, and his brother most likely cares little for me except that I am now family. I shall remain in my own confidence, and not act rashly, in hopes that I cause no pain on any side with my emotions. I wish that I weren't so illogical at the moment."

"What is irrational still ought to be discussed," Georgiana acknowledged. "It is no crime. Yet good luck in winning out over your heart. For it is quite a strange organ."

They sat there momentarily and then Georgiana randomly began to laugh.

"And what is so amusing?" Kitty smiled.

"You like my cousin. That is what is so amusing!"

❧ 13 ❧

THE MAN BEHIND THE MYSTERY

The arrival of Colonel Fitzwilliam to Pemberly was a welcome addition, I shall not attempt to deny. He not only was a comforting presence, but he was more. I never forgot how when Lydia and Wickham eloped, it was the Colonel who had roused Darcy and called him to action. Therefore, while it was safe to say that my husband was an honorable man, it was Colonel Fitzwilliam who knew how to awaken that goodness and remind Darcy that he still had it within him.

Yet blindness was not my flaw to have in this regard and when we first sat down together after his arrival, I could not deny that he and Kitty looked strangely curious about one another. Kitty observed him with nothing short of affection, he regarded her with nothing less than something he enjoyed resting his eyes on, and I was hesitant to declare what to make of it.

I decided not to mention it to Darcy as of yet, for I hoped that I was seeing things that were not there. Yet if I had been correct in my assessment, then this all would prove to be most inconvenient and calamitous.

If we all were most fortunate, Henry Fitzwilliam's attraction to Kitty would prove to be nothing more than a passing fancy, and now that she was no longer in his presence, he would forget about her.

Yet if Henry would seek her out, while his brother was forming secret designs on her, it would be the most uncomfortable and harsh of circumstances that no one would wish to confront. Brother would be put against brother, and Kitty would be the cause through which bad blood formed between them. She would, in all essentials, become their battleground. However, I attributed my conclusions to paranoia, and decided not to find a dilemma when no conflict was truly there.

All that could be done was wait. And see how all would unfold.

***

That evening, we all sat down to dinner, yet Georgiana wished to remain in bed, for all she wanted was some soup and rest. Therefore, at the table, all that remained were Kitty, Darcy, Colonel Fitzwilliam and me.

"How goes the peninsula, Richard?" Darcy asked.

"Oh, it is as it always is," Richard said. "It's a war, and it is always waiting for me."

"The Peninsular War began in 1808," I added. "And is still going on. Is there any hope for an end in sight?"

"Especially now that war between Britain and America once more seems about to break upon us," Kitty added.

"I wish that I had better news for you, other than the mere fact that the Peninsular War does not affect England much, not nearly as much as it pertains to Spain and Portugal, who are contributing the most to the War. Over the last two years, Napoleon has waged battles and campaigns in various parts of Spain and Portugal. Numerous battles."

"Yet they were inconclusive, were they not?" Kitty asked. "And therefore while the French did not lose ground, they did not gain it either."

"Yes," Colonel Fitzwilliam confirmed, eyeing Kitty keenly. "You follow the events of the war."

"Only in moderation," Kitty said. "News about the war was never much spoken of at home."

"Indeed," I added. "We came from a household where the entrance of a new arrival into our neighborhood caused more excitement and words spoken than the movement of armies, especially the Peninsular War. We never got the chance to speak of it, because no one wished to listen to what we had to say."

"That is a great tragedy," the Colonel added. "Yet it is war, and whoever wants to think on such things, I suppose? However, those of us who are involved in it, well, it makes us feel better that there are individuals such as yourself, Miss Kitty, who do monitor and care for our movements."

"It is our duty," I said.

"And yet it makes me confused," Kitty continued. "For with all the battles and campaigns, I would have thought the strength of the French Armies would be depleted."

"Oh, they have been. Napoleon's constant desire for conquest has worn down the French, in both men and in materials. He only has now roughly 200,000 soldiers left. As of this year, Napoleon has begun to direct his whole attention toward Russia."

"Russia?"

"Yes, he is determined to do it. My company is posted in the Iberian Peninsula, in hopes of keeping him at bay if he ever were to march one of his legions across that way."

The Colonel toyed with his food. "As for America, I have it upon good information that the war is coming and we shall best prepare for it. It is a foolish war, yet it has also been made apparent to me that my unit shall never be ones that are dispatched to fight them. This news makes me happy, for war in that quarter will be the more imminent danger, and it also is a matter of pride. I do not support our going to war against America, and I had hoped that all this intolerance and miscommunication ended after we lost them as colonies."

"Yet imagine if it had all ended different," Kitty said, her face pinching up as she thought on the matter. "If the revolution had never occurred. They would still be our colonies, we would be even stronger as a country, and this would not be happening. Then again, it is useless to speculate on something that has already occurred."

"It's still amusing to do so," The Colonel said. "Speculation of a past incident whose results cannot be changed is a natural thing to do. And yet, I always found that the American Revolution was unavoidable. Say that they did approve of our taxation, or that King George had responded to their pleas with reason and diplomacy, America has simply become so enormous!"

He put down his fork. "You have all seen it yourselves. It is a vast land with many people within it. And many came from other lands that were not even under the British rule. For us to think we were going to maintain them, when not only are they plenty in number, yet also separated from us by a large ocean, that was wishful thinking."

He cleared his throat and took a sip of wine. "Also, it is the way of human nature to want freedom, in whatever form you need to find it in. Do you, Kitty, never desire liberty? I can tell that you do, quite often, and if you desire it, and I know I desire it, our colonies desiring it is inevitable. Even if there was no strain between them and us, it is just simply human nature to desire independence. That is why after the war ended, all anger between both countries ceased after a while. For we all knew, in some way, that the desire for autonomy, whether it be individually or nationally, is an inevitable dream all will have."

"Then," I began, "it could also be argued, that if the American War for Independence had not occurred in 1775, then the war we face now between both lands would have become it. Think of it! Assume that America was still the British colonies, and then English vessels began to impress American sailors. And that America respected our connections and boundaries in Canada. America would be upset, angered over the injustice, they would send petitions to the king, nothing would come of it, and America would revolt."

"Sadly then," Kitty concluded, "the Revolutionary War was inevitable? We were destined to lose our colonies."

"It is a puzzlement," Colonel Fitzwilliam said. "But it is true, I believe."

"Well then," Darcy interjected, "if we lost them as a colony, due to as you so put it, the inevitable desire for independence that every individual has, then it can be argued that we shall eventually lose all of our colonies."

"It's human nature, and with human nature, all is possible. Even the last things you hope to be possible."

"And yet," Darcy said after our findings, "even I secretly desire such a thing to be undone. I am not known for being a romantic, yet I do voice an ancient wish. I wish that strife and rebellion had not occurred. I feel a connection to America. And you have all seen it. They feel it with us as well. One day, mark my words; we will regret the loss of connection. Both sides will learn to miss the other."

"Oh, we shall," Kitty said. "Yet it does not necessarily follow that the bond is broken completely. Britain and America are more than simply the people who are in it. It is the land themselves. Though they be separated by an ocean, both lands will remain linked to one another, despite the wars the people on them wage. There is a Great Connector there; we just don't see it, for we are mere mortals."

"You were in error, Kitty," Colonel Fitzwilliam said. "You are very much not a sheep."

Kitty smiled shyly and looked away.

"Richard," Darcy said, his voice icing over as he began to reprimand, "do you forget your manners? Her name is Miss Bennet."

"Oh yes," Colonel Fitzwilliam chuckled. "Yes forgive me for breaching the bounds of propriety and calling you by your first name, Miss Bennet, and I do not know of what has come over me."

"It is all very well," Kitty said, her smile warming. "No offense was taken, I can assure you."

Then they looked on each other in a way that implied significance. They were sharing some form of an inside joke. The rest of the dinner went smoothly, yet it was apparent as the Colonel gave Kitty too many significant looks that were too marked to be mistaken. He was intrigued by her as well.

As for Kitty, she smiled at him often. There was a comfort between them that was unmistakable, and she valued his words.

Unlike at Grosvenor Square, where she spoke to Henry out of innocent politeness and familiar pleasure, there was more in regards to the Colonel.

At first, I was worried that she enjoyed him because he was a soldier and many a lady has swooned over an army officer. Yet the Colonel wore no regimentals and therefore could not gather more distinction in them and appear more dashing.

No, she simply enjoyed being near Richard, for which I should not have been surprised. For even before they met, I always had the strange notion that of all my sisters, the Colonel would have the most in common with Kitty. I just did not know of to what extent it could have been, and that Kitty's curiosity could then move swiftly to intrigue and affection to the Colonel, and the man behind the mystery.

❧ 14 ❧

RUNNING FREE

The next day, Kitty found herself desirous of another morning ride after breakfast and she announced as much to the residents of Pemberly.

Darcy allowed it, given that she never leave the sight of Nicholson. Kitty naturally agreed to this and even went so far as to tease Darcy about being protective over her. Mr. Darcy blushed at this, enjoying her gradual growing comfort around him.

After Kitty left, Colonel Fitzwilliam said that he wished to take his solitary walk of the park as he had done every time that he visited, and all readily believed him. However, as he walked, he never went out of view of the stables, and lo and behold, very soon he saw Kitty walking out of the house and toward the stables.

Once she mounted and Nicholson oversaw her, Colonel Fitzwilliam left his vantage point and then made his way to her.

Once he was there, he pulled his horse Hector out of his stall, fastened the saddle and then he rode out of the stables, and began riding toward Kitty.

"Colonel Fitzwilliam!" she cried, turning her horse around and trotting toward him. "You fancy a ride this morning?"

"I find nothing finer than a good ride after breakfast. And I see that you feel the same."

"Yes, I do. And yet you knew that before."

"Oh yes, your announcement to the table. I must say, outside of Mrs.

Darcy, I have never seen another successfully tease my cousin in such a way."

"I was not erroneous, was I?" Kitty asked. "I was hoping our relationship as brother and sister-in-law was now strong enough to allow him to feel a comfort with me enough to begin taunting him affectionately."

"Oh, he enjoyed it. And yet, if you had known him so long as to wait till now to begin teasing, then I confess that I find myself gratified."

"Why so?"

"You waited till only a couple minutes after our acquaintance to tease me."

"Your presence brings ease, I admit."

"Another compliment?" Colonel Fitzwilliam laughed, an infectious sound. "And so early in the morning at that. I must be glowing."

"Don't flatter yourself so," Kitty responded, but she said it lightly.

"I don't, when you are the one who does it for me. Now, since you and I both find ourselves enjoying a morning ride, how about we journey out across the fields together?"

"I am a beginner, and therefore you shall not be able to ride with such liberty as you would wish," Kitty replied soberly. "You should ride without me, for I am certain to disappoint."

"Now you are being humble?" the Colonel replied. "You are constantly changing your mode of speech with me and it is making me quite dizzy. I would not tire of riding alongside you. If anything, this will be a great benefit. I have trained many how to ride before, and I would be apt to teach you."

"Very well then," she said, turning to Nicholson. "Nicholson, you are free, sir, and be glad that you need not babysit me any longer. I shall ride with the Colonel."

"Right, Miss Bennet."

Kitty pulled her horse near the Colonel's and they began to trot Daedalus and Hector alongside each other.

"You once said," Kitty began as they rode along, "that we are similar in our fates."

"Oh, yes, that conversation that we had when we first met."

"Yes, the improper one."

"Oh, so now you are calling it improper. That is a much-delayed reaction."

"I always thought it was so, I just found it important to have."

"And why so?"

"Because I don't want an acquaintance out of you. I want a friend."

"Then you have it, Miss Bennet."

"Do not fear. My protective brother-in-law is not present and therefore, you may call me Kitty once more."

"As long as you call me Richard."

"Thank you, Richard. You do feel more like a friend."

"I am happy to be so. Now why did you bring up our previous conversation?"

"We said much that was left open."

"Oh yes, we did indeed," he agreed. "Is there a particular aspect of our discussion, an expression, a quote that has remained with you most?"

"You either have a terrible memory, or you are intentionally acting as if you forget what I said. And I know that you have a good memory, Richard."

"Another compliment. Be careful, or I shall begin to blush."

"Don't distract me with your charm, o' you rattle! When you said that our fates were similar than you think, what did you mean?"

They cantered along easily, side by side. "I implied simply that yes, my upbringing was more luxurious, and yes, you are right; as a man, I have more liberty than you. Yet as a second son, I was born without much of an inheritance, therefore I had to become a man of occupation."

"And yet, you can earn your living," Kitty said, still smiling, however. "I do not begrudge nor belittle your pains for having a life where you must put it in danger of any kind, and I admire you officers and your sacrifice. Yet at least you never have to feel displayed like a brood mare or must be forced into being shallow and easily bought. That's also no blissful life as well."

He turned to her, quizzical. "What do you mean by all this?"

"I mean that to live in a house with five daughters, then the estate is entailed away to the next male, which means that you all have no claims to it. Since I can remember, it was impressed upon all five of us that to save the family we had to marry well, and by well, I don't mean for love, I mean solely for monetary gain. I was told to not measure a man by the size of his soul, but the power of his purse. And then, when deciding to reject the notion of that, and denying a proposal that would save the family, I was censured and despised."

"You are you implying that you turned down a wedding proposal?"

"And there is the look of disgust again, even from you."

"Indeed, I am not disgusted," he replied hurriedly, "I am simply amazed. Who was this man who thought himself worthy of you?"

"His name is Mr. William Collins, Richard, and he is the reverend to the parish of Hunsford."

"That Mr. Collins!"

"Oh, you know him? Oh, but of course you do. He is the reverend for your aunt's estate, Rosing's Park. I just never thought that you and he would have fallen into each other's paths and met before."

"Oh, I had met him before. Enough to know that you were right and just to refuse him. Why then did your parents not support your refusal? One look at the man and it only makes sense that you did."

"Because of the entail. Mr. Collins is our cousin and the next in line to inherit Longbourn upon my father's death. Therefore, if Mr. Collins were to marry one of us, then Longbourn would remain in our family, and if our father were to pass away, I would then save our family. Whether you find it selfish of me is of no consequence to me. I did not love him and therefore I could not marry him."

His expression softened. "I do not think ill of you for following your feelings at such a time. For in such matters, our feelings ought to be considered."

"My father was sympathetic toward my decision, yet my mother was merciless on me and was bitter at my decision, accusing me of ruining the family, ruining any good will we might have gained with Mr. Collins, and therefore I was a disappointment."

Kitty reached down and stroked her mount's neck. "Yet it was not simply because I did not love him. To be always told that we women only have a chance, a hope, if we marry a man simply for his wealth, should husbands and wives be selected so? It appears to be a great evil. And that is where the chains were placed upon me at the hardest. Yet when Lydia married, while it was to a questionable match, our mother's resentment abated, and Elizabeth's falling in love with Darcy has now saved us all. Therefore, there is no use for me to find my fate or not. Therefore, Richard, your fate is not mine. You are more fortunate."

"Unfortunately, I was correct in what I said before. Our fates are similar and up until your sister's marriage, it would have continued to be so. Yet now you have found luck, when I still am confined to a loveless match."

"What nonsense are you speaking, Richard?" Kitty asked, while maintaining a light demeanor. "You are a Colonel with a regiment. You have a profession and are independent."

"Am I?"

She slanted him a glance, her eyebrows arched. "Are you about to tell me otherwise?"

"Yes, a younger son, you know, must be inured to self-denial and dependence."

Kitty chuckled, amused.

"In my opinion, the youngest son of an Earl can know very little of either. Now, seriously, what have you ever known of self-denial and dependence? When have you been prevented by want of money from going wherever you chose, or procuring anything you had a fancy for?"

"These are home questions and perhaps I cannot say that I have experienced many hardships of that nature. But in matters of greater weight, I may suffer from the want of money. My profession gives me economy enough to live on, but not enough to support a wife, family and ensure that they live their whole lives comfortably. Younger sons cannot marry where they like."

"Unless where they like women of fortune," Kitty answered with a sigh, "which I think they very often do."

"Our habits of expense make us too dependent, and there are not many in my rank of life who can afford to marry without some attention to money."

Kitty blushed and looked down. *Is this meant for me? Could he be wishing to most kindly put me on my guard and let me know, without saying the words, that I am not suitable enough for him due to my lack of a dowry?* To cover her silence, however, she smiled and brightened her tone.

"And pray, what is the usual price of an Earl's younger son? Unless the elder brother is very sickly, I suppose you would not ask above fifty thousand pounds."

"Fifty thousand pounds is the minimum that I require of a partner in life."

"Oh." Kitty remained silent at first, and then she realized that her not speaking would make him believe that she was affected by his words, so she decided to turn back to the beginning of their discussion.

"Then you were correct, Richard, our lives were both very similar. We were both born with restrictions and were expected to marry someone of good fortune to save our family or save ourselves. Then I suppose, though he is merely my brother- in-law, I owe Mr. Darcy as much as my sister does. He has saved me and my sisters from a terrible fate if we do not find homes for ourselves. And has saved me from having to choose the wrong companion if the opportunity would ever arise."

"There are quite a few heroes in our family," Colonel Fitzwilliam said.

"Are there?" Kitty replied evenly. "I had not noticed."

She increased the speed of her horse and rode a little forward. Richard, seeing that she was affected, urged his horse onward.

When he reached her, his heart softened, and he looked for a way to ease the confession he gave of her being unsuitable for him.

"Kitty, have you ever run your horse across the fields?"

"I have not gone faster than a trot, on the contrary."

"Would you like to do so now?"

"But I have not the skills. And if the horse does not stop, I do not know how to rein him in if he should not listen to me."

"And yet I do," he replied, looking at her challengingly. "Do you not trust me?"

"I trust your tenacity," she replied, grinning, "yet I wonder if I am safe under it."

"I will not let you fall. Believe me, I have caught many a fellow equestrian if need be."

Kitty looked down, indecisive.

"Is Kitty Bennet afraid?"

"Yes, if you must know. And yet, I don't fear falling and receiving injury. As foolish as it sounds, I could take bruises, cuts, or even a broken arm if I can say that I bore it valiantly."

"Then what do you fear?"

Kitty looked straight at the Colonel. "I fear making a fool of myself."

"Oh... well then."

Colonel Fitzwilliam pulled his horse close to Kitty's, and in one fell action, he pulled her off her horse, raised her up and placed her in front of him on his.

"Richard!"

"Do not worry!" He laughed, reaching around her, brandishing the reins, and Hector was off, racing across the fields. Kitty grabbed onto Colonel Fitzwilliam's arms for dear life, but as they sped along, she looked out ahead of them and enjoyed the thrill of the run.

"Are you enjoying yourself now?" His voice was not lost in the wind.

"Yes," she shouted, "but I fear falling out of your embrace and on the ground. Stop so that I can make myself more secure."

"As long as you promise that you won't try to escape me."

"I promise. Do not fear. I know that you are safe. Though you can be a rattle often."

"It is a hard thing to be," Richard said, slowing down. "When we men are charming, we are accused of being rattles, yet when we lack charm, we are accused of being dull. How can you account for such hypocrisy?"

"I cannot," Kitty said as they slowed completely. "Now do not let go of me."

Kitty did not dismount, but only swung around Richard's body, not riding side saddle any longer, but with each leg apart and dangling on each side of the horse's back. Her dress rose higher to her thighs, but she thought no more of it.

"Kitty Bennet!" Richard cried. "Even you have left me speechless."

"I do not do this to break propriety any more than we have already done so, yet out of safety," she said, wrapping her arms tightly around his waist, to which Colonel Fitzwilliam immediately felt an emotional effect. "No, sir. I simply do it because this way I am less likely to fall, for only if you fall do I fall with you."

"I will not fall."

Kitty chuckled, amused. "You had better not falter, Richard, for my life depends on it. And I need not worry of you telling on me, for if you do so, you have to incriminate yourself as well, for you never should have removed me from my horse. In other words, I know you shall keep quiet, for you would not wish to get into trouble yourself."

"Then this will be our secret, then."

"I trust you, Richard."

"Ah, how foolish of you." His words were laced with humor.

Colonel Fitzwilliam urged his horse onward and then Kitty and he were racing across the acres of Pemberly, on the back of Hector, who was running free.

❧ 15 ❧

THE LAST WOMAN IN THE WORLD

As Kitty rode behind Richard, she could not help her emotions as they ran as free as the beast that was underneath them. Pressed so firmly behind Richard, she felt the warmth and strength of his body and her spirit was greatly affected by it.

Who are you to always be having me feel thus? Why can I not deny you anything as I ought? Is that how Elizabeth felt, no matter all the times that Darcy hurt her? This painful inability to reject the man because your feelings for him are so strong and prominent? It is too much, too much for my bearings. And why have I fallen for you so swiftly? Is this love, no it cannot be, and I was a fool for thinking so. My attraction to you was immediate and indescribable; therefore, I must learn that this is an infatuation and no more. Yet I cannot say no to you today. Hopefully, though this be sad to admit, I pray that I at least have the ability to say no to you tomorrow.

❧❧❧

While deep within her thoughts, Richard was overcome by his own. Colonel Fitzwilliam was aware that despite his good intentions, he was a bit of a flirt, and as Kitty called him, a rattle. He prided himself on never becoming a rake however and knew that he would never slip that far into his love for women's company to such a degree that he did not see how he hurt them.

And yet, what was he doing now? On the contrary, he was doing the exact thing that he knew he should avoid. He was taking Kitty off alone, riding with her improperly, and taking her to a secluded location. If any were to glimpse them, Kitty's reputation and her good name would be in danger. And now it was all because of him! While Richard did not agree with Darcy's kissing Elizabeth often without committing himself to her at all, Darcy at least did it in a way that they would never get discovered and Elizabeth's reputation would never suffer for his carnal desires. Richard could not offer Kitty anything, and here he was, taking advantage of her softness toward him and possibly ruining her at the same time.

And yet, he could not slow his horse down, nor turn it around and dismount so that Kitty and he would only be seen walking together. He now began to understand how Darcy had felt. People ridicule moral lapses as if they are easy things to avoid, and some are, yet not in matters such as this. When before a strong attraction, and single yourself, a person's mind can easily fall into not caring about the effects of their actions. Richard did not despise himself that day, yet he knew that he would hate himself on the next.

Eventually, they reached a stream that bordered the edge of Pemberly.

"This place is lovely," Kitty said.

"Yes, when we were children, Fitz and I would ride our horses here."

"Fitz?"

"Oh, that is our nickname for Darcy. His name is Fitzwilliam Darcy, but that's quite a mouthful of a first name, ergo sometimes we just call him Fitz."

"Fitz! I like that. Yet though I am growing more comfortable around him, I do not think that I will ever develop a close enough bond to him to call him that."

"It takes years of camaraderie, tis true."

Richard slowed his horse down to a halt, tied him up to a branch, placed his hands around Kitty's waist as she held his shoulders and he lowered her down. Then, figuring that if he were in for a penny then he ought to be in for a pound, he took her hand in his and led her along the water's edge.

"Fitz and I would also take off our shoes and stockings, and then we would wade in the water."

"Yes, that is a fun pastime."

"You've done it yourself?"

"Each Bennet girl had a childhood habit that it took us way too long to release. Elizabeth loved to climb trees, Mary loved to pick her nose, Lydia loved to, well, be Lydia, Jane loved to bite her nails, and I loved to wade in the water of streams and lakes."

Kitty then moved away from Richard, removed her shoes and began to undo her stockings.

"Oh!" Richard was taken aback.

"Well," Kitty said, "if you didn't want me to recall the fun of the habit, then you had the grave misfortune of bringing it up."

"Well, in that case," Richard said, removing his boots and taking off his stockings as well.

"We are a terrible influence on each other!" Kitty giggled.

"Yes, we are. How about tomorrow we learn to follow decorum in each other's presence?"

"Yes, tomorrow."

"But not today."

"Clearly not today."

Taking her hand again, Richard led Kitty to the water and they both stepped in.

"It's cold!" Kitty cried.

"Yes, it is."

"And it feels wonderful."

"Yes, it does."

Silence overcame them as they waded along, hand in hand, in the water.

After some time, they sat down together along the bank of the stream and looked out over the field on the other side. After some time, Kitty turned to Richard.

"How did you know that I would like this place?"

"I didn't," Richard replied. "All I had was hope."

"Ah, hope. Another Great Connector."

"If you like, I could bring you here again."

After offering it, Richard groaned inwardly. For he realized that he had promised himself that he would remember propriety the next day, and now he was offering to throw it to the winds once more.

"I would like that, but we cannot do so."

"You are correct. We should not."

"Thank you for not being offended, Richard. I like your company, yet I know its dangers."

"Dangers?"

"Richard, you know that I have this tendency to always want to please you. And I do not know if it is out of a desire to get along with you, or because we are family and I want you to like me so much, but this comfort that we have, this…thing that bonds us clearly will lead not only to my ruin, but also yours. I shall be regarded as loose and lacking discretion, making people question my family's good name."

She pushed a stone from the stream with her toe. "Now I may not care for common slander, yet my family has already suffered much under past notorious acts caused by my youngest sister. It cannot afford any more scandal. And as for you, you cannot be accused of breaching my delicacy, for you will then be forced into a bond that you clearly don't want or afford. Find your lady of the ton who has her fifty thousand pounds, Richard, and don't let any mistake we made in the past stop you from getting all that you deserve."

"You sound hurt, Kitty."

"Do I?"

"Yes," he said, looking at her narrowly. "What are you not telling me?"

"Nothing except what I have already said. I do not wish of you to compromise your chance at a fortune all because you were seen alone with me, which would compromise my name and to which you could only rectify that situation by wedding me."

She squished silt between her toes. "I am not what you want, as you have said, and so our ease of manner around each other would hurt you significantly. I know that I like you, Richard, for as my new cousin, I feel the bonds of family very quickly. Therefore, do not be angry with me for speaking about such things so bluntly. I am simply wishing to not have you regret anything and me be the reason behind that regret."

He shook his head at her, clearly puzzled. "Kitty Bennet, you are unlike any other woman I have ever met. How do you do this?"

"Do what?"

"Live every day with this sort of frankness. This honesty and refusal to confine your conversation to only talks of the weather and the state of the roads."

"I always figured that the weather is the weather without me having to comment on it."

"And it is."

"You need not worry; I don't always speak my mind with such liberty."

"And yet you do it with me?"

"Yes, I do."

"Why, might I ask?"

"Because I could tell when I saw you, that you did not fear openness. And you might even welcome it. Therefore, I took a risk and decided just to be myself in the end. Was myself enough in this case?"

"Yes, it was."

Richard looked out at the stream and watched a fish travel in the current.

"Kitty?"

"Yes?"

"You are correct, and we should not come here again. And you are right; I should do nothing to keep me from finding my lady of fifty thousand pounds. Just as you should do nothing to ruin your good reputation."

"Yes."

"However, I know that is not what will end up happening. We shall wonder what the other is thinking, feeling, until it is bursting from us. The only way to get along with each other is push through this curiosity that there is and become good friends. Let us find ourselves on the fields. Let us walk through the shades of Pemberly together, laugh at each other's jokes, poke fun at each other, and get sullen at each other when one says something that the other does not like. Let us not run from each other because we are two free spirits."

Kitty expelled a long, deep breath. "I do not trust myself with you."

"Why not?"

"Because you make me wish to run wild."

"Then let us not run away from each other. For I have learned that ignoring each other will cause more harm than good. For I will say this. Never in my life had I had a conversation with a woman in the way that I have had with you now. And I like this manner of discourse."

"As do I, though I had not known till now that I could even speak in such a way."

Richard reached out his hand for Kitty to take.

"Shall we seal this accord? No running from each other simply because we are two wild children at heart?"

Kitty took his hand and tried to hide the feeling she received upon holding it.

"Agreed. We are two children, running in the wild, and nothing more."

The next day, they met at the stables and Richard helped Kitty learn how to race her horse across the field. However, after that, Georgiana was well and Kitty spent the whole of the day with her while Richard was forced to be without Kitty, to which he felt the loss and tried to remain with Darcy the whole day and accompanying him as he inspected the farms.

However, the next day, Elizabeth and Georgiana went to visit the houses of the neighborhood and Kitty, sensing that Richard missed her, made an excuse to remain at home and they walked across the fields together, lost in conversation.

The days continued as such, with Colonel Fitzwilliam and Kitty finding a moment of peace between them, but as many words were spoken, never were they the words that had begun to form within their hearts.

Kitty, despite her apprehensions of feeling such a desire for the younger brother of Henry Fitzwilliam, mingled with her apprehensions about falling in love at all when all she initially wanted was peace and serenity, could not deny that it wasn't just infatuation. Something about Colonel Fitzwilliam's soul seemed akin to her own and was something she had sensed since the moment they had met. Time had only proven that her instincts were correct as opposed to foolish and found merely from an idle inclination.

She did not love him because she had nothing better to do. She loved him because he was her second self.

However, out of a desire to hold onto reason, she continued to tell herself day in and day out that nothing would come of her affections and the Colonel was not nor ever would be hers to have and to hold.

Kitty however would be surprised that her same thoughts and fears were mimicked in the man that she had given her heart to. Colonel Fitzwilliam, despite his best efforts, was falling in love with Kitty more and more, day by day, and he at first tried to tell himself that his desire for her was purely due to her being a novelty. She was a pleasure to be near but was beyond his reach and therefore was a forbidden fruit. Yet it was more than that. She was his match, and he grew to be more and more aware of it, for their very manners, spirits and tempers were so alike, yet different enough for them to never become bored with each other.

Therefore, Colonel Fitzwilliam began to gather the conclusion that he would rather have denied, which was that the worst thing to be afraid of had come to pass: he had fallen in love with Kitty Bennet, the last woman in the world that he should have ever felt prevailed upon to marry.

SISTERLY COMMUNION

One night, while in bed, Darcy turned to me.

"Elizabeth, we have a problem."

"Does it have to do with Colonel Fitzwilliam falling in love with Kitty?" I asked, my eyes closed and my head resting against the pillow.

"Oh...oh, I..." He stuttered, surprised at my frankness on the matter.

"Yes," I said. "I know about it all."

"Has Kitty said something to you in confidence?"

"No, I simply know my sister and all the signs were plain. She was taken with him since the moment she met him, and his manner, which is by all accounts open and charming, could not help but have cemented any regard she might have had for him."

"This is most inconvenient."

"I know. I have become aware of the fact that he cannot marry her, and as such you are afraid that he might break her heart."

"That is one of the reasons."

I turned toward him. "There is more?"

"Yes. Elizabeth...I have caught them together."

"What?!" I gasped. "Have they—"

"Oh dear, I am sorry," Darcy rushed out. "I did not mean...that. I meant that I have come upon them without a chaperone. Riding out together, walking alone, and Georgiana, who I thought would be a good companion, has actually somehow managed to always have something else to do instead of accompanying them."

"That is 'close friend pattern', which truly means that Georgiana knows that Kitty is smitten with Richard, Kitty has informed her, and they are in each other's confidence, therefore Georgiana is their accomplice."

"Oh, for god sakes, what is having two women under my guardianship if they are not suitable companions?"

"Fitzwilliam, I love you, but that is the way with them. Also, you must remember that they are not in their teens but are in their mid-twenties. Their will is set. They do not fear spinsterhood, or misfortune. Yet surely Kitty and the Colonel will not do anything too scandalous as to hinder their good names."

"I fear that they already have begun so. Too much being alone, racing horses across the plains, and the farmers and servants who see this are bound to talk on it."

"Fitzwilliam, such acts should not frighten you. Remember that they are now family, cousins, and therefore they have the right to be friendly and not fear being censured."

"Yes, I did not think of that. We must make sure to imply heavily just how they are bound by familial ties if anyone were to question their comfort around each other."

"Still, you are not wrong. Do you want me to speak with Kitty on the matter?"

"You need not do so yet. I have spoken to Richard on the matter and have warned him to cease his flirtations. He agreed that he would speak to Kitty about it as long as we gave him time to do so and did not accost her on the matter, for he would do so himself."

"While I feel it my right to confront her, for she is my sister, I would be happy to let the matter lie between them if they can learn to govern themselves."

"Therefore, nothing is left to do but wait."

"Yes, hopefully it shall all turn out for the better."

☙❧

Though not speaking on it to Kitty, I decided that it would be suitable to write to Jane about it. Therefore, one day, I sat down at my writing desk, took out a pen and paper and began to write. After I inquired after her health, telling her everything about Pemberly, I finally began to confront my fears in regards to Kitty and the Colonel.

It amazes me, Jane, how much Colonel Fitzwilliam has taken to Kitty so quickly. When she first came here a month ago, Colonel Fitzwilliam had come down to make his customary visit. Before entering Pemberly House, he saw her on the field and rushed to meet her, thinking she was me. When he greeted her, as you can imagine he was quite in for a surprise, for Kitty had replied boldly 'That she was the second youngest sister, and therefore if we Bennet girls were to be compared between sheep and goats, you and I were the goats, and she would still just be a sheep!'

Understanding her witty reference, Colonel Fitzwilliam was intrigued by her and then she went on to inquire about his horse, which she remarked to be an impressive stallion. Kitty, as you know, has taken quite a love for horses and wishes to know as much as she can about them. Unfortunately, her lively manner was enough to enthrall the poor Colonel, who despite himself, seems to always not control himself enough to keep away from her. They have begun to race horses with each other, where on occasion, he lets her win. You know how much he despises letting another person beat him at horse racing, leaving only my Mr. Darcy to be the man who is allowed to beat Richard Fitzwilliam on the field.

It is now worse, however, for Mr. Darcy has found them quite a few times alone, not in the presence of me or Georgiana as a chaperone. As much as I love our sister and am very proud of all the improvements that she has made in both her person and her behavior, I still do not trust her to make the right decision if the Colonel were to attempt...persuade her to allow certain liberties in manner and action. And for the trust I have of her, I trust the Colonel even less, for though he is a good man, he is also a 'charming and alluring' one. He is the best of men, but I cannot deny, that when it comes to a woman that he favors, I could not trust him entirely.

I know I sound like a hypocrite, for before our marriage, my beloved Mr. Darcy and I were caught in many compromising positions to the point where my father would never allow us to be in the same company for more than five minutes, but I can only argue that at that point Mr. Darcy and I were engaged, our intentions were clear, and Mr. Darcy is the most honest, devoted, loyal, and best of men. When he makes a promise, he will keep it.

When he asked for my hand in marriage, he meant to make good upon that promise and our love was simply too strong to wait till our wedding.

Yet with our dearest Kitty and Colonel Fitzwilliam, I cannot feel that the circumstance is the same, for Kitty might be inclined to kiss any man who she takes a fancy to, and Colonel Fitzwilliam, again I love him as a cousin should, he could very well be a man unable to resist breaking a woman's heart every now and again. I do not wish for our dear Kitty to be slighted or taken advantage of in any way. Write to me of your thoughts as soon as you are able.

And as for my dear husband Fitzwilliam, we still argue and bicker as a man and wife ought to, but when we forgive each other, and take comfort in each other's company, I can only say that our disagreements only enhance the happiness we feel in each other's arms.

Even in my dreams, he often feels present, a sentinel in the background watching over me. From his mind, his moods and his voice, down to his face, his form and his build, I cannot help but celebrate in my mind from day to day. How had I become so lucky, Jane? How had I met the greatest of men in a world where I thought the greatest of men were only found in stories, in myths or in legends? He is my second self, Jane. He is in my spirit, my breath, and under my skin. If we were to move too far from each other, I would feel crippled, broken, as if I was missing a part of myself and it could never be healed, or repaired to the point where I would become whole again. I know we fight with one another! As I know that a woman is not meant to war with her husband, but if the husband is in the wrong, I think it is our place to point it out. Mr. Darcy loves me for that, and that quality alone makes him greater than Achilles, Hector, or Aeneas.

But we still find peace, and that peace is priceless. I would break if I were to lose him. And so, though I know that it is vain to wish it, I pray to god every night, may Fitzwilliam Darcy never die, may Mr. Darcy live forever! For if the world were to never know him, were to never have learned that such a great man existed and a great love along with him, then they would not experience such an epic story above all. Take care Jane, and I miss you often.

Your sister
Elizabeth Darcy

I rang the bell and was surprised to see that it was Lucy who had attended me. I sealed the letter and after I wrote the address, I handed it to her.

"Oh, Lucy, please mail this express."

"Very good, ma'am."

Lucy took the letter, and within a few days, I received Jane's reply. When her letter arrived, I took it and went to my study, where I opened it up and read it in confidence.

Dearest Lizzy,

I trust that I find you well and happy, and yet a life with a man such as Mr. Darcy can be nothing less than wonderful and intriguing. Yet I still cannot imagine how you argue with Mr. Darcy. I would never have the courage or desire to argue with such a man. Besides, weren't we always told that in marriage, it is the woman's duty to always make her husband's life comfortable, without conflict and to support his every endeavor and thought?

Please, sister, do not think that I slight the manner in which you are a wife, for I do not. I am just reminding you of what we were taught, and yet, I cannot blame you for your behavior or sentiment, for your ways of being a wife have won you a husband.

My mother often looks at me in confusion, wondering how I was not the first to wed, as she had planned. Oh, Lizzy, you know not what pain and agony I go through with her unguarded speech as to my situation. I know that she means well, but her constant declarations of my beauty being a waste if no man would have me only adds to distress. I have had a couple more suitors lately, yet after writing me a few verses of poetry, a couple of times they call upon me, and then lose interest. Forgive me for asking, but is there some way that you could have Mr. Darcy invite me to Pemberly to stay for a short duration? It would be such a comfort to get away, to be in a world where I am not looked upon as a creature to be pitied, but as a woman who just simply has not found her path yet?

As for your situation with Kitty, I do not see the danger as you do, I must confess. Ever since Lydia's running off to elope with Mr. Wickham, Kitty has learned to see such a reckless and repulsive action as deplorable, and she no longer looks up to Lydia. We can therefore see the benefits of Lydia's foolishness as an action that forced Kitty to open her eyes to more rational and sensible thoughts and actions.

Kitty has become such a better person now, especially now that she is under your guidance, and I don't think she wishes to lose the progress that she has made. As for Colonel Fitzwilliam, having met him, I do believe that he can be quite alluring even though he's not that handsome. And yet, he is Darcy's cousin. Would he do such a thing to his own cousin's sister-in-law? What are your thoughts on my assertion?

Please write to me soon, with favorable word or no.

Your loving and affectionate sister,
   Jane

I closed the letter, stood up and thought of how to form my reply. Wishing to write my letter later, for I wanted to see Darcy first before so that I could obtain his permission, I left and made my way to his study. However, very soon, I was stopped at the door when I heard voices coming from within, and I knew them to be the voice of my husband and his cousin.

"Tell me in earnest, Darcy," Richard said. "What do you complain of?"

"You know very well what I am angry of!" Darcy replied, irate. "Richard, you promised me that you would behave yourself."

"I know, and I am aware that I have failed you. Yet I have also failed Kitty, and Elizabeth. I have broken confidence with all of you, and I am ashamed of myself."

"Your words mean nothing. One moment you promise to be more considerate of Kitty and bend to propriety, and then the next moment, I come upon you swimming with her in the lake wearing nothing more than your undergarments!"

I practically fell over! I had to lean against the wall to prevent myself from doing so!

"Richard, please tell me that you have not taken her?"

"No more than you took Elizabeth before you were wed," Richard said coldly. "And yet, Darcy, how am I any worse than yourself? You know how love is, Fitz, and during it, sometimes one can lose oneself."

"You admit to being in love with Kitty then?"

"Yes," Richard said, sounding tired. "I tried to deny it to myself for too long, yet now I cannot. Fitz, I love you and Georgiana very much, but why do you think I found a way to extend my stay here? I cannot be away from her for long. I think of Kitty always. She is different, Fitz."

"I know all too well. She is similar to Elizabeth, and therefore, I do understand your tendency to forget yourself. Yet you must understand, she is my sister now, and protecting her is something that I desire to do."

"You need not worry. I am resigned. All the money in the world does not matter. She has no dowry, I know this, but wealth is not something that Kitty needs. And economy is something I have learned to exercise more throughout my life. I can provide for us."

"Don't be a fool. You know perfectly well that with the little bit of dowry her father gives, I shall add to it as well."

"Oh, Darcy, I had not known that. Thank you, truly."

"Yet this does not solve the other problem."

"What other problem could there be?"

"Oh, nothing substantial," Darcy scoffed, sarcastic. "Just the tiny matter of your brother also liking her, but I'm sure that does not affect you at all."

"What!" Richard said, sounding alert and angry.

"Yes, it is true. When dining at Grosvenor Square, Henry and Kitty met, this you know, but what you don't know is that he was quite taken with her."

"That…that is nonsense! If he liked her at all, would he not be here now, trying to woo her? It is all in his head."

"Love usually is in the head. Besides, he would be here now if I had accepted his request to come, which I have not."

"What? What did you say?"

"I have not told Elizabeth yet, but I soon shall. Your brother has written to me a couple of times, asking me to let him visit Pemberly. I wrote back both times telling him that Kitty has been ill, and she was not able to receive visitors, so he would have to wait till she recovered before he should come down. I was hoping if I put off his visit for a long enough while, he would eventually get distracted by the attentions of another woman, yet he has not so far."

"Why have you not wanted Henry to come?"

"For your happiness and hers, of course. I knew that you liked her, Richard, and I knew that if he came, you would grow jealous and despondent. However, now that he has not come, I still worry over the events. Richard, when Henry finds out that you are engaged to a woman he was thinking of courting, how do you think he shall receive the news?"

"Oh, god. My own brother. To like her is to betray him."

"Oh, Richard, it was not your fault, and you have not betrayed him."

"But if I continue to pursue Kitty, then I would surely hurt him."

"If Kitty loves you, and you love her, then while I am sorry for Henry, he holds no claim to her. You have broken no vow."

"Yet, Fitz, does it follow that if she chooses me, she will be content with her lot? Henry is the heir to my father's estate; he has the wealth, and the prestige. In marrying him, she can become a gentlewoman of rank, a Lady."

"You know Kitty does not care for such things."

"But I do, if by choosing me, she will regret it forever."

"Richard, what are you saying?"

"I'm saying that I need to speak to her alone. I know that you will tell Elizabeth all of this. Please tell her that I am sorry for my behavior, and that I shall do everything to make it right in the end. Though if she were to lose respect for me, I would not blame her."

"Very well, Richard. Just please, whatever you do... do not break Kitty's heart."

"Believe me, in the end, it is only my heart that will be sacrificed."

⚜

I moved away from the door and rushed down the hall, disappearing around the corner before Colonel Fitzwilliam exited.

When I knew that he was gone completely, I came to a decision and made my way to Kitty's room. When she was not there, I then went to Georgiana's room and found them both looking at which gown they would like to wear if they ever had to go to a dance. When I met them, I told Georgiana that I needed to borrow Kitty for the moment because I needed her opinion about something I wanted to buy for Jane.

Georgiana believed my fib, Kitty followed me out and then when we arrived at an empty room, she followed me inside and I shut the door behind her.

"Kitty," I began.

"What is it?"

"I know about you and Colonel Fitzwilliam. I know everything."

"Elizabeth," Kitty said, sitting down after I told her everything that I had overheard. "I am sorry to have caused you pain, and I know what you must think of me."

"I do not judge you as severely as you would have expected, Kitty. I know how love makes you forgetful and oblivious to propriety sometimes. Yet Kitty, when it begins to become public, then you will be labeled as reckless and rash."

"I know." She picked at nonexistent lint on her gown.

"Kitty, you truly are in love with him, aren't you?"

"Yes, very much. As much as I don't wish to hurt his brother in any way, I cannot help myself. I love Richard."

"Has he made an offer to you?"

She looked away. "No, he has not."

"When he does, he will not have the chance to always enjoy what others about him have, and he will not be able to maintain the life that he was used to."

"You think me not worthy of him?" Kitty rose, getting roused.

"No, I do not think that at all. I just don't want him to grow to despise his love for you. I don't want you to have to suffer such a fate."

"Richard is different, and you know that I do not care for luxuries all that much. All I will require is one cook and I can maintain the rest of our living quarters myself. We can marry modestly, and I will economize."

"You need not worry. Our family will always help you, especially Darcy, and you will not struggle. Yet Kitty, while I know that I am a hypocrite in this way, please, you must cease to allow him to take such liberties with you."

"Elizabeth, I know it's wrong. I will not even act coy on the matter. Yet for some reason, when I am with him, I forget myself. I know that this is affection, yet I could not imagine just how much of an effect it would have on me. Elizabeth, I cannot deny him anything."

I sat down in a chair, resigned.

"I know that you can't," I said closing my eyes. "I understand."

Kitty sat down beside me and took my hand.

"The sadness," she said, "in knowing that in the face of love, one forgets oneself. Even if I knew that he would not be able to offer me anything, it's heartbreaking for me to admit this, but I still could not hate him, at all. I would always wish to make him happy. I am sorry for it, yet I know that he is my second self, and I will always love him."

"Well then," I said, "if he offers anything, which I know that he will, I know your answer, what you will say. And I cannot deny that if I was in your position, my path would be the same."

"Yes, yes it would. Or rather, yes it was."

That night, Darcy and I were lying in bed, holding one another in each other's arms. He had told me everything that had transpired between him and Richard, while I told him about my talk with Kitty.

"So, he didn't know about Henry's love for Kitty?" I repeated.

"No, he didn't. And now I'm afraid of the effects that knowledge will have on his decisions toward her."

"As am I. Yet this all is beyond our control now."

Then I began to chuckle.

"And what is so amusing, Mrs. Darcy?"

"That you found them bathing in the lake. While I should be upset with them, I am only upset with us."

"What?"

"I am upset with the fact that we never thought to do it ourselves."

Darcy chuckled and hugged me closer.

"Yes, I can see your frustration in that corner."

"Yes, you should. Oh, and I have another matter to discuss. Yet this is about another sister."

"And by *other* sister, please let it not be about Lydia. I do not think I can survive such an ordeal."

"Of course you could survive it. You're like the rocks of Stonehenge, Fitzwilliam. You'll always stand. Yet, you need not worry, it is about Jane."

"Oh, how is she?"

"She is well enough in body, yet not in mind. Our mother keeps hounding Jane about suitors, pressuring her to marry. And it is vexing her. She was wondering, in hopes of being free from such pressure, may she come and visit Pemberly for a while?"

"I don't understand. You and I married, Lydia is wed, albeit horribly, so why would your mother need to taunt and torment Jane into being wed now that your family's fate is secure?"

"My mother has two daughters wed. Therefore, she has nothing else to do but wed off the rest of them. You remember your Cousin Emilia from America. Well that is my mother, in a lesser light."

"Tis true."

"And Jane, who is without doubt the loveliest of us Bennet girls. Therefore, my mother naturally is confused."

"Confused?"

"Yes, since Jane was in her teenage years, our mother had assumed that Jane would be the one to save the family. And that Jane's beauty would be the one to make a good match, a wealthy match, and to see that it was me who did so confuses my mother. She was correct that one of us would catch a wealthy and wonderful husband, yet she bet on the wrong daughter. And now, to cover her error, she must also prove it to herself that Jane still is the one to make an excellent match."

"Oh...good god that is horrible."

"Yes, it is. Therefore, can Jane please stay, for as long as she needs?"

"Of course. I didn't mean for my hesitancy to imply that I did not allow it. Yes, Jane may come to stay with us."

"Thank you. I shall write to her on the morrow."

⚜

The next morning, it was raining, and I began to write my letter to Jane.

Dearest Jane

Forgive my delayed response, and Mr. Darcy has willingly granted you the allowance to visit Pemberly for the rest of the year if you wish it. I actually am of the suspicion, that except for our mother and her 'lively' and 'impertinent' ways, he is growing quite fond of our family. For he has grown to love Kitty and Mary, and both have grown to have a great respect for him. I think he likes to have my sisters around him for it makes him feel paternal and responsible for their welfare. I think he likes having many women to look after actually, for I believe he wished he had more than one sister for a sibling all his life, and you all fill that void of sibling compassion that he was never allowed to experience. Therefore, if you were to stay with us, that would only satisfy his need to provide for and take care of those that he loves.

As for the more serious of our discussions, my dear sister, you proved right in one way, and wrong in another. As I had proved right in one way and wrong in another. Colonel Fitzwilliam's feelings for our sister are genuine and strong. Yet for as strong as is his attachment to her, her love for him has

150

grown to be even stronger. They have turned out, to the surprise of all around them, to ardently admire and love one another.

This is no summertime affection however, that will stop as soon as fall and winter begin, for as you know, Colonel Fitzwilliam is a man of the world in every respect. He has had his share of lady companions, and has enjoyed his manhood to the fullest extent, and yet he has never felt for a woman in this way before. Kitty, when around him, only has eyes for him. She understands what it means to be a soldier's wife, has taken an interest in his tales of being in battle, has begun to follow the events and battles from the war with Napoleon, and wishes to understand all his feelings and sentiments in regards to politics. She wishes to be right for him! I have never seen such a marked change in someone's attitude and yet hers is fixed. In that, sister, you were right, and I was in error.

In the manner of which you were in error and I was correct was in that they could not be trusted to act accordingly. My beloved Mr. Darcy caught them swimming in the pond together that's hidden and on the edge of Pemberly, and they were in their undergarments! They were in an intimate embrace, perhaps with the potential to go further, when my Mr. Darcy came upon them.

Colonel Fitzwilliam valiantly tried to defend Kitty, stating that he practically carried her on his horse to the lake where he proceeded to take off her dress even at her protests, and then threw her in the water. But then Kitty replied that she eventually began to enjoy his attentions and could not resist him due to her heart's attachment.

Jane, it's all become a mess! Mr. Darcy is embarrassed because of his cousin, I am embarrassed for it's our sister, and yet there is comfort above all things. Colonel Fitzwilliam has strongly declared that he wants to marry Kitty at the earliest convenience of all, and Kitty wishes to as well. I swear it's Darcy and my dilemma all over again. Is this the Darcy curse or the Darcy luck? That both my husband and his cousin have a certain way about them that all they need to administer is a simple touch around a woman's waist, one kiss, and we give way to them? I cannot judge our sister, for I know how these Darcy men get when their passion is ignited.—Sister, please burn this infamous letter after you are done reading it—they become possessed, lift the woman up and will her to see the beauty of their rash actions. They can make a woman see the overwhelming loveliness of a gentleman ceasing to be... a gentleman.

There is a crisis however, with Colonel Fitzwilliam's desire to marry Kitty. Being the second son in his family, his older brother will inherit the family fortune which, as you know is why he has a profession as a soldier. He must earn an income, and so his family has always desired him to marry a wealthy heiress of some kind with 50,000 pounds to her name at least so that Colonel Fitzwilliam can support his wife comfortably.

Yet Kitty practically has no dowry, as none of us did, and so she can bring nothing to the marriage. Mr. Darcy has agreed to help him when needed, but I feel the pain of their situation, that the Colonel must choose between wealth and true love. I know Kitty can live without luxury, for as long as she has the Colonel, she feels as if she has a luckier lot than most. Yet the Colonel is used to a certain lifestyle that he might not be able to provide when marrying Kitty. It would injure my soul to see Kitty hurt because the Colonel might one day turn away from her because she would become a financial burden to him. I do not want Kitty to undergo such pain, for she deserves better. We all do.

Yet despite this crisis, everything else could not be better suited. For though the Colonel is ten years older than Kitty, his liveliness and confidence suit her own and they are two people whose hearts are the same. They are two people whose persons are not more perfectly matched, and yet their purses could not be more at odds with one another. I do so hope that when they do marry, may their economical class not make them regret their love for one another. There is nothing worse, Jane, than when two people no longer love because that love turned sour due to poverty.

As for controlling their urges, Darcy has threatened to sew the colonel in a satchel sack to restrain him from trying to further his flirtations and indiscretions with Kitty, who admits that she would allow him any liberty as long as she could never be parted from his side. I admit that her love for the Colonel shows our sister's good taste.

And as for you Jane, I am sorry for what our mother has put you through. I know her temperament, disposition, and inability to censure her words accordingly, and I must offer you my condolences for having to be the victim of such vulgar comments that must fall from her mouth. Remember, you have not failed by not catching a husband. The rise and fall of a woman's success should not depend on her ability to get a husband, but rather on the state of her mind. Marriage is an event that cannot be experienced by all because life does not work out in such a way always, and *happiness in marriage is almost entirely by chance. Therefore, I say this Jane, please; I do not care how the world looks at you or perceives your station in life: never marry without affection. If you cannot love him and he does not love you, never EVER get married. I did not marry Mr. Darcy because it was a convenience. I married him because I was irrevocably in love with him, and I would never love another. Remember, we shall always take care of you if you wish, and never look on you as a burden, for you are not. Here, you will simply be Jane, as you always were.*

Your affectionate sister,
  Elizabeth

A few days later, Jane's reply arrived.

I am coming to visit in a fortnight and shall stay for as long as you and Mr. Darcy allow me to. And your words did not fall on deaf ears, Lizzy, for I fully agree with you and your example has led to me making up my mind: I shall never in life marry without love. If the man never comes, then he never comes. And no matter his wealth, or his position, if I do not love him, then never shall I marry! You, my sweet sister, have guided me in this, and I believe you to be fully correct! Thank you so very much Lizzy!

Your loving sister,
  Jane

I felt elated in knowing that Jane would be joining us, and Darcy also seemed to enjoy the concept of her coming as well. Thus, ending our sisterly communion in knowledge that at least three Bennet sisters would be reunited once more.

❧ 17 ❧

DEPARTURES & ARRIVALS

The rain came suddenly as Kitty and Colonel Fitzwilliam were walking along the grounds and therefore, to protect themselves, they retreated under a copse of trees.

After they arrived there, both of them placed their hands on their shoulders and gasped for air.

Kitty moved away from Richard and looked out at the rain.

"Kitty?" Richard asked.

"Say that I wanted to marry you," Kitty said, avoiding his gaze. "What would you say?"

Richard blinked, startled by her frankness.

"I know that it is not the woman who should begin to announce it," Kitty said, "but it has been four days, and I am afraid that you will never say it. So, I figured that I should."

"You are fearless."

"I know that it is not desired, and men would be frightened by the idea of my eagerness, but you are not like any other man I have met, Richard," Kitty pleaded. "You are unique. Richard, I wish to marry you. Won't you say yes to me?"

Richard moved forward and looked away from her.

"Do you know what I cannot stand, Kitty? What vexes me to no end?" Then he turned to her. "I cannot stand that I am madly in love with you. I cannot stand how everything I feel, you say it first, and you know what is within me, and I don't know how you see it. I cannot stand how I never wish to be away from you."

"Why does this frighten you?" Kitty asked, somber.

"Because it is too much of a pain, to look on you, and see a woman that I cannot have, and should not allow herself to waste herself on me."

"What?"

"Kitty... I know how my brother feels about you."

"I... I have never promised him anything. And while I do not wish to cause him any pain, he and I have only met a few times! I owe him no devotion, and I have the right to give it to you."

"You have broken no vow yet let me do right to you."

"Right? You call this right?" She was vexed.

"I call it prudent. If you marry my brother, he can give you everything, wealth, a comfortable and luxurious home, a title, prestige and a secured future. What can I give you, Kitty? Nothing. Just a small domicile, living from month to month in hopes of always being comfortable enough, having to be given money from our relatives, and death.

"Kitty, don't you understand? I am a Colonel in a regiment. And there is always the chance that I will pass away on the battlefield. Then I will surely leave you with nothing."

"So, I am to turn away from you because of monetary gain? Is this how you would have a woman weigh you by? And so, you are now telling me to marry your brother! Say all that is good and fortunate in this world were to take place, and you lived, and your life were to turn for the better. You would have to watch me with your own sibling. You would have to spend your life seeing me unhappy with Henry!"

Richard looked at Kitty with sorrow.

"Kitty, my regiment has been called to the Peninsula. I received the letter yesterday. Napoleon is on the move and our generals have ordered some of our militia to march to support Spain. Now I have no choice and can no longer delay my leaving."

"You... when do you leave?"

"I must leave in two days' time."

"And you fear that you will not return."

"I know there is a chance that I might not."

"Then let me be loyal to you. If you go off, let it be known that I am bound to you, and I shall wait. If you pass away, only then shall I move on."

"I cannot have you put your life on hold for me. I love you too much to have you do this, not when I know that there is a chance for you to have all that I could never give."

She was near grief. "You break my heart in denying me this."

"Do I?"

"Richard, if you do not propose to me now, then I will never forgive you."

"Oh, Kitty!" Colonel Fitzwilliam grabbed Kitty, raised her toward him and kissed her passionately. "Must you be so stubborn," he cried, "and must I be so weak?"

"The only weakness that you will display is if you deny me the right to love you."

"I will be the failing of you," he said. "My love can give you little!"

"Will you give me yourself?"

"Yes, of course I shall. You already have me!"

"Then your love gives me enough."

"Dear god, if only I were stronger. Yet I am not. Do not marry my brother, Kitty, and forget all that I said. Marry me! Promise yourself to me now, to me always, promise that you will wait for me to return. And if I don't return, then be free."

"And even then, I would never forget you. Richard, of course I promise myself to you. I've always been promising myself to you and I always will. So, won't you say yes to me?"

"Of course, my love! I never should have tried to do otherwise, and I apologize for it. I just wanted to be prudent."

She caressed his cheek. "Oh, don't talk to me of prudence!"

"I know. What a foolish thing to be at the moment."

He kissed her again.

"Kitty Bennet, will you marry me?"

"I thought that we covered that already?" She laughed, a light, gay, happy laugh.

"In times like this, I wish to be redundant. So, you must be as well. Will you marry me?"

"Of course, Richard Fitzwilliam."

Richard lifted her up and twirled her around.

Colonel Fitzwilliam and Kitty made the announcement to Darcy, Elizabeth, and Georgiana, who were both equally happy and equally apprehensive about the match that was being made. They were content for they knew that Kitty and Colonel Fitzwilliam were the perfect match for one another, yet there was the fear of how Henry Fitzwilliam would feel about it, as well as Lord and Lady Fitzwilliam.

Darcy wished that they would be married before Richard left, but time was too short, and there was the plus of the Colonel and Kitty not being wed. With the Colonel's leaving, Kitty and he, though devoted to each other, would still be not bound by each other. Therefore if one of them were to transfer their affections to another, they would be breaking no vow. Also, they would have more time to forego announcing anything to the Fitzwilliam clan, and they could avoid telling Henry Fitzwilliam of it for as long as possible. If worse came to worse, and the poor Colonel suffered a terrible fate in battle, Kitty would be grieved. Yet she had never committed herself, therefore she would suffer for his passing, but would still be free to easily love again.

Therefore, with all the conflicts that would arise with their love, there equally would be something to cause benefit to it.

Yet between all of the happiness and fears, the day for Colonel Fitzwilliam's departure soon came, Darcy and Elizabeth allowed Richard and Kitty a private moment to allow intimacy and loving words to be spoken.

Richard then climbed his horse, Kitty kissed his hand and then he was off to London, driving down the pathway of Pemberly and disappearing into the distance.

As soon as he disappeared, Kitty found herself overcome with the loss of him, ran into the house, to her room and denied company for the rest of the afternoon.

However, where one loss came to the company, so did the occupants of Pemberly gain another.

A week after Colonel Fitzwilliam had gone, a carriage pulled down the road to Pemberly, and the exchange of departures and arrivals went hand in hand.

Jane Bennet, for the first time, had come to Pemberly.

AN INDEPENDENT JANE BENNET

"My goodness," Jane said as she stepped out of the carriage and we all greeted her. "Elizabeth! Kitty! Georgiana! And Mr. Darcy!"

Accompanied by Mrs. Reynolds, we all were lined up as her carriage had rolled in, and when the door opened, Darcy was there to open the door for her, helped Jane down, and we all embraced her. After we all hugged, Jane looked up at the house and her eyes grew wide.

"Well, in all my life, I never would have imagined such a place. So, this is Pemberly?"

I hugged her again. "Yes, yes, Jane, it is."

"Such an overwhelmingly beautiful place," Jane said in awe. "More than I could have imagined it to have ever been."

Mrs. Reynolds came forward, they were introduced, we all went inside, had tea and Jane told us how her journey had gone.

"The roads were very good, and my journey was quiet and comfortable," she acknowledged. "The only thing that I could say was a mishap was that a carriage that was driving on the road almost hit a cow, but since it did not happen, it was more comical than it was tragic. Therefore, enough about me, I am desirous to know how you have all been here at Pemberly."

Instinctively, all eyes turned to Kitty, who had been feeling the loss of Colonel Fitzwilliam very keenly. Her spirits had been quite low since he left, yet she did her best to make herself merry, it was just very apparent that it was forced. We did not blame or be angry at her though, for she handled it with much grace, never turned toward the dramatic, or broke down and cried. Yet, despite it all, we could not help at the moment but turn to her, and Kitty felt our eyes on her.

"We have been enjoying very good weather," Kitty said, taking the initiative. "And we have every cause for cheer. Mr. Darcy has given me a horse named Daedalus, Georgiana has taught me how to ride, Elizabeth has become the mistress of Pemberly very well, we have met many of the tenants, and we were given much amusement at the arrival of Colonel Fitzwilliam."

"Oh, Colonel Fitzwilliam. How is he?"

"He is...very well. Or as well as a servant under our majesty's regiment can be. He has been called away to the Peninsula and shall aid the Spanish against the French."

"Oh, poor Colonel."

"Poor Colonel and poor country," Georgiana said. "It is very hard that Napoleon has made himself into a constant threat onto the rest of Europe."

"I have been doing some more research on the matter," Jane added, "And it has led me to believe that the only way that the fighting will cease is only if he is stripped from power and, well..."

"Restrained," Darcy finished for her. "Or exiled."

"It is sad that it has had to come to such a case. However, yes... but onto lighter subject matter, Mr. Darcy, really, thank you for letting me stay here at Pemberly. For it is quite wonderful and I needed such a retreat."

"It is my pleasure," he said warmly.

Mrs. Reynolds and I showed Jane to her room, which Mrs. Reynolds had already prepared, and she left as soon as it became clear that I could supervise from there.

"You shall learn to love her quickly," I said to Jane, referring to Mrs. Reynolds. "She is quite invaluable."

"Oh, she seems so. Now Elizabeth, tell me, how is Kitty? I could see the way you all looked on her. It was as if you were worried that she would break at any moment."

"Because we are waiting for her to. Yet she has born it well and better than could have been expected."

"Yes, she has grown tremendously. And you and I both know why."

"Because she is away from Longbourn?"

"Precisely. I will go and see her soon and do my best to offer her any solace, but to fall in love and lose your love to the army, well, that must be hard for her."

"It is, but what of your hardships? Jane, was mother so pressing that she frightened you all the way to come to Kent?"

Jane sighed deeply. "Elizabeth, you know our mother means well, and her heart is full, just as her love for us is tremendous. Yet her methods, well, you know that they are not the best by any means. She constantly references Mr. Darcy, claiming that I should be so lucky myself one day. She also has hinted at her anger for me not drawing in Mr. Bingley."

"What?"

"Yes, it turns out that when we had gone to America, she thought your marriage would not only throw me into the paths of other rich men, but she had one man in particular in mind: Mr. Bingley. She was expecting me to return as his fiancée."

"I cannot deny her some sense in that regard," I allowed, "for your tempers are so much alike."

"Yes, though one might even argue that they are too much alike."

"I see that argument as well. Jane, you were always good, too good, I often thought, and sometimes I was worried about your tendency toward having such a generous candor. Yet now I see that you have grown wise."

"I have become more acquainted with the ways of the world and as it has altered Kitty, so it has altered me. Yet the alteration is even more marked and to my utter surprise. Elizabeth, unless I feel a deep and binding affection for a man, I... I do not wish to marry."

"You do not?" I asked, surprised.

"No, I mean, why should I? I am content now, and there is something I do want, but knowledge of that is just out of my reach. And I want to find myself before I arrive at it. And when I went home and knowing that you were wed, as was Lydia, I felt that the pressure to marry was lifted from my shoulders, and therefore I could just be at peace to read, do home theatricals with the Austens, maybe even write a book myself, or join a committee. But all mother spoke of was me meeting man after man."

Jane pressed her palms over her skirt, as if to iron it. "She would introduce me to any new person who came to the neighborhood, mentioning our relation to Mr. Darcy, and while her efforts displayed her pure love for me, it all grew so tiresome. I want to be able to discover myself, Elizabeth.

Do you think under the shades of Pemberly that I will be able to search for me?"

I had to chuckle. "Well, I have not polluted them the way that Lady Catherine said that I would, therefore, I hope that you may."

⚘

Jane proved to ease herself into the home of Pemberly with speed. She immediately wished to meet all the residents on the farms of Pemberly, so we rode out with Kitty and Georgiana and then became acquainted with them all.

As she met them, we came upon one farm that belonged to the tenant named Mr. John Wilkins, who was married to a woman named Loretta and they had—

"Ten children!" Jane cried when she met all of them. There stood Mr. Wilkins, Loretta next to him, and their ten children who were all still less than twelve years old.

"Oh, you heard right!" Loretta cried, holding the youngest in her arms, who was still a baby. "And something tells me that that number might be liable to change any day though. With our luck, that's what I seem, too right."

"What are their names?" Jane asked.

"Oh, the oldest one down there is Bridget, that one is Thomas, then there is John, James; aye, three boys in a row, then Catherine, Amelia, Abigail, Christopher, Molly, Charles and Peter is my baby here. As you can see, Catherine and Amelia are twins."

"They all look wonderful," Kitty said. "So tell me Catherine, is that with a 'C' or a 'K'?"

"Oh, um... I don't know," Catherine replied.

"It's with a 'C'," Loretta said, looking down while she held Peter.

"Oh, that's wonderful," Kitty said, trying to cover the awkwardness of the moment. "I only asked out of camaraderie. I am one with a 'C' as well, and it was just nice to have that in common."

After a few moments, we all left and travelled to the next farm. As we had done so, Jane turned to me.

"Elizabeth, did the children not know how to read?"

"No, I suppose they did not," I answered. "This is the first time that I had met the whole family, and it was hidden from me till now."

"Oh."

Jane grew quiet and reflective, looking out of the carriage window as we approached the next farm.

❧

Over the next couple of days, Jane, though proving a good addition to our household, seemed to be preoccupied with something that she did not speak of. Even Kitty noticed this, who was so attentive to Jane's demeanor that it began to help her forget her owe woes.

One day, Jane asked me if she could take Nicholson and have him pull her along in a coach to look over all the grounds. Darcy and I, who trusted Nicholson completely, allowed this, and Jane set out with him, and did not return until an hour before dinner. This continued for a couple more days, and I grew apprehensive.

"She is up to something," Kitty said to me in confidence. "Pemberly is large, and while there is much to see, surely there cannot be that much? I know that she would never do anything to hurt herself or cause alarm, therefore do no misinterpret me. Yet there is some scheme afoot. This I do know."

One day, I went to her room before she set out with Nicholson, but she had already gone. My curiosity was so extreme that I wanted answers immediately. Thinking of how would be the best way to find out what was underneath all that Jane was not telling me, I came upon recalling the one person who always knew everything that occurred in Pemberly, no matter how much of a secret it was.

Knowing that Darcy had ridden off to visit a tenant farmer who was disputing with another farmer, I went to his study, opened the door and saw who I was looking for.

"Mrs. Darcy," Jefferson said, standing up. He had been pouring over a map and then took his glasses off, standing up and bowing to me. "I was just looking at the neighboring farms and wondering which one would be most suitable for Mr. Darcy to purchase."

"He is wishing to expand Pemberly?"

"Pemberly is the beating heart of Kent in regards to agriculture. There is always room for expansion."

I entered the room and stood before him.

"So," he added, "what can I do for you?"

"I was wondering if you had noticed that my sister has continued to drive about the countryside."

"Yes, I have definitely noticed. This day, she has taken the path that she has taken for the last five days."

"You know where they travel towards and they have a set destination?"

"Yes," he said. "When your sister came and Nicholson began to escort her repeatedly, I worried that he might think himself at an advantage and though a good man, I did not want him to think he could take liberties in any way. Paranoia, Mrs. Darcy, is necessary for my trade. Therefore, I made it quite clear one day that I wanted to know their whereabouts. He informed me of such, but just to be certain, I followed them the next day."

"You did?"

"Yes, you must forgive my precautions, but when ladies and their good names are concerned, it has always been part of my duties to preserve them."

"Except for where my sister Kitty was involved?" I replied, archly.

"Are you certain on that one?"

"Pardon?"

"Who do you think was the one who told Mr. Darcy where they were when they decided to go for a swim in the lake that bordered the estate? How do you think he was able to find them?"

"He ordered you to watch them?"

"He ordered me to keep Miss Kitty safe."

My surprise and relief were evident. "Well, then please do so again."

"I have and I always will. Miss Bennet is perfectly safe, I can assure you. If anything, you have a remarkable sister."

"How so?"

Jefferson just smiled.

"Well, I could tell you, but I find it might be more beneficial if I were to show you."

"Why so?"

"Because some things should not be told, Mrs. Darcy. Some things should simply be seen."

Taking a phaeton, Jefferson urged the horse onward, following the path that he claimed Jane and Nicholson used, and I was seated next to him.

"It is moments such as this that I feel I should learn how to ride a horse," I said. "I love walking, but now I am becoming aware that learning how to ride makes me more independent."

"You don't like not controlling the moment, do you?"

"No, Jefferson, I do not." I turned to him, eyed him keenly and he noticed.

"What is it?"

"Is there anything that you don't know, Jefferson?"

"I do my best to make sure that there is little that I do not know. I would be a terrible valet and friend to your husband if I did not."

"Yet your experience at such things requires a history. What were you once?"

"Everything, Mrs. Darcy. I was once everything."

"Everything good, or everything bad?"

"Everything that a man has to be in this world. Do not worry, Mrs. Darcy, there is no bad in me. Only what has been mistaken."

"Either way, I would never judge you."

I silenced myself and let him drive me on with no more questions, for it seemed a delicate matter.

We reached a familiar path.

I pressed a hand to my mouth. "Wait, I know this way. We are going in the direction of Mr. Wilkins's farm."

"Yes, that is where she is going all the time."

He stopped the horses, Jefferson helped me down and we walked the rest of the way so that we could get a look without being seen. Through the trees, I saw Wilkins's farm and there, in the enclosure was the Wilkins children, with Nicholson setting up some desks, papers and quills. Jane stood over them and began to speak.

"As of yesterday, I showed you the letters individually, and I shall show them to you again before I shall allow you to all try and trace the letters themselves."

The children all nodded as Jane took out a paper that had all the letters on them and began to sound them out to refresh the children's memory.

"She is teaching them how to read and write!" I gasped.

"Yes," Jefferson said, "Yes, she is."

After watching her for some time and helping the children trace the first eight letters in the alphabet, I turned to Jefferson.

"I should not walk in and interrupt their lesson, should I?"

"No, you should not. Even though I can see that you are supportive, you should not accost her just now. It is clear that this is a part of her life that is all her own and that she likes it that way."

"And how do you see that?" I asked him, surprised. Jefferson looked down and avoided my gaze.

"You were married once," I realized. "Weren't you?"

Jefferson smiled gently. "Yes, yes I was."

"Very well. We have lingered here long enough. Come."

Jefferson followed after me.

⁂

"She is teaching the tenant children to read?" Darcy said.

When he had returned to Pemberly, I sought him out and told him immediately about where Jefferson and I had gone.

"So far it has only begun with the Wilkins children, yet Fitzwilliam, you should have seen it. Jane looked happy, and I could not believe that she had even come upon such an idea. I know that you would not naturally allow such a notion of hers to continue, but please, Fitzwilliam. Tomorrow let me take you to her lesson and you will see it."

"I do not like her not seeking my approval first, but very well, I will come with you."

"Thank you, Fitz."

"Right and...wait, did you just call me Fitz?"

"Oh, yes, I heard that was once your nickname," I replied archly, teasing him.

"Yes, I recall those days."

⁂

When Jane came to dinner, we did not question her, for a plan had then been set in motion. Rather Georgiana had some news and she began to share it.

"More of the militia has been set in motion," Georgiana said. "I have heard from Mrs. Pratt that another regiment has been sent to aid the defenses against Napoleon's advancement into Russia, and her son has joined that regiment."

"Which son?" Darcy asked, "Joseph or Nicholas?"

"Nicholas. That makes him the thirteenth man amongst our acquaintance in Kent who has taken up the army as a profession. This number has increased the number of women who wish to follow their unit and become civilian nurses."

"Civilian nurses?" Kitty asked. "Do they have experience with aid and healing injuries?"

"A couple of them have some experience at it, but the rest shall go there and learn from the surgeons and doctors who are there at the base camps."

Kitty's sigh was reflective. "Oh. They are fortunate in that they will see their sons or husbands again. Yet won't it be dangerous for them as well? Isn't it too dangerous of an adventure?"

"There are always safe houses for civilian nurses that are meant to keep them safe."

"And they will have safe passage for when they are to return as well?" Kitty asked. "Sorry, I am starved of knowledge is all. I had not known that mothers and sisters followed the militias."

"They shall be safe if they need to return, that is a guarantee."

"Then I should not fear for them," Kitty said.

I looked at her with curiosity, and yet I could see that she was simply envious of the other women who would be travelling to the Peninsula. She would never think of joining them herself however, for she knew that we would not permit it.

"Oh," Kitty said. "And I have received a letter from Lydia today."

"Did you?" Jane said. "And how does she enjoy Newcastle?"

"Her words imply that she both likes and hates it."

"Truly?"

"Yes, I have listened to her enough to understand what is hidden beneath the words that she uses. And yet, I don't know how to reply to her requests. Nor am I certain that I even want to."

"Why, what did she write?"

After supper, Kitty retrieved the letter and began to read it aloud.

"Dear Kitty, also dear Elizabeth as well,

How are you? I've heard that you are now living at Pemberly and I find that such a joke. I never thought, you who loved looking at the soldiers of the militia with me, would want to willingly go into Kent. Do you recall all the times we ran and dined with the officers in Meryton? I remember it as if it were yesterday, don't you? It was all so simple back then. However, I know

that you must miss me terribly, and I confess myself far too merry to miss
any of you. As for Newcastle, I love it for I have many friends who favor me;
I am a great favorite of the officers, which is well, because Wickham seems
to always be too occupied with other duties to be home often. We have had to
transfer to a different lodging than before, for I did not like the previous one,
and nor did my dear Mr. Wickham!

Kitty lowered the letter and turned to us.

"That truthfully means that she and Wickham had to move to another home because they could not afford to live in the one they had."

"Of course it does." Darcy glowered. "Damned Wickham."

Georgiana chuckled to herself, which was a good sign. After the trial duration of time where a woman feels loss over a man, a woman begins to hear the mention of his name with annoyance, then she eventually begins to enjoy the idea of hearing him ridiculed. Georgiana was clearly at the third stage. This meant that she no longer was in love with him and truly regretted her mistake.

Kitty continued reading.

"There are often parties occurring, I dare say that another man I have met
quite fancies me, and if I were not married, I would think him quite worth my
attentions. However, now that I am curious, I too would like to see Pemberly.
And say that I was to come there, we can be as we once were. Lydia and
Kitty Bennet together once more. I can barely speak for laughing! Therefore,
if you do not understand what I mean, then you must be a simpleton. Ask
Elizabeth to ask Mr. Darcy to let me come to Pemberly. My dear Mr.
Wickham will let me remain there for as long as I wish. Do so and write back
to me with a ready reply.

Kitty lowered the letter.

"We cannot let her come," Kitty said.

"Of course not," I said.

"Very much not," Jane said.

"Thank goodness," Georgiana said.

"Over my rotting corpse," Darcy said.

"You must understand," Kitty said. "I love Lydia, I do, but she has not changed."

"Or only worsened now that she is beginning to see that Wickham is not in love with her by any means," I said.

"What do you mean?" Georgiana asked.

"It's in her wording."

"Elizabeth is correct, Georgiana," Kitty said. "Our sister, without saying so, has begun to learn that Wickham does not care for her one way or another and is doing her best to hide that truth from herself. She is therefore trying to seek favor out in other places, yet that is not helping, therefore she wishes to take refuge here. Yet I do not know how to reply."

"Say that you are content in being in Pemberly," I offered, "that you are happy that she enjoys Newcastle and that you shall speak with me in turn. Then I shall write to her myself about how she cannot come at this time."

"Very good," Jane said. "Even I am resigned in her case. The only way that Lydia will ever learn how to overcome her own nature is if we don't indulge it. There are others who were born without her opportunities and now if she is to have a better life, she needs to earn it."

"But for now," Georgiana said, "if you would forgive me." Georgiana stood up, took the letter from Kitty, walked over to the fireplace and threw the letter into the fire. She turned around to see us all staring blankly at her, and then she walked back to the sofa and sat down softly.

"That felt so good to do," was her only reply.

Kitty stifled a chuckled and sat down.

Then we all burst out in laughter, even Darcy.

After dinner, I went to the bedroom and found Darcy staring at our fireplace.

"What is it?" I asked. "You look as if you are thinking hard on something."

"I am. I am simply recalling how my little sister just walked up to Kitty, took the letter, simply threw it in there and just let it burn. My love, I truly did not see that coming."

"Nor did I. It was all quite amusing."

I sat down and began to undo my stockings.

"Which reminds me, tomorrow we must leave to spy on my older sister around one in the afternoon."

"Oh, yes, that other surprising thing that our sisters are doing. Well, it will be amusing if anything."

The next day I had taken Fitzwilliam to the hiding spot where we could spy on Jane as she was teaching the Wilkins children. After no more than fifteen minutes of watching her, Darcy had quite made up his mind.

We left and returned to Pemberly to discuss the matter.

"You are correct, my dear, for it was quite an admirable thing. She looked positively heroic in her efforts."

"I know. Fitzwilliam, I think that we should admit to knowing about her activities and show our support in this. And not only our support, yet also our help."

"Help, how so?"

"I have a plan."

I began to unfold my plans to Fitzwilliam and afterwards, he only had one thing to say:

"Inconceivable."

"Are you certain that you are using that word in the correct way?" I replied, laughing.

He chuckled. "Of course I am, woman. Don't mock me."

"Oh, I mock you, sir. I mock you very much."

The next day, before Jane wished to leave, Darcy and I asked Jane to join us in his study. Jane entered behind us, worried that we must be angry with her, yet we assured her of the contrary. When she sat down, we acknowledged that we had learned of her teaching the Wilkens's.

"I hope that you are not angry with me," she said, "yet I felt as if I needed some occupation of some kind, and I felt pity for those children."

"Jane," Mr. Darcy began, "we are not angry with you. At first I will admit to being slightly angry for you not bringing me into your confidence of your plans."

"I was worried."

"Worried?" I said. "Over what?"

"That if I let anyone know, then word would reach Longbourn. You know how angry it would make the rest of our family, who believe a lady should have no occupation of any kind. Even when that occupation is not truly a profession, for I do not get paid to do it."

"Precisely," Darcy said. "Since you receive no pay, it is not a profession of any kind. Rather now it is a charity. And charity must always be admired as the best of activities. And even if it were not the case, if you so desired to take it on as a profession, I would not judge you, for I have grown to respect the need for work."

"Mr. Darcy, do you truly mean it?"

"Yes, I do."

"And Jane," I said, "we have not brought you in here for the sake of reprimanding you in any way. We have called you here to tell you that if you so need, you can use one of the spare rooms here in Pemberly and bring any children who you wish to teach here. You can give them lessons in the comforts of the room where you shall be protected from the elements, have more supplies at your disposal and I can have the servants bring the children food in between lessons."

She was dumfounded. "What? You... Mr. Darcy and Elizabeth. Could this be true? Do you really mean this?"

"Yes, we do," Darcy said. "We have the perfect room for it."

Jane rose, hugged me warmly and then turned to Fitzwilliam.

"Mr. Darcy, sir, you truly are quite heroic in a unique way."

Darcy looked down and blushed.

"My contribution is little," he said. "I give the children a room, but you give them an education. I can take no praise."

"You can and you shall. Not many gentlemen of such rank would care for those less fortunate in such a way, yet you do. Rejoice Mr. Darcy, you are a good man."

Darcy blushed again. Jane then took my arm and smiled at me.

"I must go to the Wilkins Farm and let them know this. They shall be delighted."

Jane left us alone.

"Well, my dear husband, did you hear that?" I smiled. "You are a good man."

"It's a nice compliment to have. Now hopefully I can keep it."

The room was quickly set up in a way where there were many chairs, sofas and we found some writing desks in the attic from when Georgiana and Fitzwilliam had to use them when they had governesses. We also borrowed some other desks from servants who could allow them to be spared, and in three days' time, the Wilkins children were brought in to the room of Pemberly, and it was equally surprising to know that this was their first time in the actual house, for they had mostly seen it from afar.

Their mother Loretta joined them, and once they overcame the daunted feel of being around such grandeur, Jane began her lessons.

After two hours of her teaching, Mrs. Reynolds had Lucy and some other servants bring in refreshments while I helped serve them.

By the end of the day, Jane's lesson was declared a success, and Darcy saw how beneficial her work was.

When Sunday came and we all attended services at Acton, I mentioned Jane's free lessons to teach children how to read and write, asking our fellow church members to spread the word that Jane was willing to give lessons to the children of the destitute and tenants of Pemberly.

By the end of the week, Jane had over fifty children as pupils and she taught five days a week, for four hours of the day and she would have no more than twenty pupils per day.

Work of her educating them while I oversaw the classes and fed the children spread rapidly and the lessons became the talk of Kent.

Her good deeds caused much elation, and were spoken highly of except for Kitty, who it made sullen.

One time, I overheard her speak to Georgiana.

"Is it possible to feel so useless?"

"You are not useless, Kitty," Georgiana said.

"I cannot help but feel so. You oversee the welfare of the poor around the village, Jane is a hero who teaches their children, Elizabeth is the beloved mistress of Pemberly that everyone admires, and I am simply... Kitty. Where is my use in the world?"

I felt bad for her state, for I understood what she was feeling, and I did not know how to rectify her need for importance. Not greatness, just importance. Thus, Kitty took more and more time to ride her horse Daedalus alone, and I hoped that the peace she achieved in her solitary journeys would help her find solace.

Yet, to maintain communication of our actions at Pemberly, I sent letters to Hampshire, to Longbourn, to Charlotte Collins at Hunsford, and to the Austens.

Our mother was filled with anxiety over Jane's actions hindering her finding a perfect match. Charlotte Collins, Maria and Cassandra admired her actions, yet what was most amusing was Jane Austen's response.

"An independent Jane Bennet," she had written. "I confess, even I didn't think of that one."

❧ 19 ❧

MOST SHOCKING NEWS

One day, while I was feeding the children in between lessons, I immediately felt sick. I had to excuse myself, rushed to the washroom and managed to make it there just in time before I keeled over and vomited up my breakfast.

There was a knock on the door.

"Mrs. Darcy," Came Lucy's voice from behind the door, "are you all right, mistress?"

"I must be sick, Lucy. Can you come in and clean up after my accident?"

She entered and saw my purgation in the wash bin, though she recommended walking me to my bedroom before she cleaned up after me.

"It is fine, Lucy, I promise that I can make it to my room on my own. Please inform Miss Bennet that I cannot come back to the lessons and inform Mrs. Reynolds to bring me some tea and bread."

"Of course, Mrs. Darcy."

Lucy proceeded to clean as I left the room, made it to my bedroom and lay down on the bed. Lucy entered with the tea that Mrs. Reynolds had made for me and she asked to remain with me, yet I told her that I was feeling better already, which I was. I spent the whole time in my room, yet the sickness passed swiftly, therefore when Darcy arrived to inquire after my health out of concern, I had felt well completely and could put his mind at ease.

Therefore, all was well with me, yet time would show that I had spoken too soon. There was a crisis, it would turn out, yet it had naught to do with my health.

❦

The next day, when all came down to breakfast, all were in attendance, except for Kitty. I prepared to send Lucy to wake her, assuming that Kitty had simply overslept, but Georgiana offered to go and rouse her.

As she had left, Jane and I inquired after the Fitzwilliams, for we knew that they had sent Darcy a letter.

"Oh, they are all well, and there is good news, we hope. My Aunt Fitzwilliam has informed us that their youngest son, Acton, who you still need to meet, is having the good fortune of beginning to court an heiress."

"That is wonderful," Jane said, "And—"

We were interrupted by a shout. We all stood up, surprised and Mr. Darcy walked forward, but Georgiana burst into the room, carrying a letter.

"She is gone," she cried, "Kitty is gone."

"What do you mean?"

"She was not in her room when I went to wake her," Georgiana stammered, "and I found this letter."

I snatched the letter and began reading.

Dear Elizabeth, Georgiana, Jane and Mr. Darcy,

I know that my actions will make you irate with me to say the least, and I do not blame you for your feelings. Just as I am sorry for how my absence will make you appear. If our parents call you out to blame for my choice in running away, then show them this letter to inform them that even I confess to you being wonderful guardians, and this is my fault and mine alone.

You may recall Georgiana telling us of the women in Kent who would be traveling to the Peninsula and become civilian nurses. Well, weeks ago, I had contacted those women, with Mrs. Pratt in particular, and I began to set into motion my plans to join them. This is not a sudden scheme, yet one that I have been planning for quite some time and only now have undergone.

Yesterday, due to delays, the carriages going to the location where we would brook passage to the continent left late, which made me able to stay for dinner, though I silently crept from my room and crossed the grounds where I rode Daedalus to the meeting point and joined the party of women before we left. You need not fear, for I will be in the company of many others, I shall be quite safe, for man servants accompany us for protection, but I am resolute in this matter.

I do not know whether it is love or adventure that drives me more, or a combination to pursue both. I know Richard's militia, and I will find him. He shall be angry with me, that much is certain, yet by his side I shall remain, to aid him in mind and spirit, to help him if he ever gets hurt, and to aid the soldiers around him as well.

I hope my plight does not impair the greatness of your reputations of any kind, nor drive away your affection of me. Yet please understand that this is something I must do. I cannot explain it, yet this is where I feel my path is headed towards, and if destiny can be called so, then I shall pursue it.

I will not tell you of the destination of our carriages, for fear that you all shall pursue me. Please, try to understand, or at the very least, remember that I love you all and that I hope that I will not make the same mistake as Lydia, or to become like her.

I do not flee because I am running away with a worthless libertine. I simply go to help those who deserve it. Elizabeth and Mr. Darcy, please forgive me, and the voice that within calls out that this is my destiny, and I should meet it.

Remember the better parts of myself,
Kitty

I closed the letter, handed it to Darcy, who read it as well, and then he called for Jefferson.

Once Jefferson was informed of Kitty's plight, he and Darcy themselves secretly left to find out where the destination of the civilian nurses was. They did not entrust the mission or any details to anyone else, because they did not wish for it to be made public and ruin Kitty in any way. Her actions were admirable to say the least, yet the way she went about it was what would hinder her.

While they rode on through Kent, Jane, Georgiana and I waited in anticipation, hoping there would be a happy end to this most shocking news.

✻ 20 ✻

LIVING FROM DAY TO DAY

Four days' time had passed, and Darcy and Jefferson had not returned to Pemberly.

My fear had now enhanced from not only the fate of Kitty, but also fear for Fitzwilliam. This was the first time since we were married that we were separated from each other for so long, and I was not certain that I could sustain being away from him any longer. Not only was I missing his presence, yet also much had to do with loss. And fear. Fear does play strange tricks on the mind and it was doing so with mine. I worried that they had been ambushed by highwaymen, that Fitzwilliam had fallen from his horse, or that some other calamity had befallen him.

After so long an absence, I sat with Georgiana and Jane and once more, we began to deliberate over the matter.

"I feel as if this is my fault entirely," Georgiana said.

"How could you think such a thing?" I argued, "Kitty would do what was in her will."

"No, but I am the one who taught her how to ride, of the women who were traveling to the Peninsula, and I also... I knew that she was unhappy of late."

"She misses Colonel Fitzwilliam," Jane concluded.

"Yes," Georgiana said. "Yet it's more than that. Kitty wanted something to define her. Colonel Fitzwilliam's arrival and her falling in love with him was simply a diversion, or a distraction from something that was already beginning within her. Kitty wanted something to show her importance in the world, and to have an adventure of some kind, whether it be an emotional one or a physical one. My cousin gave her an emotional one and now he has given her a physical one to undertake."

"She has read too many novels, then, and wants to be a hero."

"Who doesn't at one time or another, Jane?" I said. "If you think on it, we were raised to be so in a manner of speaking."

"What?"

"Think of it. Our mother raised us to believe that we had to marry well to save the family, or at least marry at all to do so. She just did not foresee, or no one could, of having five daughters who would grow up, keeping that notion of being heroic in some way, and yet they would have five different definitions of what being a hero was.

"You've grown to wanting to educate others, I married for love, Lydia married recklessly and out of sensibility as opposed to sense, and Mary is a devoted philosopher, keeping to her studies and being serious. When one stops and looks on it, Kitty always wanted a direction, and always was a little creative, making her idea for how to be a heroine not suitable for our way of living, which is why she probably had the hardest time of finding an identity.

"Georgiana, this is not your fault, nor is there anything that anyone could have done. This action, it can be argued, was inevitable, and is not coming from the worst parts of herself, but the better half that she was never allowed to express."

"I cannot despise her ever," Georgiana said, "even though we should be expected to. I am simply angry and confused as to what we ought to do."

"I agree. It's been four days and her absence will be noticed very soon."

"Maybe that is the problem," Jane said, "is that we are saying nothing."

"What do you mean?"

"If you think on it," Jane said, standing up and beginning to pace while she began to consider the situation in full, "What bad has Kitty done except for leave for a place without getting her family's consent, which is something that only we know about? She has traveled with a group of women, who we are acquainted with and are excellent chaperones, to be a civilian nurse in a public setting where she will hopefully find and look after someone who is now her own family."

She twirled around and looked at us. "Think on it! If we only say to everyone that we all gave Kitty our consent to leave and travel to the Peninsula, and we approved of it once we saw that she was in a company of reliable women companions, then there will be no problems. For, when you think on it, her actions, as long as we show that we allowed them, are by all accounts admirable."

Georgiana and I looked at each other.

"Do you think Fitzwilliam will like that we have said something to the people without gaining his consent?" Georgiana asked.

"We do not have time to think on that," I said. "We have already lost time with these four days. Tomorrow is Sunday and after the services will be a perfect time to let this slip amongst those in the neighborhood, the word will spread, and all will be well. Besides, in the absence of Fitzwilliam, I have no choice but to take up his mantle. And therefore, I shall do just that." I then turned to Jane. "Thank you, Jane. Now it's time that we save this on our end."

The next day, we attended Sunday services, and after the ceremony was ended, we began to speak and converse with everyone else in the laity. When they inquired about the absence of Kitty, we casually told them of how she joined the Kent nurses to embark to the Peninsula to look after our soldiers. Then we apologized for not speaking of it before, for we had assumed that it was common knowledge amongst the tenants of Pemberly and the village of Acton.

They were overjoyed in hearing news of her deeds and cried out in admiration of her selflessness.

"It is amazing," Mr. and Mrs. Wilkins said after we finished our narration. "Between Miss Bennet here teaching our children, you looking after them and allowing them in your home as equals, Miss Darcy attending to the poor and now Miss Kitty going off to tend to sick and injured officers. You are a collection of gentlewomen who are made to be heroes then!"

More in the laity echoed her sentiments and we were left blushing, for never before had we known that our actions affected so many in a beneficial light.

On the fifth day of our waiting, I was looking out the window and my heart was elated when I beheld a carriage driving down the lane.

I rushed down the steps.

"A carriage is coming down the road," I said to Mrs. Reynolds, who was walking by with a vase of flowers.

"What!" she cried, putting the vase down and following after me.

We rushed through the halls and burst through the front doors, coming down the steps and awaited the carriage drawing nearer. When it did so, my heart rose. The door opened, then one boot appeared, stepping down and then another.

"My goodness," Henry Fitzwilliam said, climbing down and closing the carriage door behind him. "Your hurry to meet me is most refreshing."

My stomach felt as if it dropped to my knees.

"Mr. Fitzwilliam," I gasped, feeling utterly at a loss. "Welcome to Pemberly, sir." Then I remembered myself and curtsied. "I had not expected you."

"Yes, forgive my sudden appearance, yet it is of no fault of mine. I had sent a letter to Darcy three days ago, I expected him to have received it, and yet one look in your eye confirms what I have expected, which was that he has not told you."

"Oh, I can assure you that it is through no intention of his own. He has been away for five days."

"Away? Good heavens, and he has left you here alone?"

"I am not alone I can assure you. I am here with my sisters."

"Of course. I had heard of such, it is only..." then he turned to Mrs. Reynolds. "Mrs. Reynolds, it is pleasing to see you again."

"It is an unexpected pleasure, Mr. Fitzwilliam." she answered as she curtsied. "And I am happy to see you as well."

The door opened, and Jane and Georgiana emerged.

"Dear Georgiana and Miss Bennet." Henry bowed. "Your beauty grows with more bloom every day. And yet, where can the other be?" he asked, his eyes beginning to glow, revealing his anticipation. "Where is Miss Kitty?"

We escorted him inside, I ordered tea to be brought and while it was being prepared, Georgiana informed him of Kitty's joining the company of civilian nurses to the Peninsula. While she did so, I secretly wrung my hands behind me in frustration. Of all the things that could not be expected, Henry's arrival was the most unwelcome.

When Georgiana finished telling him all, Henry leaned back, both annoyed and amused.

"I must say that I do not know whether I should be amazed and impressed by her or ashamed."

"Ashamed, sir?" I repeated, coldly.

"Aye, Mrs. Darcy and I mean no offense. A woman such as Kitty Bennet, of such genteel manners and current rank should not take it upon herself to travel as if she were no more than a commoner."

I balled my fist, and then released it so to hide my inner anger with his response.

"And yet," he continued, "I cannot deny being marveled at her. It has not fallen below or above my notice that she has left so to see to my younger brother, and the compliment is most keenly felt. For it means that she feels a binding tie to my family. And she will ride to assist us if need be. I therefore cannot deny to be flattered by the gesture. Yes, I feel her actions most keenly indeed."

Jane, Georgiana and I looked at each other with apprehension. This all was beginning to come together, and we were about to heal the damage that Kitty's disappearance had done, and now with Henry's arrival, it had all fallen to the worst once more.

When realizing that we were alone, Henry offered to remain at Pemberly until Darcy's return. His reasons for having come to Pemberly were because it was along his way. He had received an invitation from a friend who was hosting a hunting party and ball at their great home in a county that neighbored Kent, and since Pemberly was along the way, Henry thought it was suitable to break his journey here.

I pointed out that his stay might affect his arrival time at this other home. Yet it turned out that he was early in his journeying and therefore could stay at Pemberly for a whole week complete, as long as he wrote to tell his friend that he would arrive at the last minute.

I could not deny his presence, nor ignore the well-meaning stance behind it, therefore Henry remained.

⚜

One morning, after breakfast, I found myself feeling ill once more. I was sitting in my room and I was successful in making it to the chamber pot on time, where I forced up my meal once more.

When I summoned Lucy in the dispose of it, she took the pot and looked at me.

"Mistress, please allow me to send for Mrs. Reynolds, who will call the apothecary."

"I am well now," I argued. "Do not fear, it was merely something about the food that upset me."

"Begging your pardon, Mrs. Darcy, but you are not fully well. And this is not sickness you are going through. I could be wrong, yet I have seen it before many times."

"Seen it before? Well, what do you think this is? What has befallen me?"

When Lucy told me of her suspicions, she went to Mrs. Reynolds, who sent for the doctor immediately.

He came swiftly, within two hours, took in my condition and then gave me a diagnosis that he said was undeniable. I was surprised and frightened to say the least, for being exposed to something new and harmful.

However, to not cause alarm, I made Mrs. Reynolds and Lucy promise to secrecy, and I did not tell anyone. Not Jane or Georgiana. When Darcy arrived, he would be the first one that I would tell. I owed him that much.

Therefore, in anticipation, I waited, living from day to day in hopes that my husband would return to me.

21

WONDERFUL NEWS

C an a person fully describe agony? A poet can attempt it, yet I do not believe any description would explain the word properly.

Darcy and Jefferson had been gone for nine days at that point, and I was growing fearful.

Therefore when Mrs. Reynolds burst into my room, I was overwhelmed beyond my wildest dreams.

"Mrs. Darcy," she cried, "two men on horses ride down the lane. It was too far away to know for sure, yet I know that it must be them! I would know Darcy anywhere."

"I..." was all that I got out before I jumped up and ran out of the room, with Mrs. Reynolds following behind me. Georgiana, Jane and Henry were already waiting in the hall when I came down.

"It is him," Georgiana cried. "I can tell."

"It damn well had better be!" I cried in desperation, running past them and out to the beginning of the road. When the two riders had gotten close enough for me to see that it was Darcy, I began running toward him.

"Darcy!"

"Elizabeth!" he cried, slowing his horse down to a halt, jumping down and opening his arms to me. I rushed into them and we almost toppled over as he wrapped his arms around me and kissed my cheek.

"You cannot leave me for so long again!" I cried. "Yes, I am selfish for it, but so it is!"

"I know my dear, I know."

We stood there for a while, simply holding each other while I was heedless of all who looked on us.

Then I looked at Jefferson, who looked resigned.

"Did you not find Kitty?" I asked.

"We were unsuccessful," Jefferson said. "They traveled swiftly, and by the time we reached London, they had already boarded a ship for the continent. They had departed, yet we did learn that she is well, safe, as long as the ship passage goes as planned, then she will progress easily to the Peninsula."

"Then she cannot return unless of her own free will," I said. "Well, there is nothing we can do for her now except wait. And we have another pressing matter at hand."

"What matter?"

I turned my head, Darcy followed my gaze and he saw Henry Fitzwilliam gawking at us from across the lawn, standing next to our sisters.

"Good god, what is he doing here?!"

"Fitzwilliam, look at me." He did so and then I did my best to convince him of the urgency of obeying me.

"Right now, you are going to hear me lie about everything. All you can do is nod your head and follow my story."

"I—"

"Fitz!" Henry Fitzwilliam called out. Darcy took his horse by the reins, led him onward and we approached Henry and the rest of them.

"Henry," he said, "it is good to see you. Your arrival simply has startled me."

"As had your sudden adventure."

"Oh," I said. "Forgive me, Henry, for not telling you of the proper reasons for his leaving. Darcy left because of a fear that my sister's journey might not go as smoothly as we believed, so he followed the company to see to her welfare and return when he was certain of it. Yet now he has." Darcy looked at me.

"Oh, you need not worry, dear," I continued. "I already told him of how Kitty has received our permission to travel with the soldiers' families to follow the regiments who were deployed to assist Spain, and how by doing so, she has earned the goodwill of everyone on the estate and in Acton. He feels all the flattery of her wishing to look after his brother."

"Yes," Henry said. "Though I still am uncertain if I approve of her going, Darcy, I admire your liberty in sending her, for her concern for our family truly is touching."

Darcy turned to me again and I winked at him. Taking my hint, he turned back to Henry.

"Right," he said "Yes, it is all most touching."

"Well," Darcy said when we were alone. "This is all most... aggravating."

"Yes, it must be hard."

"Very hard. My cousin, Richard, has gone off to the Peninsula to fight in the war, Kitty flies after him to be with her one true love, and Richard's brother is here, and in truth, for breaking his journey here is clearly a fib he gave just so that he had a harmless way of coming to see Kitty, he has come to clearly woo her, when she actually is in love with his brother. Has it all come to this?"

"Yes," I answered with some humor, "I believe that it has."

Darcy sat down and kissed my forehead.

"Though I must commend you and our sisters for spreading the news of Kitty's plight as if it were something we all intended. That was well done."

"Thank you. Therefore at least, for the moment, all that we can say is that any problems that are in the family are internal ones that could affect the peace of the family, but not external ones that can ruin anyone's good name. The entanglement of Kitty, Henry and Richard is out of our hands, or if I might say so, completely not in need of our hands."

"What do you mean?"

"I mean that Kitty has left and gone off to the continent. She will be gone for months. Absence is said to make the heart grow fonder, but I've often found that it can make the heart grow forgetful. Maybe, by her being away, Henry might begin to cease caring for her. Therefore, if there is a problem, then we need not worry ourselves over it, for we have all the time in the world."

"Oh," Darcy said, lightening up. "While I am truly angry for the run-around Kitty has put me through, that is one plus. And one only. If she ever returns, Lizzy, I will undeniably lose my temper with her."

"I think she knows that."

"Brilliant. But it is truly good to be home again, Elizabeth."

"And I am happy you are returned. I worried about you all too often, and I wished to have you with me, now more than ever."

"Well, you need not fear, for I am returned, and I plan to stay."

"And Henry?"

"Now that I am home, Henry shall depart tomorrow morning for his friend's home, and we shall have nothing else to worry over."

"Well, that may not be necessarily true."

"How so?" Darcy snapped, afraid. "Elizabeth, I have just returned home. Please do not tell me that there is something else for you to worry over."

"Yes, there is something else. And you best prepare yourself."

Darcy sat down and folded his hands. "I am prepared,"

"Fitzwilliam, the most extraordinary thing has occurred, and I hope you are agreed that it is the most wonderful of news."

"Wonderful? Then this news is not of misfortune then?"

"If I know you, which I believe that I do, I think this might be the perfect announcement for you and everyone to boost up your moral, and that of the rest of the household."

"Will it?"

"Yes. Fitzwilliam, I am pregnant."

Darcy froze, and then he stood up slowly.

"What did you say?"

"I said that I am pregnant. And you and I are going to have a child."

❧ 22 ❧

THE NEXT TIME

"W-we..." he stuttered. "We...we are going to have a child?"

"Yes, Fitzwilliam. And you are going to be a father."

Darcy faltered, smiled, and then embraced me.

"I cannot believe it."

"Oh, you had better!"

"It is only, this is perfect."

"Yes, and in the wake of all this confusion and calamity, we now have hope, don't we?"

"Yes, the best hope in the world. I do not want you to do anything that will strain yourself, promise me, Elizabeth."

"I am stubborn, but not that much. I shall do everything to keep our baby healthy."

"We must send out letters," he said. "For this is news that I want the whole family to be aware of."

"My husband wants to be social?" I laughed. "That is an incredible thing."

"Because, unlike usual, I have incredible news. Oh, Elizabeth."

He kissed me once more.

"The happiest day of my life was when I married you."

"And I with you."

The next day, we announced the news to everyone, and it turned out to be the best thing to have done.

Henry offered to remain a day to celebrate with us, but we all encouraged him with alacrity to press on, under the excuse that it would be unwise to delay seeing his friend any longer. In truth, we just wanted him to depart, for every day he was there, every day we worried that he might overhear news from the servant's gossip of Kitty falling in love with his brother.

Determined to avoid that conflict for as long as possible, we wished him a safe journey, and he was on his way across the roads of Kent once more.

Upon his leaving, we all gave a sigh of relief.

"Well," Darcy said after the departing carriage, "'til the next time you are in the middle of a love between three, cousin, till the next time."

23

THE LIGHT THAT ECLIPSES
THE DARK

"Just this way, Miss Bennet," the Lieutenant told Kitty as he led her along.

"Right, thank you," Kitty replied, rubbing her dirty hands down the front of her already stained dress. Wearing nurse attire that had seen worse and better days, Kitty turned to the man who she was already helping.

They were the first of the wounded who had been brought in from the battlefield and Kitty had to hold that particular officer down while the surgeon had removed a musket ball from his shoulder. Once the surgery had gone successfully, Kitty helped cauterize the wound, then she cleaned it and wrapped it in bandages.

"Rejoice," Kitty smiled down at the soldier. "It could have been much worse. You live another day. Now rest."

As Kitty stood up and began to follow the Lieutenant, the wounded officer grabbed her arm. Kitty turned around and looked down at the officer whose deep brown eyes were filled with pain and sorrow.

Without so much as a word spoken, Kitty understood all that he wanted to communicate to her with the solitary glance.

He wants me to know that he is grateful. That I see him for what he is. And that he wants to hold a woman one last time, in case he never gets the chance to do so again.

Kitty leaned down, ran her hand down the soldier's face and stood up again.

"Rest now," she said.

Kitty turned to the Lieutenant and followed him out of that section of the medical quarters.

⚜

"Are you certain, Lieutenant?" Kitty asked.

"Yes," Lieutenant Dunlap replied. "It is the 43rd Regiment and the militia has just arrived. Why is it this regiment in particular that you sought knowledge of?"

"A family member of mine is in that regiment," Kitty said. "I was hoping to see him again."

"Well, it is not as you would have it, then."

"What do you mean?"

"The regiment fought in the Battle Albuera and now they have just been able to collect their wounded from the battlefield. We will also get some wounded from the Spanish and Portuguese units in as well. For this is the only camp with the largest medical facility."

Kitty's heart beat with trepidation. "Were you given the names of the wounded?"

"A list has not been made as of yet, but soon an inventory will be drawn."

"Do you perchance know if their Colonel was among the infirm?"

"Are you referring to a Colonel Fitzwilliam?" Lieutenant Dunlap replied, turning to her.

"Colonel Richard Fitzwilliam, yes," Kitty replied eagerly.

"That is your relative?"

"Yes, he is my cousin."

"Then I'm sorry."

Kitty looked at the Lieutenant, stricken with fear.

"He has been injured," the Lieutenant said. "He was shot in the stomach and they are performing the surgery as we speak."

"No... Where is he housed?"

"Miss Bennet?"

"Lieutenant! Where is he? And more importantly, take me to him."

Dunlap nodded to Kitty and led her onward. As she followed him, her mind thought back on all the weeks that had passed since she had come to Spain. She had learned how to tend to the soldiers, sew up the battle wounds and assist the doctors, and for the past two months, she had been in agony, hoping to grow closer and closer to where she heard the Colonel's regiment to be.

Finally, having arrived at the safe houses in Albuera, she had hoped the rumors were true, that his army would arrive to assist the British regiment that her company followed.

She followed the Lieutenant into another medical house and the first thing they were greeted by was the surgeon as he came from the other room, wiping his hands down with a rag.

"Doctor," the Lieutenant saluted.

"Lieutenant." The surgeon's eyes fell on Kitty. "If you have come to assist me in the surgery, then there is no need. I have finished the operation."

"And how is the Colonel?" Kitty asked, keeping her voice strong in spite of her fears.

"We were fortunate. The musket ball did not puncture any of his major organs, and we have sewed up his wound, yet that does not stop the fact that there will be potential for much internal bleeding. Either he shall die of it, or a cyst will fall and clot the area. He is in the hands of God, now."

"Yet the man we speak of is Colonel Fitzwilliam?" Kitty confirmed.

"Yes," the surgeon said, "It is."

Kitty rushed past him and entered the room.

"Miss Bennet!" Lieutenant Dunlap cried, yet Kitty took no heed as she rushed into the room to find two nurses looking after a man who lay on a cot. Kitty moved forward and soon saw that the man who they tended to was Richard.

"I cannot believe..." Kitty whispered.

Falling in between being awake and being asleep, Richard rolled his head and his eyes opened slightly. Lieutenant Dunlap entered and tried to pull Kitty out of the room, yet she pushed past him, rushed to Richard's side, fell on the ground and placed her arms around his shoulders.

"Richard," Kitty cried, happy to have seen him finally, after weeks in desperation. "Richard please, open your eyes for me just a little."

Richard looked around, opened his eyes and squinted.

"Kitty?"

"Yes," she sighed. "Oh, my love," Kitty said, kissing him on the lips. "Here you are."

"But... no, you are not here," Richard said, delirious. "Kitty is not here with me now."

"Yes, she is. Believe that I am here."

"She is far away from me now," Richard said, his eyes glazing over. "She is above me as if she is of the heavens."

His eyes closed slowly, and Kitty began to weep while the nurses pulled her away.

"He needs to rest, miss," they cried. "He needs time to recover."

Kitty allowed herself to be dragged away, in fear of having to see the Colonel pass away before her very eyes.

"The battle proved to be in our favor," Lieutenant Dunlap said as Kitty and he were at a table, eating the little bit of rations that were theirs for dinner. After a couple of hours to settle her nerves, Kitty had been persuaded to eat something. "The French forces were the *Armee du Midi.*"

"That means Army of the South, correct?" Kitty asked.

"Yes, it does. The battle took place roughly 20 kilometers from the frontier fortress-town of Badajoz. Marshall Soult led a French expedition from Andalusia into Extremadura in a bid to draw Allied forces away from the Lines. Lucky for us, Napoleon's information was outdated, and Soult's intervention came too late. Soult was able to capture the fortress at Badajoz on the border between Spain and Portugal from the Spanish."

"I know about these complications, difficulties, and specifics already," Kitty said. "The French were forced to return to Andalusia due to some other defeats."

The Lieutenant continued. "However, under the demands of Soult, the French left Badajoz strongly garrisoned. Last month, news of Masséna's complete withdrawal from Portugal reached everyone, and that's why we are here. We sent our armies, along with the Portuguese, to retake the border town. The Allies drove most of the French from the surrounding area and began the Siege of Badajoz. Soult then gathered an army from the French forces, and marched to relieve the siege. Yet under the General Joaquin Blake, the Spanish army and ours allied and we were able to force the French back, winning this battle."

"You know I follow the news, Dunlap, so why do you tell me this?"

"Because there is something I must warn you about."

"What is that?"

Lieutenant Dunlap rolled his shoulders and looked away from her.

"Dunlap," Kitty said, "what is it?"

"I fear...this whole battle was pointless. Our armies may have won, but both sides suffered heavily. We were too battered and exhausted to even pursue them. We can resume the investment of Badajoz, but we won't be able to hold it if the French return."

"And they will return," Kitty concluded.

"Yes, they will. They always do." Lieutenant Dunlap leaned forward. "Miss Bennet... Kitty. You have been a nurse in this company for three months now, and in all that time, you have never spoken of this Colonel till recently."

"I did not think to see him so soon," Kitty replied quietly.

"He is your cousin?"

"Yes."

"And I must ask, is he more than a mere cousin?"

Kitty looked at Dunlap, unafraid.

"Yes, he is." Dunlap looked down at the table. "Is this where you tell me that seeing him is inappropriate? That I should watch myself, and remember myself?"

"I am too far from society to be a gentleman, Kitty. I just simply...Kitty, if I am correct, and the French do return to Albuera, we cannot hold them at bay. And your cousin, the Colonel, must be moved even when he is recovering."

"Even when moving him would be dangerous for him," Kitty said.

"Yes."

Kitty hunched over and looked at the table before her.

"What you are saying is that my cousin could eventually die. That was the whole point."

"No, that wasn't the only point. Sometimes we officers' stop speaking because there is no way that we can voice the terrors that we have seen. And then there are some of us, who believe that if we continue speaking, we are aware that we are still alive."

"Do you forget sometimes?"

"When one is in the presence of tragedy so much," Dunlap added, "one begins to feel as if they are dead themselves."

"I will not lose faith or hope," Kitty argued. "Until Richard's eyes close permanently, I will hope that he will live."

Lieutenant Dunlap eyed her keenly.

"You clearly are very much in love with him?"

"Yes."

"Then... enjoy your hope. Yet prepare yourself for the worst."

Dunlap stood up and began to walk away.

"Lieutenant Dunlap? Jason?"

The lieutenant turned toward her.

"Thank you, for everything," Kitty said.

Dunlap smiled and walked away.

⚜

The next morning, she went to visit the Colonel's tent. When she entered, she saw that his eyes were closed, yet she was content to sit by his side and wait with him.

As she had done so, she could not have been in his company for one full minute before he began to speak.

"Kitty?"

Kitty leaned forward and moved by his side.

"Richard!"

"Kitty..."

Kitty took his hand in hers and kissed it.

"You are awake. I have been looking for you for months."

His eyes opened slowly.

"It was an odd thing. When I woke up this morning, I called out for you. And when the nurse said you would come soon, I almost wept. I thought you had been in a dream of mine, for you are there often, but never more than a dream. And to see you now, to feel you, you still seem no less real. No less beautiful. Yet still you seem so far beyond me, like a light in the dark, and you walk with the sun behind you, bringing me toward you. You are here, aren't you?"

"Yes, I am right here," Kitty whispered, beginning to cry.

"And are you going to leave me?"

"Never. I'm going to look after you. Every day, I am going to look after you."

And to that promise, Kitty held fast and determined. In less than a month, the French did return, and by that time, the wounded had to be removed. Kitty became Richard's personal nurse, seeing to his comfort and health as he was transported with other injured officers of high rank, across Spain and to the harbors where they would be transported back to Britain.

"The one luxury of being wounded almost to the point of dying," Richard said bitterly as he was being transported in the carriage. "We are not fit for fighting any longer. Therefore, one can make the argument successfully that the only way to escape the pains of war is to almost die."

"Oh, don't be so morbid!" Kitty tried to lighten his mood.

"Then what should I do instead?" Richard asked.

"You should kiss me, and that is all."

Richard took her hand and pressed it against his lips.

"That is how high I can get, for moving my chest hurts terribly."

Kitty leaned down and kissed him.

Once they reached a safe village in Spain, the injured rested there before progressing back to Britain. Kitty bathed the Colonel to keep him from getting dirty as well as rebound his wounds with fresh clean bandages. As she did so, he pulled at her hair.

"What?"

"Nothing. I just cannot believe that I almost did not choose to marry you."

"You thought you were doing the right thing. You and Mr. Darcy are too similar at the strangest of moments."

Kitty smiled as she re-fastened the bandages.

"And you came out here, traveling this far, for me?"

"You were worth the adventure. And I owed you."

"How?"

"You taught me how to feel alive again. And you gave me courage. I never would have been brave enough to undergo such a journey as this until I had met you. I daresay that if there was something that would create Kitty Bennet, then it would be you."

"Kitty, you've always been brave."

"Yet because of you, I have my goodness now, and my purpose. And it shall not be taken from me. You shall not be taken from me either."

"Then I dare say that I have it in me to fight to live."

"You had better."

⚜

Once the injured rested enough, their journey continued. They boarded a ship that would take them back to Britain and Colonel Fitzwilliam, now almost recovered, stood next to Kitty and looked out at the war that was behind him, amazed that destiny had something else in store for him.

"What are you feeling?" Kitty asked the Colonel as he stood on the deck, looking in the direction of England.

"I feel born again," he said, "or fortunate. I was close to death, Kitty. I felt it at my heels, pulling me downward. And yet here I stand, walking towards the destiny where the light that eclipses the dark lies. It is with you, Kitty. It is with you."

❧ 24 ❧

SO IT BEGINS

P emberly was all astir with the awaiting of their arrival.

"I cannot believe that it all has turned out for the better," I said, making certain that their bedrooms were ready.

"Elizabeth," Darcy said, "please dear, everything is perfect, so don't move around so."

"Fitzwilliam, do not worry on my account, I am perfectly well."

"I know, it is just...I cannot help but be cautious of your state."

"I am as healthy as a horse."

"I've seen some unhealthy horses in my time."

"Yet not today, hopefully."

A month ago, we had received word from Kitty that she had found the Colonel, he had been severely wounded and thus he was given leave and was being brought home where he would be allowed to recover.

When he arrived in London, he was retrieved by Mr. and Mrs. Bingley, for his parents were no longer in London, but in Derbyshire. Upon coming home, Mr. Bingley would let him remain at his townhouse and then once he was rested, they would journey into Kent, where Colonel Fitzwilliam would remain at Pemberly indefinitely until his recovery was fully complete.

What we did not foresee, however, was that the Fitzwilliams had wished to come to Pemberly as well, in hopes of convincing their son to come to

Matlock instead to recover. Little did they know that there was no reason he would go there, and the reason why was going to come forward in due time.

"Fitzwilliam," I said. "While I am happy in knowing that Kitty and Richard will be returned to us, I wish they would be met with a more fortuitous outcome. This day is going to end poorly either way."

"Yes, it is. Yet we have no choice in the matter."

We walked downstairs where everyone was assembled. And that whole company was Darcy, Jane, Georgiana, Lord and Lady Fitzwilliam, their other son, Acton, who had come down from Northampton, and Henry Fitzwilliam himself.

Yes, that was the rotten outcome, and the reason that Richard did not want to recover at Matlock. He knew he would have to face Henry, and now his homecoming would have to be marred by giving the news that he had come home to recover, and to marry the woman that Henry still fancied.

All of us sat together, waiting for the arrival of our officer and his love, for Mr. Bingley had announced that they all would arrive on that day.

Darcy, out of anticipation, began to pace back and forth. In between his footfalls, I heard something.

"Fitzwilliam?" I said. He stopped and turned to me.

"What is it?"

Then we all heard the hooves of horses trotting down the road. We all stood up and walked briskly out of Pemberly and waited along the lane.

The carriage pulled up, parked before us, the carriage door opened...

"Elizabeth!" Kitty cried, jumping out of the carriage. "Jane, Georgiana, and Mr. Darcy!"

"Kitty!" we all cried, actually overjoyed to see her. Despite her rash actions, it was undeniable that Kitty did act quite heroically. We were stopped from embracing her because she then turned around and began to help Colonel Fitzwilliam step down from the carriage. He clearly was humiliated in needing her assistance, yet it was apparent that he needed her support all the same. It was quite heartbreaking to see that the Colonel, who was so strong a man, needed to rely on another, but Kitty was proud to stay near him.

As he climbed down, Kitty remained with her arm around him while he also leaned on a cane. I turned to Henry, who looked at their embrace and his face froze over.

Mr. Bingley and Miriam climbed down as well and beheld us.

"Well," Kitty said. "We are here, and our hero is home."

"Yes, he is," Darcy said. "It is a wonder that you are both returned to us."

Darcy walked up to Kitty and kissed her on the forehead.

"While you are still in trouble," he whispered, "I know we owe you much."

"Thank you, Mr. Darcy."

"Though I am still angry."

"I know."

Darcy turned to Richard.

"And you, stay here as long as you like."

"Thank you, Fitz."

Kitty looked down at my stomach, which was large and looked as if I had swallowed a watermelon.

"And if I didn't know how long I had been away," Kitty said. "Your progress says it all. You are truly with child. Oh, Elizabeth, that is wonderful. You shall be an excellent mother."

"Thank you, Kitty."

"And Darcy," The Colonel said. "Congratulations. I know fatherhood is meant for you."

"Yes," Darcy said, "I believe that it is."

Once our words of goodwill were spoken, we turned to the rest.

Now seeing that the moment had come, Jane, Georgiana and I went to them and we all had a warm embrace.

Next, Lord and Lady Fitzwilliam hugged Richard, happy to see that their son was alive, yet Henry remained where he stood.

"Come inside," I said, happy that all was well, and our family was returned to us. "I have some tea and refreshments prepared for you all."

We all entered, and I began my duties as hostess with alacrity. I knew I missed Kitty, yet I did not know it was to such an extent before. And the Colonel, who was always a wonderful addition to our household, was clearly missed by all.

"As we journeyed here from London," Miriam told me in a whisper, "Kitty told me her whole story. I never knew she possessed such nerve."

"I did not know either, yet I should have."

As Lucy and some other servants brought the tea in, Mrs. Reynolds helped serve it, happy to be around the family. As we all sat down, Kitty remained close to Richard, as if they were tied to one another by an invisible string.

Many questions were asked about Richard, and his time overseas, but Lady Fitzwilliam dominated the conversation, for Richard, though the middle son, had clearly been her favorite, and Henry and Acton were their father's.

"For god sakes mother," Acton said. "Richard is recovering from a fatal injury. Give him time to breathe at least, for you bombard him with questions to the point where he must feel as if he is under social fire."

"Oh, I do not mind it, Mother and Acton," Richard said. "Though I do, admittedly require some quiet, not because of silence, but because I have an announcement to make."

"Oh," Henry jeered. "You have just returned home, and you already have the strength to give a speech. Nothing stops you, does it, Richard?"

"Clearly not, Henry, for I survived the worst of battle. Words don't hurt me anymore."

I looked in between them, and I saw a bit of rivalry in their eyes; however I knew that that reaction would be little compared to the reaction that was soon to come.

Richard stood up and placed his hands behind his back.

"One can say that fighting in a war makes you appreciate life, and that it makes you wish to undergo all the beauties that it has to offer. However, this was not the case with me. Rather, it occurred before. While here, under the beautiful shades of Pemberly, I had met my destiny in the shape of a magnificent woman. Before setting out for the Peninsula, this wonderful creature gave me no choice but to fall in love with her."

I looked at Kitty, who blushed while Richard spoke.

"And I did," he continued. "I fell hopelessly in love. Then I went off to fight, in fear that I would never see this magnificent woman again, but I was wrong. I underestimated her courage. She followed me, came to me in a desperate hour, cared for me, and gave my will a reason to fight to live. And now I am here, still a full man. And I am not afraid. I almost lost her once, out of resignation that I could not offer her the best life. However, I will not lose her for the world. Therefore, I announce that I have proposed to Kitty Bennet, asking her to be my wife, and she has accepted."

My sisters cheered, Darcy and Acton did as well, Mr. Bingley and Miriam also exclaimed their joy at the bond, but Lord and Lady Fitzwilliam sat there transfixed, while Henry looked murderous.

Standing up, he took a step forward.

"Richard," Henry cried. "What did you say?"

"I said," Richard continued, "that Kitty shall be my wife. Please, brother, be happy for me."

"What!"

"I said please, Henry, be happy for me."

Filled with anxiety, I turned and didn't need to look far, for Darcy was at my shoulder.

"It is as I feared," he whispered to me. "And so it begins."

Yes, so it began.

THE END

Don't miss out on your next favorite book!

Join the Satin Romance mailing list
www.satinromance.com/mail.html

THANK YOU FOR READING

Did you enjoy this book?

We invite you to leave a review at your favorite book site, such as Goodreads, Amazon, Barnes & Noble, etc.

DID YOU KNOW THAT LEAVING A REVIEW...

- Helps other readers find books they may enjoy.
- Gives you a chance to let your voice be heard.
- Gives authors recognition for their hard work.
- Doesn't have to be long. A sentence or two about why you liked the book will do.

ABOUT THE AUTHOR

Ney Mitch has been a long-standing Jane Austen enthusiast, having written forty novels that were inspired by her various works. Since stumbling on Miss Austen's books after graduating from college, she has always dabbled in Austen inspired literature, ranging from writing works for teens to adults. Originally, her desire was to adapt Jane Austen's writing in a way to help young adults connect with her, however over time, she has spread her aims to other genres and styles.

Having received her BA Degree at Desales University, she is a writer, both literary and dramatic, as well as being a Historic Reenactor.

 facebook.com/courtney.mitchell.589

 twitter.com/CMMitchelPsyche

pinterest.com/shebaanna

ALSO BY NEY MITCH

WITH SATIN ROMANCE

Pride, Prejudice, & New Adventures

Rapture & Rebellion

Fortune & Misfortune

Desire & Destiny

Memory Series

Moments of Moments Past

Moments of Moments Present

Moments of Moments Future